Once Upon a Time in December

ALYSON ROOT

J&M BOOKS

Human Authored™, Reg #: 5606711, https://authorsguild.org/human

For permission requests, write to a.rootauthor@alysonroot.com

Published by J&M Books

483 Green Lanes, London, N13 4BS

Print ISBN: 978-1-917785-35-8

Ebook ISBN: 978-1-917785-34-1

Developmental Edit & Cover design by:

Tara Sullivan, The Write Gal Co.

www.thewritegal.com

Line & Copy Edit by:

Linda Slate

Proofed by:

Crystal lee-Wren, COLProof

&

Morgan Bonito

Once Upon a Time in December is written in American English. However, the narrative includes British characters who use authentic British slang and colloquialisms where appropriate to their dialogue and voice.

1

Baubles & Breakups

Whitley held her breath as she waited for Anthony's answer, the silence stretching between them like a taut wire ready to snap. Should he be taking so long? The question echoed in her mind as precious seconds ticked by, each one feeling like an eternity. She felt the shift in the atmosphere around her as she continued to wait, the festive chatter of the Christmas party fading into a distant hum. The weight of the engagement ring box in her trembling hand felt heavier with each passing moment, and she could feel the curious stares of the party guests burning into her back like tiny flames.

"Ant?" She chuckled nervously, hoping to sound less worried than she was, though her voice betrayed the anxiety coursing through her veins like ice water.

He rubbed the back of his head awkwardly, his usual confident demeanor cracking as he eyed the crowd of elegantly dressed people witnessing Whitley's proposal attempt. The soft glow of the Christmas lights reflected off the crystal champagne glasses held by onlookers, creating a surreal backdrop to what should have been the most romantic moment of her life.

"Shit, Whitley. I mean, thanks for asking...but no. Um, I don't want to marry you."

The words hit her like a physical blow, each syllable cutting through the warm, festive air of the ballroom. Wait, that wasn't right. This couldn't be happening. Not here, not now, not like this. Whitley pinched her brows together, confusion and disbelief warring across her carefully made-up features. "But..."

"Let's go talk, okay?" Anthony's voice was strained, uncomfortable, as if the words were being dragged from his throat against his will.

The sudden reality of what was happening slammed into her with such force it was almost physical, like being hit by a freight train of humiliation and heartbreak. She tensed her muscles to keep herself upright, fighting against the overwhelming urge to crumble right there on the polished marble floor of the DuPont family's annual Christmas gala.

"Okay." It was all she could get out of her mouth, the single word barely audible above the thundering of her heartbeat. There she was, on her knee in a dress that cost her an entire month's salary, the deep emerald velvet fabric pooling around her like a puddle of expensive regret, still holding out the leather-bound engagement ring box like a fool.

Gasps and whispers reached her ears even through the blood pounding with every beat of her heart, the sound of her social humiliation spreading through the crowd like wildfire. She could practically feel the smartphones being discreetly pulled out, ready to capture her mortification for posterity. This couldn't be happening. Not at her family's most important social event of the year.

Gritting her teeth until her jaw ached, Whitley finally dropped her hand and awkwardly maneuvered herself into a standing position, her four-inch heels wobbling slightly on the smooth floor.

Taking Anthony's proffered hand, she kept her head held high with practiced dignity until they were safely out of the ballroom, away from the prying eyes and barely concealed excitement of the gossip-hungry guests.

"Fuck," Anthony moaned, dropping her hand the moment they were alone in the marble-lined corridor, his fingers running through his perfectly styled hair. "I didn't think you'd do it tonight, Whit."

The casual way he said it made her stomach lurch, as if her proposal was some inconvenient surprise rather than the culmination of months of planning and dreaming.

"Anthony, you need to explain what's going on. I...I thought you wanted me to ask you to marry me?" Her voice sounded steadier than she felt. Years of DuPont training in maintaining composure under pressure served her well, even in this moment of personal crisis.

"I did," he began, before dropping his eyes from Whitley's face to the overly polished floor, unable to meet her gaze. The silence stretched between them, filled only by the distant sound of the party continuing regardless of their presence. "But then..."

"But then, what?" Whitley's mind buzzed loudly, a thousand thoughts and fears colliding in her head like bumper cars at a carnival.

"Well, then I met someone." The words fell from his lips like stones into still water, creating ripples of devastation that spread through her entire being.

"You...met...someone," Whitley repeated slowly, as if saying the words might make them make sense, might transform them into something less shocking than they were.

Anthony scrubbed his face with both hands, the gesture making him look younger and more vulnerable than she'd seen him in years. "Yes. I met someone, and I think I'd like to see where it goes."

Feeling utterly confused, hurt and...confused some more, Whitley stood silently in the opulent hallway, surrounded by oil paintings of long-dead DuPont ancestors who seemed to be judging her from their gilded frames. Anthony, the man who'd shared his life with her for the past six years, who knew how she liked her coffee in the morning, and which side of the bed she preferred. The man who only last week confessed how much he wanted to make things permanent between them, his eyes bright with what she'd thought was love and excitement, and that he'd like it if Whitley was the one to propose because it would be "so romantic and modern." *That* man was now standing in front of her, fidgeting with his bow tie, telling her he'd met someone else.

"But I love you, Whit. Like, so much. I don't want to end things." His voice took on a pleading quality that made her skin crawl. "Maybe...I don't know...we could try an open relationship for a while?"

Dumbfounded, flabbergasted, rendered speechless—all adequate descriptors for Whitley's current state as she processed the absolute audacity of his suggestion.

"I..." How the hell was she supposed to answer that? Less than half an hour ago, she was sure they'd be engaged by now, already mentally planning their spring wedding and looking forward to the next part of their lives together. An early Christmas present to her parents, who'd made it clear they wanted her to marry as soon as possible and pop out some grandchildren to carry on the DuPont legacy.

Taking a small step back, Whitley shook her head in disbelief. Her heels clicking against the marble with a sound that seemed to echo her breaking heart. "You...you want me to be in an open relationship so you can sleep with other people?"

"It was—"

She held up her hand, cutting him off before he could say anything more. The gesture was sharp and final. "After making me believe we were on the road to marriage and kids, you're now asking me to give you my blessing to sleep with other women? After I've just made a fool of myself in front of my parents and their closest friends, you want me to what? Waltz back in there and tell them it's all okay, because even though you don't want to marry me, I've quite happily agreed to be in a non-monogamous relationship. Is that about the long and short of it, Anthony?"

"Whit, come on. Look, I know it's a lot to process and I'm so sorry I didn't say something before you—"

"Got down on one knee and proposed publicly. Like you'd always dreamed." The bitterness in her voice surprised even her, cutting through the air like a blade.

He swallowed hard and winced, the sound audible in the quiet corridor. "Yeah."

Dropping her gaze to the intricate pattern of the marble floor, Whitley took another step back, putting more distance between them. "I need to get back in there and smooth things over with Mom and Dad."

She needed a hell of a lot more time to deal with this than a ten-minute chat in the corridor outside the DuPont Christmas Gala. She'd need a long fucking time and plenty of booze to make any kind of sense of it all, and maybe a few sessions with her therapist...and possibly a complete life overhaul.

But the one thing Whitley didn't have tonight was time to fall apart. She was the eldest DuPont child, heir to a fortune and a heritage that stretched back generations. She had responsibilities and an image to uphold—expectations that had been drilled into her since childhood. Not that her parents would expect it—they'd probably be shocked to see her return to the party after such a public humiliation—but Whitley wouldn't let them down. She couldn't.

"Whit, are you really going back in there? Don't you think we should talk?" Anthony's voice held a note of panic, as if he finally began to understand the magnitude of what he'd done.

Taking a third step back, Whitley straightened her spine with the regal bearing that had been bred into her bones. "We will talk, but not now. I suggest you go home." Her voice was ice cold, each word precisely enunciated.

Adjusting his bow tie nervously, Anthony peered over her shoulder at the entrance to the party, where the sounds of laughter and music continued to spill out. "Would...would you have a word with your dad? You know, smooth things over?"

Insanely, she automatically nodded, the people-pleasing response so ingrained it happened without conscious thought. That was Whitley: the woman who acquiesced to anything Anthony asked of her, who bent over backwards to make his life easier. Would she do the same regarding his request for an open relationship? Internally, her stomach rolled at the thought, bile rising in her throat. But she was a people-pleaser by nature and upbringing. She hated conflict with every fiber of her being, and her life was so fundamentally entwined with his after six years together. The thought of not being in a relationship—any kind of relationship—felt wrong, like losing a limb.

Twirling on her heels, Whitley donned her mask—the carefully constructed facade she'd perfected over the years, which had protected her many times in the past. She wouldn't let people see her vulnerabilities; wouldn't give them the satisfaction of witnessing a DuPont fall apart, especially not tonight. If she were to face these people with any sort of dignity intact, it would be with her head held high and her composure unshakeable.

2

Mistletoe & Meltdowns

Pausing by the double doors that led back into the ballroom, Whitley took a second to perform a breathing exercise her sister Aubrey had taught her a few months ago during a particularly stressful period at work. Whitley was prone to stress, being in the position she was in. She was in line to inherit the DuPont fortune, and all the responsibilities that came with it—the foundation, the business interests, the social obligations. Occasionally, she needed a little help to calm her anxiety, and breathing techniques worked wonders for centering her scattered thoughts.

Smoothing down the velvet material that made up her dress, feeling the expensive fabric slide beneath her palms, Whitley walked back into the party. Mercifully, the band played with a little more gusto, presumably because one of her family members had told them to keep the guests entertained by any means necessary and distract from the drama that had just unfolded.

Spotting her parents across the crowded ballroom, standing near the towering Christmas tree that dominated the center of the space, Whitley ignored the pointed stares and barely concealed whispers that followed her path and headed straight for them. As she stepped up, her mom and dad parted seamlessly, allowing her to slip into the newly formed guarded space. They stood back together immediately, creating a shield from the curious guests, and Whitley couldn't have loved them more for it. Seconds later, Aubrey and William joined them, forming a DuPont family circle of protection around her that felt like a fortress against the outside world.

"Darling, are you okay?" Lucienne DuPont, Whitley's mother, was the epitome of regal elegance in her midnight blue gown, her silver hair perfectly coiffed. But right now, concern etched lines around her usually serene eyes as she looked worriedly at her daughter.

Whitley reached for her mother's hand and patted it gently, drawing comfort from the familiar warmth of her mom's touch. "I'll be fine. We need to talk some more."

"What the blazes is going on?" Lucas, her father, asked in his deep, authoritative voice that commanded boardrooms and charity galas alike. "I thought the pair of you—"

"Me too, Dad." Whitley could perfectly understand their confusion. She had plenty of it herself—enough to drown in.

"Do you need me to kill him?" William asked without a trace of humor, his protective instincts as her younger brother kicking into high gear.

"I'll help him bury the body," Aubrey tacked on with deadly seriousness, her eyes flashing with supportive fury.

"I appreciate the homicidal protection, really I do, but there's no need. Anthony and I will work it out." She couldn't bring herself to tell them what he'd asked of her, how utterly humiliating his suggestion had been. It was even more humiliating that she couldn't tell them she'd outright refused.

"Has he gone home?" Lucienne peered around the room subtly, her practiced social grace allowing her to scan for Anthony without appearing obvious. "I don't see him."

"I told him it was best if he retired for the evening," Whitley replied with a level tone that belied the churning chaos inside her. Her guts were tumbling like a washing machine, and she felt on the cusp of vomiting, but she'd hold it together through sheer force of will. "I'm sorry about this," she added, meeting her parents' eyes with genuine remorse. "I didn't mean to embarrass you or the family."

Lucas scoffed, his expression softening with paternal love. "My darling, I couldn't give a fig what anyone thinks. Our concern is you, sweetheart."

Whitley would not cry. She would not!

Clamping her jaw to the point of pain, Whitley gave him a small smile as a reply, not trusting her voice to remain steady any longer. "Should I do the rounds?"

It would be torture making polite conversation and pretending everything was fine, but if it meant saving face for her family and the company, she'd do it. Half the guests at the party were rich benefactors of the DuPont Foundation for Musicians, a foundation Whitley herself had set up and was immensely proud of.

"No. Have a drink," Aubrey said firmly. "You don't owe them anything, Whit."

"Aubrey's right, sis. Come on, let's get wasted," William declared, already steering her toward the bar.

"Maybe not *too* wasted," Lucienne called as her youngest children dragged Whitley over to the bar, signaling frantically for shots.

The burn of alcohol helped breathe some life into her lungs, the familiar warmth spreading through her chest. She hadn't realized how numb she felt over it all, as if her body had gone into shock.

"So, what did the asshat say?" William asked bluntly after sinking his third shot of bourbon, the amber liquid disappearing with practiced ease. It was no secret her younger brother had felt no love for her partner. Anthony had a way of rubbing people the wrong way with his casual arrogance and entitled attitude, but Whitley had always found his boyish charm...well, charming.

"Please don't call him that." Whitley sighed, draining another drink and feeling the alcohol begin to dull the sharp edges of her pain.

"Whit, come on. You were both set on marriage. We all knew it, and then this," he said, waving his hand vaguely in the direction of where Whitley's disastrous proposal had taken place.

Her eyes sought the spot where she'd kneeled in front of him, and she was hit again with an almost physical force, like being punched in the gut. This time, though, it was anger rather than hurt. A raw and unadulterated wave of ire burned through her veins like molten lava. "I made an idiot of myself," she hissed.

Aubrey curled an arm around Whitley's sunken shoulders, her touch warm and comforting. "*He* is the idiot, Whit."

"He asked me for an open relationship," she confessed, the words tumbling out like a dam bursting. "He's met someone else."

William cursed him out immediately, his vocabulary impressively colorful, and Aubrey growled low in her throat. "You've got to be shitting me."

If only she were. "Nope. I...I had no idea." Jesus, she was pathetic. "All this time I thought our lives were on the same track, heading for the same destination."

"Well, yeah," Aubrey scoffed, indignation radiating from every pore, "because he made you believe that! This is not your fault, Whitley."

Shaking her head, she sneered at the rogue tear rolling down her perfectly made-up face, probably taking her expensive mascara with it. "I can't believe it." Wiping the offending tear away with force, Whitley signaled for more drinks. "He asked me to propose," she muttered. Clearly, this was her way of wading through the quagmire that was this evening's turn of events. "He wanted a romantic proposal, and I gave him one."

William dropped his head on her shoulder in a gesture of brotherly comfort. "It was beautiful, Sis."

"It was stupid. I was stupid. I didn't even say no!" The admission burst from her lips like a confession she'd been holding back.

Aubrey and William shared a confused look over her head. "Didn't say no? What do you mean?" Aubrey asked tentatively.

Whitley chuckled bitterly at the lunacy of it all, the sound hollow and broken. "I didn't say no to the open relationship. He's left here tonight, after humiliating me, thinking I'm actually considering it."

"Are you?" William asked carefully, his voice gentle but concerned.

"No. I mean..." She trailed off, uncertainty creeping into her voice.

"No, Whit. Just no. End of sentence. There is no way you're letting that asshole turn you into somebody you're not." Aubrey's voice was fierce, protective, cutting through Whitley's confusion.

Sniffing, Whitley looked at her sister with watery eyes. "But I don't know how to be without him."

Aubrey scoffed, her expression softening with understanding. "Yes, you do. Six years is a decent amount of time, Sis, but in the grand scheme of things, it's nothing. You had a life before Anthony. You just gotta remind yourself of it."

"She's right, Whit. Unless you can categorically say you'd be happy and fulfilled in a non-monogamous relationship." William's words hung in the air between them, heavy with implication.

Whitley knew she wouldn't be. It wasn't how she was built; it wasn't who she was at her core. She wanted a partner who only wanted to be with her—who chose her every single day. "No, I wouldn't be happy," she whispered sadly, the admission feeling like another small death.

Dabbing her face with a napkin, careful not to smudge what remained of her makeup, Whitley pulled herself together with visible effort. She knew people would be watching, probably hoping for a little more drama to spice up their evening, but she wouldn't give them the pleasure. Tonight was about celebrating and raising money for the foundation. Clearing her throat, she plastered on a smile that didn't quite reach her eyes.

"Okay, I need to stop talking about him. Just for now. Tomorrow you can help me deal, but tonight I need to focus on the party."

And what a party it was! The DuPont Christmas bash was the social event of the year, the kind of gathering that people talked about for months afterward. Anyone who was anyone hankered to be on the guest list, and invitations were coveted like precious gems. Whitley's mother was in charge of the event and always managed to upstage herself every year, creating experiences that left guests breathless. Tonight's party was all about elegance and magic, a winter wonderland brought to life in the most opulent way possible. It certainly wasn't a *costume-themed* shindig, but there *was* a theme, and most people had dressed to match, creating a cohesive visual feast. Greens, golds, and reds were the overall esthetic: the primary colors of Christmas, but in sequin form and smelling of expensive perfume.

Turning from the bar, Whitley took in the beautifully decorated hall with fresh eyes, trying to see it as her guests did rather than through the lens of her personal catastrophe. Twenty-foot Christmas trees lined the room, each one a masterpiece of decoration, perfectly decorated with thousands of twinkling lights, elaborate ornaments in shades of gold and silver, and delicate ribbons that caught the light as they moved in the gentle air currents. Whitley was in the midst of admiring one such tree, trying to lose herself in its beauty, when she spotted Anthony across the room.

Why is he still here?

"I thought douche canoe went home," William so very helpfully observed, his voice dripping with disdain. Aubrey craned her neck to see what she and William were looking at, her expression darkening. As the three DuPont siblings looked on in growing horror, Anthony—not so subtly—kissed the woman next to him, on the lips. It was brief, but noticeable enough that several other guests had turned to stare. The woman was petite and bleached blonde—everything Whitley wasn't—and she giggled like a schoolgirl at something Anthony whispered in her ear.

"Is he for real?" Aubrey gasped, snatching her gaze to Whitley with wide, disbelieving eyes.

Placing her glass on the bar with more force than necessary, Whitley's feet moved without conscious thought, her body operating on pure instinct and rage. Her mind went utterly blank as she glided over to the space where Anthony and whom she presumed was his new love interest stood huddled in the corner, laughing and giggling like teenagers at a school dance. The sound of their happiness grated against her raw nerves like nails on a chalkboard.

"Are you fucking kidding me?" Whitley heard herself say, her voice carrying across the immediate area and causing several heads to turn. She saw Anthony pale and the woman shrink back like a frightened animal. "You couldn't even do me the courtesy of seeing her in private? You felt I needed to be humiliated a little more?"

"No, Whit, it's not like that," Anthony stammered, his face now flushing red with embarrassment or guilt—she couldn't tell which and didn't particularly care.

Turning her face, Whitley scanned the Christmas tree immediately to her left, her vision narrowing with laser focus. In another fit of unconscious movement, her hand reached out, almost of its own accord. Whitley plucked off the biggest ornament she could reach—a heavy, ornate golden orb that felt substantial in her palm—and launched it at Anthony with all the force her anger could muster. The satisfying thunk as it hit her target sent a surge of vindictive pleasure through her system. As soon as it connected, Whitley reached for another ornament, and another, and another, her movements becoming more frantic with each throw. Silver bells, crystal snowflakes, delicate glass ornaments—all became ammunition in her arsenal of fury until Anthony was shrinking behind his new girlfriend like a coward.

"Get. Out!" Her voice was ice and fire combined, her body shaking with the force of her rage and humiliation. The words echoed through the suddenly quiet ballroom, cutting through the festive atmosphere like a blade through silk.

The silence that followed was deafening, broken only by the soft tinkling of ornament fragments hitting the marble floor. Every eye in the room was on them now, phones discreetly raised to capture the spectacle. Whitley stood there, chest heaving, surrounded by the glittering debris of her destroyed composure, finally feeling like she'd found her voice.

3

The First Noel in D Major & Festive Fury

Layla stilled her bow for the second time this evening, the horsehair trembling slightly against the strings as she processed what she'd just witnessed. The first pause was a well-timed, planned break arranged by the event coordinator, a sharp-eyed woman in an impeccable black suit who'd briefed them earlier. The quartet had been advised of the upcoming proposal and were ready to play a celebratory jaunt, their sheet music for "Wedding March" at the ready. However, that hadn't happened.

Instead of a happy announcement followed by Champagne toasts and congratulations, Layla watched in absolute horror as the guy floundered like a fish out of water and then rejected the absolutely stunning woman on her knee. The woman's emerald dress pooled around her like liquid silk, and even from across the ballroom, Layla saw the way the light from the crystal chandelier caught the tears threatening to spill from her eyes. Like, what the hell? Was he a complete moron?

Okay, looks weren't the greatest reason to say yes to a marriage proposal, but if Layla had a woman that stunning on her knee holding a ring—especially one that gorgeous, with those killer cheekbones and that regal bearing—she'd already be halfway down the aisle, planning their honeymoon.

Layla, Simon, Reena, and Puck watched with barely concealed fascination as the crowd gasped collectively and then began whispering behind gloved hands and champagne flutes, the sound rippling through the ballroom like a wave. They saw the good-looking man, his bow tie now slightly askew, whisk the stunning woman out of the room with what appeared to be urgent desperation. Only then did the four musicians regard each other with raised eyebrows and shared looks of disbelief.

They'd come to the conclusion they just had to do their job and maintain some semblance of professionalism, so the four-piece group started playing again with renewed vigor, hoping to distract the onlookers from the social catastrophe they'd just witnessed. Their efforts earned them a heartfelt nod from the lady in charge, an elegant woman with silver hair swept into a perfect chignon, and a dress so stylish she had to be in contact with Vogue directly. Layla had no idea who she was, except that she was obviously very rich. That much was clear from the diamonds dripping off her like expensive raindrops, and the natural air of...a sort of nobility that seemed bred into her very bones.

Layla had been stateside for two months now, and this was her first real paying gig that didn't involve standing on street corners with her violin case open for tips. Her three roommates, who were also the musicians sitting next to her playing their respective instruments, had told her these sorts of high-society parties were usually snooze fests filled with stiff conversation and lukewarm canapés, but they offered a decent paycheck that could keep them in ramen noodles for weeks.

As far as Layla was concerned, this Christmas wonderland was far from a snooze fest. Disregarding the drama of the proposal that had just unfolded like a car crash in slow motion, the people were all stunning in the effortless way that money seemed to buy, and the drinks were flowing like water. The Champagne alone probably cost more per bottle than Layla made in a week of busking. She'd seen more than one heated argument conducted in hushed, civilized tones and at least two hook-ups since beginning the mini concert, couples having disappeared behind towering Christmas trees for stolen moments. It was like watching a soap opera from inside the studio—absolutely fascinating and completely addictive.

They'd just hit their stride on "The First Noel in D Major," Layla's favorite arrangement she'd spent months perfecting, when she saw the gorgeous woman return to the party. The transformation was remarkable—she was ramrod straight now, her spine like steel, and her face had become a mask of...nothing: complete and utter composure that revealed absolutely no emotion. She must be a lawyer or something, because it was one hell of a poker face that would make professional gamblers weep with envy.

Layla watched with growing fascination as the woman glided over to whom she presumed were family members. They all looked kind of the same, with that aristocratic bone structure and confident bearing that spoke of generations of good breeding and old money. Then the three younger ones, including said gorgeous woman, whom Layla presumed were siblings based on their similar features and protective body language, headed for the bar with determined strides. If Layla didn't know the music like the back of her hand, every note and rhythm ingrained in her muscle memory from years of practice, she'd probably have fluffed it up by now with how completely invested she was in the unfolding drama.

Snapping back into professional mode with visible effort, Layla began to play again, losing herself in the music, letting the familiar melody wash over her like a warm embrace. The violin sang under her skilled fingers; each note pure and clear in the acoustically perfect ballroom, until a weird sort of whimpering sound, like an animal in distress, made her stop mid-note and stare in confusion. This was no well-timed gap in their carefully planned concert. Oh, no. There was an audible screech of their bows against strings as they stopped suddenly to see what was happening, the harsh sound cutting through the elegant atmosphere like nails on a chalkboard.

In the far corner of the room, near one of the magnificent twenty-foot Christmas trees that dominated the space, Layla could see the lovely lady plucking baubles off the perfectly decorated branches with increasing fury. She couldn't help the snort of surprised laughter which escaped her lips as the woman proceeded to use the expensive decorations as projectiles, firing them in rapid fashion with the accuracy of a trained marksman at...oh, at the good-looking man who had just rejected her so publicly.

Obviously, things weren't hunky-dory then, and the woman had reached her breaking point. The entire room had come to a complete halt, conversations dying mid-sentence, champagne glasses frozen halfway to lips, as everyone watched in fascination as the guy got thoroughly pummeled by flying Christmas ornaments.

There was no point in pretending they weren't watching this spectacular meltdown, so Layla carefully laid her violin in its velvet-lined case with practiced precision and stood to get a better look at the show. An older gentleman, distinguished and clearly someone of importance based on how others deferred to him, stepped up beside the hottie and said something Layla couldn't hear from across the room. Whatever it was made the good-looking guy visibly pale and fidget with his bow tie like a nervous schoolboy.

God, she wished she had popcorn for this entertainment.

Eventually, two strapping blokes in all black—clearly professional security—escorted the good-looking guy from the room with the kind of efficiency that suggested this wasn't their first rodeo. Hot Lady deflated like a punctured balloon, her rage seeming to leave her all at once, and allowed the two younger ones she'd been necking shots with earlier to lead her away from the scene of destruction.

"Jesus," Puck muttered, his voice filled with awe, "I've never been to a party like this."

Puck, a man with weirdly long limbs that seemed to go on forever, was their cello player and looked like he'd been stretched on a medieval rack. He was Layla's best friend and actually called Puck—it wasn't a nickname his mates had given him. His dad really loved Shakespeare and had a twisted sense of humor when it came to naming his children.

Puck was from England, as was Layla, but his parents were dual citizens who'd moved back to the States for better opportunities when Puck turned seventeen. They'd always kept in touch, though, exchanging letters and emails across the pond, and when Layla mentioned she was looking to start an adventure and escape the suffocating predictability of her life, he instantly told her to get her bum on a plane and get to New York as fast as humanly possible.

So she did, with nothing but two suitcases and a head full of dreams.

They lived in a tiny apartment that could generously be called cozy but was more accurately described as cramped, with Simon and Reena, who had been playing at a tiny jazz bar when Puck was having a drink one night. They'd become fast friends, and the rest was history—completing their quartet of dreamers. The place was barely big enough for four people, with paper-thin walls and a kitchen that could fit maybe two people if they were very friendly, but it was theirs.

None of them wanted to be a part of the classical world via the usual methods—the stuffy conservatories, the rigid hierarchies, the soul-crushing auditions where one wrong note could end careers. They wanted to make a name for themselves by bringing their beloved genre into modern times, making it accessible and exciting for people who'd never set foot in a concert hall.

They busked on street corners and in subway stations, and picked up jobs like tonight's as often as possible, building their reputation one performance at a time. All four had crappy bar and café jobs to keep a roof over their heads and food in their bellies. Layla worked at a dingy coffee shop that smelled perpetually of burned espresso and broken dreams. But none of them would change a thing, especially not Layla.

This, being here and playing her music, was her dream: the vision that had sustained her through countless rejections and empty violin cases. Moving out of her parents' comfortable but suffocating house in the English countryside and forging her own path, in America no less, where anything seemed possible if you worked hard enough. She'd done London first, of course—played the streets and underground stations, making somewhat of a name for herself in the busking community. But it hadn't been enough to quench the restless feeling she had inside, like a fire that refused to be extinguished; like she was made for more than just surviving on tips and the occasional wedding gig.

Right now, though, she was made to sit back down by a glare so cold that Layla thought she'd physically freeze on the spot. The woman whose party this was—Mrs. DuPont, she'd heard someone call her—was boring holes into her with eyes that could cut glass, and for good reason. Layla *should* be playing the violin and maintaining the elegant atmosphere, not partaking in what was clearly a case of schadenfreude. Yeah, people could suck sometimes, but she didn't want to be one of them; didn't want to lose her compassion in pursuit of personal entertainment.

Retaking her seat with as much dignity as she could muster, Layla picked up her violin and gracefully placed it on her shoulder, feeling the familiar weight settle against her collarbone, and began a haunting rendition of "Silent Night." The melody flowed from her instrument like liquid silver, each note carefully crafted and emotionally charged. It was the only thing she could think of doing to turn the attention back on the musicians and away from the drama that had just unfolded. Puck, Simon, and Reena fell into the melody seamlessly, their instruments joining hers in perfect harmony, allowing Layla to lead them through the familiar carol with the confidence born of countless hours of practise.

She was a talented violinist even as a child, showing an aptitude that had her teachers calling her parents with excitement. In her formative years, she became somewhat of a prodigy, winning competitions and earning scholarships, but she always rebuffed the rigid rules of classical training that tried to box her creativity into acceptable forms.

The stuffiness of it all, the way they wanted to strip away everything that made music personal and meaningful, had driven her away from traditional paths. But she loved the violin with a passion that bordered on obsession. It was almost an extension of herself, as natural as breathing, and she couldn't imagine life without it cradled against her shoulder, so she continued to learn and play, but on her own terms.

Her parents, bless their supportive hearts, were just proud she'd found her passion so early in life. When Layla had told them she was off to London to busk and make her own way in the world, they'd cheered her on with an enthusiasm that brought tears to her eyes. When she then told them she was jumping on the next flight to New York to chase an even bigger dream, they'd hugged her close, told her how proud they were of her courage, and gave her a thousand pounds to help her get started in a new country.

Her body swayed naturally as she allowed the music to completely encompass her, the familiar trance-like state washing over her consciousness. The world could be on fire around her and she wouldn't notice, not when she was in her element. The ballroom, the drama, the watching eyes—all of it faded away until there was nothing but the music flowing through her fingers and the pure joy of creation.

4

Projectiles & Alley Encounters

Christmas carols were Layla's specialty, the genre that had become her calling card on the streets of London and now, New York. She'd learned early on that December was her best month to earn cash when busking, as people's hearts opened, along with their wallets, during the holiday season. So she'd concentrated on learning them all by heart, every traditional carol and modern Christmas song she could get her hands on, until she could play them while watching TV or having a conversation. Best of all, she was a talented composer in her own right and liked to mess with the old songs, adding a bit of flair and modern sensibility. It usually went down well with audiences who appreciated fresh takes on familiar melodies.

As she opened her eyes and cast a look around the room, Layla instinctively knew the song was a hit. The majority of the room had surrounded them in a loose circle, their faces enraptured by the magic Layla and her group were producing. The earlier tension had melted away, replaced by the warm glow of a shared musical experience. Hopefully, it meant the scary lady would forget Layla's earlier transgression and maybe even rehire them for future events.

With the drama over and normalcy restored, the night progressed as it should have from the beginning. The quartet completed their set list flawlessly and enjoyed every moment of it, playing everything from classical pieces to jazzy arrangements of holiday favorites. The audience was appreciative, applauding enthusiastically after each piece, and several people approached them during breaks to compliment their performance. At around half-past twelve, the guests began to filter out, getting into expensive cars and hired limousines, allowing Layla to breathe a sigh of relief. They could finally set their instruments down and think about going home to their cramped but beloved apartment.

Puck went and sorted out the payment with Mrs. DuPont while Layla, Simon, and Reena took advantage of the leftover Champagne on offer; the good stuff that probably cost more per bottle than they made in a week.

"Wanna come for a drink?" Reena asked, her cheeks flushed from the Champagne and the excitement of a successful gig. They often went to a bar to decompress after performances, dissecting what went well and what could be improved.

Layla shook her head, suddenly feeling the exhaustion of the evening settling into her bones. She was absolutely knackered and needed a good night's sleep more than she needed another drink. Tomorrow, she'd be up and out early to snag a decent spot in Central Park before the other buskers claimed the prime real estate.

"Not for me, ta," she said through a yawn she couldn't suppress. "My bed is calling, and I'm ready to answer."

"I'm up for it," Puck called, heading towards them with a rather fat-looking envelope that made Layla's eyes widen. "We made bank tonight, guys. Serious bank."

Layla peered into the envelope and gawped at the contents, her jaw practically hitting the floor. Jesus, were those hundred-dollar bills? She'd never seen so much cash in one place. "Shit, how much is there?"

"Too much," Puck replied with a grin that threatened to split his face in half. "I think Mrs. DuPont was happy we kept our shit together and got through the night without any major disasters."

"We are definitely celebrating," Simon blurted, his eyes wide with wonder at their unexpected windfall. It wasn't like the foursome saw a whole lot of money on a daily basis—they mainly lived on instant noodles and whatever was on sale at the corner bodega, for crying out loud.

"It's still a no from me," Layla added firmly, though she was touched by their desire to include her. "You guys shoot off and have fun. I need to use the loo, and then I'll be heading home to my lovely bed."

"Sure you don't want us to stick around and walk you to the subway?" Puck asked, concern creeping into his voice as he hefted his cello case up and onto his shoulder.

Layla shook her head with a grateful smile. "Nope, I'll be fine. Just be careful with your instruments, okay? And don't get too pissed."

"We'll go to Pink Pearl," Reena announced. "Parker will let us stash them in her office like always."

Pink Pearl was their go-to bar—a dive that had become their second home. It was cheap, cheesy, and full of queers—absolutely perfect for their little found family. Plus, Parker, the rather sexy owner with her sleeve tattoos and infectious laugh, had befriended them quickly and gave them open season on the little stage in the corner. Not a vast audience to play to, but an audience all the same, and every performance was practice.

Carefully tucking her violin case behind a heavy velvet curtain where it would be safe, Layla nipped to the bathroom to freshen up before the journey home. She'd only been in there for a few minutes, touching up her lipstick and finger-combing her hair, but the ballroom was completely deserted by the time she came back out. The silence was almost eerie after hours of music and conversation. Rolling her eyes at being abandoned, she collected her precious instrument and headed for the main doors, already mentally planning her route home. Locked—she was fucking locked in.

"Well, shit," she whispered to the empty ballroom, her voice echoing slightly in the vast space.

Not wanting to spend the night alone in an unoccupied building that probably had a security system she didn't want to tangle with, she turned tail and headed for the employee area she'd noticed earlier. There had to be an emergency exit somewhere—these old buildings always had multiple ways out for safety reasons. She'd risk setting off an alarm if it meant she got out of there and made it home to her warm bed instead of sleeping on a ballroom floor.

With a skip in her step and renewed energy at the prospect of escape, Layla grinned to herself as the green neon light of the exit sign lit up the service corridor like a beacon of hope. Without pause, she pushed through the heavy door and braced for a siren or alarm to start wailing. Nothing but blessed silence.

"Jesus, fuck it's cold," she chattered through gritted teeth, her breath forming white clouds in the frigid December air. Her teeth clacked together like castanets as she gingerly stepped through a pile of snow that had accumulated by the door. A set of footprints in the pristine white caught her attention, and against her better judgment and every outcome of every horror movie she'd ever seen, she followed them around the corner of the building, where she was definitely about to be murdered by some psycho killer.

Instead of a psycho killer, though, Layla stumbled upon a rather irate goddess launching...yep, Christmas decorations at the brick wall with impressive force and accuracy. They smashed on impact with satisfying crashes, showering the narrow alleyway with shards of glass and glitter that caught the streetlight like fallen stars. But that didn't deter the hot lady one bit. Nope, she just kept throwing with increasing fury, her face marred with a mixture of anger and deep sadness that made Layla's heart clench with unexpected sympathy.

It was only when a particularly large bit of shrapnel hit Layla square in the head, causing her to grouse and curse under her breath, that the woman registered her presence. It didn't go down well at all. She shrieked in surprise, lost her balance on her ridiculously high heels, windmilled her arms frantically in a futile attempt to stay upright, and then fell flat on her bum in the snow with a very undignified thump.

"Fuck, are you okay?" Layla asked with genuine concern, stepping carefully over the treacherous mess of broken glass and scattered ornaments to reach her.

"Great," the lovely lady mumbled sarcastically, her carefully constructed mask finally cracking. "Just fucking great." Her face crumpled like tissue paper, tears springing from her eyes as if a dam had burst, and she began to weep with the kind of raw, ugly crying that came from deep emotional pain. The sound left Layla completely unsure of what to do with her hands or her words.

Looking around the deserted alley, she made a quick decision. She couldn't leave this person on her own, in this state, in an alleyway in New York at nearly one in the morning. That was just asking for trouble, and despite being a stranger, Layla's conscience wouldn't let her walk away.

"Let's get you up, yeah?"

With a bit of muscle and some creative maneuvering around the expensive jewelry, Layla managed to get the mystery pissed-off lady to her feet. She was slim and elegant, but the damn bling she was wearing—the diamonds, the heavy necklace, the ornate earrings—must have weighed a ton and made the process more complicated than it should have been.

The woman flashed a small, watery smile that transformed her face completely. "Thank you. That's very kind."

"You're welcome," Layla replied, brushing snow off the woman's coat. She nibbled her lip nervously, weighing her options. "Um, would you like to get a cup of hot chocolate or something? You look absolutely freezing, and there's a decent all-night diner about three blocks from here."

She fully expected the woman to say no and politely decline. After all, they didn't know each other from Adam, and accepting invitations from strangers went against every safety rule ever written. But maybe that anonymity, that lack of judgment from someone who didn't know her story, was exactly what led her to take Layla up on her unexpected offer.

"I'd like that actually," the woman said with surprising firmness. "It's been quite a night, to put it mildly."

Huh. Should Layla admit she'd witnessed exactly how much of a "night" it had been for her? The proposal rejection, the bauble-throwing incident...all of it?

"Um...yeah, I was there. At the party, I mean. Playing violin."

The lady closed her eyes and breathed deeply, as if centering herself for whatever came next. Was she about to start launching shit at Layla now for being a witness to her humiliation?

"I see," was all she got, delivered in a carefully neutral tone.

"If it's any consolation," Layla said carefully, "I think he's a right tit for saying no. Anyone with half a brain would be lucky to have someone like you."

Two ice-blue eyes snapped open and fixed on Layla with laser intensity, studying her face as if trying to determine her sincerity. Holding her breath, she waited to see if her forthrightness was about to get her into trouble or earn her a slap across the face. The woman's grin started slowly, like sunrise creeping across her features, until it filled her face with genuine warmth and transformed her from beautiful to absolutely radiant.

"Yes. He is quite the tit, isn't he?" she agreed with a laugh that held the first notes of real joy Layla had heard from her. "I'm Whitley, by the way."

"Layla. And I know just the place for hot chocolate and emotional breakdowns."

5

Midnight Mass &
Musical Miracles

Why was she following a complete stranger through the deserted streets of Manhattan at nearly one in the morning? Whitley knew it was absolutely idiotic, potentially dangerous, and went against every safety rule her parents had drilled into her since childhood, but she still trundled along the sidewalk next to Layla in silent contemplation. This was a woman who had witnessed her at possibly the lowest point in her life, both socially and privately, and yet somehow didn't seem to judge her for the spectacular meltdown she'd just displayed.

The city felt different at this hour—quieter, more intimate, with only the occasional taxi cutting through the darkness and the distant hum of late-night revelers echoing from nearby bars. Streetlights cast long shadows on the snow-dusted pavement, and as they walked side by side, their breath formed white clouds in the icy December air.

"We're overdressed," Whitley mused, taking in her elaborate ball gown that now felt ridiculous outside the opulent ballroom, and then Layla's less flashy but still elegant dress. It was plain black with a slight shimmer that caught the streetlight, creating subtle patterns as she moved; a nice cut but not tailored to her body like Whitley's custom-made creation.

"It's from a charity shop," Layla said matter-of-factly, causing Whitley to snap her eyes up in surprise. "The dress, I mean. I can see you trying to figure it out, doing that thing rich people do when they're trying to place designer labels." Layla's smile was warm and without malice. "I picked it up for like twenty quid back home, just before I came to New York. I guessed I might need something smart to chuck on if I managed to get a posh gig like tonight."

"I...I'm not sure I understood most of that," Whitley admitted with a grin, finding Layla's directness refreshing after years of carefully coded social conversations. Layla's accent wasn't especially thick, but she spoke fast and used a lot of Britishisms that flew right over Whitley's American head.

Layla smiled back, her eyes crinkling at the corners with genuine amusement. "Thrift store dress. Twenty dollars. Better?"

"Much better. And it's lovely, by the way. You look beautiful in it." The compliment slipped out before Whitley could stop it, and she felt heat rise in her cheeks despite the cold air.

They fell into comfortable silence again, their footsteps creating a steady rhythm on the mostly empty sidewalk. Whitley sucked in some frigid air, hoping it would inject some feeling back into her emotionally numb body. The evening played over and over again in her mind like a broken record, but she still couldn't make sense of any of it. They'd been happy, hadn't they? Anthony had said he wanted to marry her and have children. He'd encouraged her to propose in the romantic way he'd always dreamed of. So how did they get from there...to this nightmare of humiliation and betrayal?

"Are you okay?" Layla's voice was soft, concerned.

Whitley looked around wildly, suddenly realizing she'd completely zoned out and stopped walking in the middle of the sidewalk looking like some kind of statue. Layla stood close by, close enough that Whitley could smell her subtle perfume—something floral and warm that seemed to cut through the cold night air. Her eyes were laden with genuine concern, and the kindness there made Whitley's chest tighten unexpectedly.

What could she say? Of course she wasn't okay. Nothing was fine. Nothing made sense anymore. Whitley's life as she knew it was irrevocably changed, turned completely upside down in the span of a few devastating minutes, and for the life of her, she didn't know how to navigate this new reality where everything she'd planned and hoped for had crumbled to dust.

"I..." She had absolutely nothing; no words to explain the chaos in her head or the hollow feeling in her chest.

"Hey...so this might sound weird, but...could I take you somewhere before we go to the diner?" Layla's voice was gentle, almost hesitant. "It's not far from here, maybe a ten-minute walk, but I think it might help you...decompress. Clear your head a bit."

Feeling her body begin to tremble, whether from the cold or the emotional shock she couldn't tell, Whitley nodded without hesitation. Why the hell not? What did she have to lose at this point? If she didn't follow Layla, her options were bleak and depressing. She couldn't go home to the penthouse—not when Anthony would be there waiting to ambush her with more manipulation and twisted logic.

Staying with her parents and siblings sounded awful in a different way. They'd overcompensate and drive her nuts with too much love and support, treating her like fragile glass that might shatter at any moment.

"Okay. Lead the way." She wanted to ask Layla what exactly she'd seen in the ballroom and how much of her humiliation had been witnessed. There was no need to ask why she'd been there—the violin case slung over her shoulder gave that away clearly enough. It was sad she hadn't had the chance to really listen to Layla play. The beginning of the evening had been spent worrying over the proposal, rehearsing her words and trying to calm her nerves, and well, the rest of the evening had been spent trying not to completely break down or actually murder Anthony with her bare hands.

Now she was worried about what the other guests had witnessed and what they were already saying in their cars and limousines on the way home—what Layla had witnessed. They weren't friends, barely knew each other at all, but Whitley still found the idea of this kind, straightforward person seeing what had happened nearly unbearable.

"We're here," Layla commented quietly, once again rousing Whitley from her intrusive thoughts that seemed determined to torture her. Lifting her head, she gazed up at the church that rose before them, its Gothic spires reaching toward the star-filled sky. The building was beautifully lit by ground lights surrounding the perimeter, casting dramatic shadows on the stone facade and making the stained-glass windows glow like jewels in the darkness.

"Oh, um...I'm not religious," Whitley said uncertainly, suddenly wondering what she'd gotten herself into. The last thing she needed was some kind of religious intervention or well-meaning sermon about forgiveness.

Layla smiled, her expression mischievous and knowing. "Me either, to be honest. But this ain't no ordinary church service, or midnight mass. Will ya trust me, practical stranger?"

The cheeky grin that accompanied her words made Whitley chuckle despite everything; the first genuine laugh she'd managed since the disaster began. Shrugging, she gestured for Layla to step through the large wooden doors that looked like they belonged in a medieval castle. With a quick inhale of the cold night air, she followed, not knowing what to expect.

The sound hit her first—voices raised in perfect harmony—a choir belting out Christmas carols like there was no tomorrow. Not unusual given the time of year and the setting, but there was something different about these voices; something raw and powerful that made her pause just inside the doorway. It was the ragtag bunch of kids she saw making the angelic sound that made her breath catch in her throat.

"Come and sit down," Layla whispered, her voice barely audible above the soaring melody.

The church was lit by what seemed like hundreds of candles, their flickering flames casting dancing shadows on the ancient stone walls and creating an atmosphere that was both sacred and magical. Sinking onto the nearest wooden pew, its surface worn smooth by countless worshippers over the decades, Whitley turned her entire body toward the altar. Some kids were sitting cross-legged on the floor, others lounging against pillars or meandering around the space as if it were their living room, but they were all singing with voices that seemed to come straight from heaven. "O Come All Ye Faithful" had never sounded so beautiful, so pure, so filled with genuine joy and hope.

They sat there in reverent silence for several more carols, each one more beautiful than the last. Whitley's mind, for the first time all evening, was solely focused on the present moment, soaking up the raw talent being displayed by these unlikely angels. The music seemed to wash over her like a healing balm, easing some of the tension from her shoulders and the ache from her heart.

When the voices finally faded, the silence was palpable, heavy with the lingering echoes of their performance. The other people dotted around the church—and Whitley now noticed there were maybe a dozen others, all sitting quietly and listening with the same rapt attention—held their collective breath until one of the kids whooped in pure delight. The spell broken, the group immediately burst into raucous clusters of conversation and laughter, their voices echoing off the vaulted ceiling.

Turning to Layla, Whitley sat with her mouth hanging open for several seconds, completely speechless. Layla laughed at her expression, clearly delighted by her reaction.

"Good, right?" she said with obvious pride, as if she'd personally trained each young voice.

"They were absolutely fantastic. I..." Whitley struggled to find adequate words. "Are they a professional choir? Some kind of youth program from a music school?"

Wrapping her coat a little tighter around her slender body, Layla shook her head with a sad smile. "Nope. All homeless kids, every single one of them."

Whitley turned back to the group with fresh eyes, her heart clenching as she took in details she'd missed before. On closer inspection, she could see they wore clothes that were far too big or far too small; hand-me-downs and charity donations that didn't quite fit. Most looked like they hadn't had access to proper washing facilities in days, their hair unkempt and their faces bearing the telltale signs of life on the streets.

"All of them?"

"Yup. They come here most nights after the usual midnight mass is finished, when the church is supposed to be empty."

"And the priest doesn't mind? He allows this?"

"Nope, he doesn't mind at all. Actually encourages it, from what I understand." Layla's voice was warm with admiration. "Keeps the kids safe and warm for a few hours and gives them something positive to focus on instead of just surviving."

"How am I only just finding out about this?" Whitley asked, genuinely bewildered. She thought she was pretty well versed in the comings and goings of the city, including the various programs and initiatives that served the community. After all, her family owned a significant portion of Manhattan real estate, and she was especially knowledgeable about anything related to the arts. But these kids were completely new to her, and they clearly deserved so much more than a drafty church to keep them safe at night.

Standing with practiced grace, she smoothed down her ball gown, the expensive fabric rustling softly in the hushed atmosphere, and tried to ignore the curious stares from the other late-night visitors scattered throughout the pews.

"Excuse me for a moment, Layla."

Walking down the aisle with the confidence that had been bred into her from birth, she met the eyes of several teens who regarded her with immediate caution and suspicion—understandably so. She probably looked like some kind of fairytale princess who'd wandered into their world by mistake, all diamonds and designer silk in a place where survival was the primary concern.

"Good evening," she began, waiting patiently for them to quiet down and give her their attention. It took a little while, conversations gradually dying as word spread through the makeshift choir that the fancy lady wanted to speak, but finally the entire group turned their full attention to Whitley with expressions ranging from curious to openly hostile.

"Your performance was absolutely outstanding," she continued, her voice carrying clearly in the acoustically perfect space. "Truly extraordinary. Do you have any kind of representation? Management? Someone helping you develop your obvious talents?"

A young woman, probably close to eighteen with fierce eyes and protective body language, scoffed loudly. "Lady, does it look like we have representation?" Her tone was sharp, defensive, clearly expecting some kind of condescending charity pitch.

"Would you like it?" Whitley asked simply, cutting straight to the heart of the matter.

The teen squinted suspiciously, moving protectively in front of several younger kids who couldn't have been more than twelve or thirteen. "Who are you, exactly? What do you want from us?"

"My name is Whitley DuPont," she replied, letting the weight of that name settle over the group.

"Shit, Jas, she's like super rich!" a boy around twelve shouted from the back of the group, his voice echoing off the stone walls. "My mom used to clean one of their buildings before she got sick!"

Whitley laughed, the sound genuine and warm. "Indeed, I am quite wealthy. I also run a foundation specifically for gifted musicians such as yourselves. Young people with extraordinary talent who need support and opportunities."

Another scoff from Jas, but Whitley could see interest flickering in her eyes despite her defensive posture. "We're just messing around, keeping warm. Nothing special about it."

"How would you like to stop *just messing around* and do this for real?" Whitley asked, her voice filled with the kind of quiet authority that came from years of boardroom negotiations and charity galas. "Professional training, proper venues, recording opportunities, the works."

The group exchanged meaningful looks, a complex web of silent communication passing between them. These kids had clearly been together for a while and had developed their own family structure and hierarchy with Jas as their obvious leader and protector.

"Here, take my card," Whitley said, pulling out an elegant business card from her small evening purse. "Think it over carefully. If you're interested, we'll meet somewhere comfortable for you, discuss exactly what's on offer, and then decide together if we want to move forward. No pressure, no strings attached."

"Just like that?" Jas said, her voice heavy with skepticism born from years of disappointments and broken promises from adults.

"Just like that. I know talent when I hear it, and you all have it in spades—more raw musical ability than I've heard in some professional venues." Whitley's voice was completely sincere. "The foundation can help you with housing, proper clothes, education, healthcare, whatever you need to succeed. If you want it."

She watched Jas look around the group, clearly the decision-maker despite her young age. Several kids were nodding eagerly, their eyes bright with hope, while others looked more cautious, probably having been burned before.

"We need to talk about it," Jas said finally, her tone slightly less hostile but still carefully guarded.

"Of course. That's exactly what you should do." Whitley smiled, reaching into her purse again. "Here's some money to use if you decide to call. For phone cards, food, whatever you need while you're making your decision."

"We don't need your charity," Jas said sharply, but her eyes lingered on the bills in Whitley's outstretched hand.

Whitley laughed, the sound echoing warmly through the sacred space. "Jas...may I call you that?" The girl gave a small, grudging nod. "This isn't charity, it's an investment in your futures. You have something special here, something that could change your lives completely. Please take it, and I genuinely hope to hear from you soon."

Taking a step back, Whitley tried to make eye contact with every child in the group, smiling warmly at each young face. Some smiled back tentatively, others remained guarded, but she could see the wheels turning in their minds.

"Have a wonderful night, all of you. Keep making that beautiful music."

Whitley was passionate about the program, and she hoped Jas took her up on the offer. She'd started the foundation in memory of her childhood best friend, Malory James, who had been a gifted savant on the piano. Malory had come from privilege, like Whitley, however her father lost the family fortune as Malory was on the cusp of becoming great. Malory's once-guaranteed future suddenly became unattainable.

Unfortunately, Malory had passed away at only fifteen years old from a drug overdose when she'd been refused entry into one of New York's top musical schools due to her lack of funding, and frankly, the family name being blacklisted in society. The snobbery made Whitley feel sick.

When Malory's dreams were shattered, she'd spiraled. Whitley had never forgiven herself for not being able to help Malory. She'd not grasped the severity of what Malory was going through. As Whitley got older, she made a promise to help as many young musicians as she could. She couldn't solve the world's problems, but she could do *something*, and the music foundation was her contribution and way of keeping Malory's memory alive and thriving.

6

Really Bad English Tea & Unexpected Comfort

L ayla was waiting by the heavy wooden church door, her violin case slung over her shoulder and an expression of curious admiration on her face. "What was that about? You looked like you were conducting some kind of business meeting."

"Just having a chat about possibilities," Whitley said mysteriously, not wanting to jinx anything by talking about it too much. "Now, how about that hot chocolate you promised? I think I could use something warm and sweet right about now."

They walked through the quiet streets to the closest all-night diner, a classic New York establishment with red vinyl booths and fluorescent lighting that had probably looked exactly the same for the past thirty years. They slid into a booth near the window, and Whitley ordered a hot chocolate while Layla requested a cup of tea.

"I don't know why I keep ordering it," Layla said with a rueful shake of her head as the waitress walked away. "You Americans make absolutely piss-poor tea. It's like drinking flavored water with delusions of grandeur."

Whitley smiled, finding Layla's bluntness refreshing after years of polite social niceties. "Maybe you need to switch to coffee? When in Rome and all that?"

"Nah, never. It's tea all the way for me, even if it tastes like dishwater." Layla leaned back in the booth, studying Whitley's face with those perceptive eyes. "Anyway, how are you feeling? You look better than you did an hour ago."

Miraculously, she did feel better—not good, not whole, but definitely more stable than she had since Anthony's devastating rejection. "Thank you for taking me to see those children sing. They were absolutely magical and exactly what I needed to put things in perspective."

"Told ya it would help you decompress," Layla said with a satisfied grin.

Whitley regarded Layla through fresh eyes, really seeing her for the first time. This woman had unselfishly given up her evening to help a complete stranger, had shared something clearly meaningful to her, and was always smiling with genuine warmth. She was refreshingly forthright in a world full of people who spoke in coded language and hidden agendas.

"You *did* tell me, and I honestly can't thank you enough. You didn't have to do any of this."

"Eh, it's no worries at all. You had a right old banger of a night, didn't you? I would've been neck deep in eggnog by now if I were in your shoes."

"*A banger of a night*," Whitley repeated slowly, testing the unfamiliar phrase on her tongue. Suddenly, a laugh rumbled from deep in her throat, starting small and growing until she was genuinely giggling. Everything just felt so absolutely ridiculous when she looked at it from the outside. Here she was, sitting in a dingy diner with a British musician, after watching homeless kids sing like angels, because she'd completely lost her shit and thrown Christmas ornaments at her cheating ex-boyfriend in front of New York's social elite.

A sweet, infectious giggle came from across the table. Layla was watching her with dancing eyes, laughing along with obvious delight. "Sorry," she spluttered between her giggles. "When someone starts laughing, I literally can't stop myself from joining in. It's like a reflex."

Wiping a tear from her eye, Whitley impulsively reached across the small table. "Laugh away, please. If I don't laugh about this, I think I'll cry, and I absolutely refuse to waste any more tears on him."

The waitress appeared with their drinks, her voice cheerfully oblivious to the emotional conversation she'd interrupted. "Here you go, ladies. One hot chocolate, extra cream and mini marshmallows, just like you ordered. And one pot of tea with milk on the side. Or would you prefer cream?"

Whitley bit her lip to suppress another laugh as Layla physically recoiled from the steaming pot. "Milk is fine, ta."

They waited for the server to leave before continuing their conversation. Whitley licked off a giant glob of whipped cream, savoring the sweetness, as Layla poured out her tea with the resigned air of someone about to drink medicine.

"Fucking hell, it's like drinking piss," she grumbled after taking a tentative sip, her face screwing up in disgust.

"You should really switch it up if you're planning to stay here long term," Whitley suggested, amused by Layla's stubborn loyalty to terrible tea. "Is that what you want? To stay in New York City permanently?"

"Sure, I think so. I mean, I haven't got a solid five-year plan or anything like that. My roommates and I work as many gigs as we can get our hands on. We record sessions and post them online, trying to build a following. It's all very day-to-day at the moment." Layla waved her hand dismissively. "Anyway, this isn't about me and my musical dreams. You don't have to tell me anything about what happened tonight, obviously. We don't know each other from Adam."

"We don't." Whitley sighed, wrapping her hands around the warm mug. "But maybe that's what makes it easier to talk about. Lord knows my family is going to be a veritable nightmare of good intentions."

"Don't you get on with them?" Layla asked, genuine curiosity in her voice.

"We absolutely do, that's the problem. They'll over-support me, if you know what I mean. Hovering and fussing and treating me like I might shatter into a million pieces at any moment."

Layla laughed knowingly. "Got it completely. My parents can be a bit like that at times, bless them. Although it helps that there are a few thousand miles between us right now. I don't mind them fretting from afar—it's the up-close fretting that drives me mental."

"God, I wish that were the case for me. I'm probably going to have to move back in with them until I get this whole mess sorted out."

"Right, you live with the guy? Anthony, was it?"

She nodded, taking a moment to savor the smooth hot chocolate before answering. "We have a penthouse together on the Upper East Side. I presume he's there right now, either wallowing in self-pity or celebrating with his mistress."

"So he definitely cheated then? Is that why he said no to your proposal?"

Jesus, this was painful to talk about, but somehow necessary. "He..."

"Crap, you don't have to tell me," Layla interrupted quickly. "That was super rude of me to ask. I'm sorry."

"No, it's fine. I think I need to say it out loud to make sense of it." Whitley took a deep breath. "He wanted me to agree to an open relationship. He met someone else but still wanted to be with me too."

Layla scoffed and then waved her hand apologetically. "Sorry, but that's like the oldest play in the manipulative bastard handbook."

Whitley cocked her head, intrigued. "Meaning what, exactly?"

"Well, I'm guessing he's not of the same financial means as you, right?"

"You're referring to my wealth." Layla gave her a "no shit, Sherlock" look that made Whitley smile despite everything. "He has a good career as a corporate lawyer."

"Yeah, but I doubt he's as loaded as you and your family. I mean, I've no idea exactly who you are beyond the name, but judging by the size of that Christmas party and the fact that your surname is plastered on half the buildings in this city, I'm gonna hedge my bets you're all gazillionaires."

Whitley laughed, appreciating Layla's directness. "Close enough to gazillionaire status, yes."

"Right," Layla continued, punctuating her point with her index finger like she was delivering a closing argument. "So he ain't gonna let go of his meal ticket, is he? Not willingly."

Oh, that stung, but it also rang with uncomfortable truth. "I guess not."

"Shit, sorry." Layla winced, clearly seeing the pain that flashed across Whitley's face. "That came out harsher than I meant."

"No, please continue. I want to hear your theory." No one else in her life would be this brutally honest with her, and maybe that brutal honesty was exactly what she needed right now.

"Your family gives him access to money, power, and social status he could never achieve on his own. He's a cheating arse who, instead of doing the decent thing and leaving, wants to manipulate you into an open marriage so he can have his cake and eat it too. That's my guess, anyway."

Whitley sat back hard against the vinyl booth, the air leaving her lungs in a rush. Wow. Layla was absolutely right, and hearing it laid out so starkly made everything crystal clear. Whitley already knew Anthony was a creep after what he'd pulled tonight, but Layla had just shown her exactly how calculating and manipulative he truly was. He'd probably been sleeping around for years, and why this particular woman was the one he'd decided to come clean about was suddenly obvious.

"Oh my God." She laughed, but there was no humor in it. "He wanted to avoid a prenup."

"Um, what?" Layla looked confused.

"Anthony. The Tit, as you so colorfully named him earlier. By coming clean now and talking me into an open relationship, he hoped to avoid the whole prenup conversation entirely. I can see his strategy now: he'd wait for a while, let me get comfortable with the arrangement, and then bring up kids and marriage again. He'd be in the clear to sleep around, with legal protection."

"You weren't planning to have a prenup?" Layla asked, nearly choking on another sip of terrible tea. "Christ, I really can't drink this swill."

"I wouldn't have forced one on him. I trusted him completely."

"Wow, so if you'd divorced later, he would've been set for life. You really think he was that calculating?"

"He's a corporate lawyer who specializes in hostile takeovers. Of course he's that calculating. I can't believe I didn't see it before now."

It was Layla's turn to lean forward and offer a comforting hand, her fingers warm against Whitley's cold ones. "To be fair, it sounds like he knew exactly what he was doing and had been planning this for a while. Don't blame yourself for trusting someone you loved. It sounds like you dodged a massive bullet."

"Why couldn't I have dodged it a little less publicly?" Whitley sighed, thinking about all those phones that had undoubtedly captured her meltdown. "What an absolute mess."

"Pfft. It'll circulate the gossip mill for a few weeks, then something else will take the spotlight. Some celebrity will have a breakdown, or a politician will get caught in a scandal, and everyone will forget about your bauble-throwing incident." Layla's voice was matter of fact and oddly comforting. "What's more important is that you saw him for what he really is before you said 'I do.' Now you can get on with your actual life instead of wasting more years on a manipulative tosser."

"I'm really glad I agreed to have hot chocolate with you, Layla. Truly. I can't thank you enough for tonight."

A yawn stretched across the violinist's face and she covered it with her hand. "Damn, sorry. I'm absolutely pooped. It's been a long day and I've got to be up early tomorrow to claim a good busking spot before all the prime real estate gets taken."

The reminder of their very different circumstances hit Whitley like a cold splash of reality. "Where will you go tonight? Back to your apartment?"

"Yeah, back to our shoebox with my three roommates. It'll be fine." Layla stood and stretched. "Where will you go? Not back to the penthouse, I'm guessing?"

"To my parents' place. I'll be fine, too, just probably smothered with concern and hot soup."

Layla nodded, shouldering her violin case. "Well, it was really nice meeting you, Whitley, despite the circumstances. I hope life treats you well from here on out."

Whitley smiled up at her new friend—because that was what Layla felt like now, despite having known her for only a few hours.

"You too, Layla. Good luck with whatever musical adventures await you."

7

Pinstripes & Purple Hair

Layla had exactly twenty minutes to get to the Lower East Side, and she was absolutely going to be late. Flying in from Los Angeles at the last minute had been a colossal mistake, especially because she knew from bitter experience the weather in New York during December was notoriously unpredictable. And of course, because the universe had a twisted sense of humor, there'd been a massive blizzard that had swept across the East Coast, delaying her plane's landing by hours and turning what should have been a simple journey into an endurance test of cramped seats and crying babies.

So instead of arriving refreshed and ready to perform, she'd crawled into the tiny apartment she shared with her three roommates a full six hours later than expected, exhausted and jet-lagged. Mercifully, it left her with enough time for a quick shower, an unsatisfying nap, and a return to the streets to busk the life back into her soul before her next gig.

As she stood on the familiar street this crisp morning, soaking up the sounds and smells of the city she'd fallen head over heels in love with, Layla was so incredibly happy to be back. Back with her favorite people, back in the place that felt more like home than anywhere she'd ever lived. The honking horns, the smell of hot dogs from street vendors, the constant hum of eight million people living their lives—it all felt like a warm embrace after months of LA's artificial perfection.

It had certainly been a whirlwind of a year, one that had changed her life in ways she never could have imagined. A week after the bizarre DuPont Christmas party where she'd witnessed the most spectacular public breakup in Manhattan social history, Layla found herself with a job offer that seemed too good to be true. She strongly suspected Whitley had something to do with it, pulling strings behind the scenes with her family's considerable influence, but considering they hadn't exchanged contact information during their late-night heart-to-heart, she couldn't exactly ask for confirmation.

Puck, Simon, and Reena had practically shoved her out the door when she'd hesitated about accepting the West Coast gig, insisting she'd be crazy to turn down such an opportunity. So Layla had accepted the job, which was supposed to be a short contract in LA, recording film scores for independent movies—the kind of work that could make a musician's career if the right people noticed.

One score had turned into several more, each project leading to new connections and bigger opportunities, and before she knew it, she'd been living in LA for close to a year. The work was steady, the pay was better than anything she'd ever imagined, and she was building a reputation in the film industry that could have set her up for life. She could have stayed even longer if she'd accepted the permanent position they'd offered her, complete with a fancy title and a salary that would have made her parents weep with pride.

But Layla had missed New York with an ache that felt physical. She missed the freedom of busking on street corners, the unpredictability of never knowing who might stop to listen, the raw connection with her audience that studio work could never replicate. She missed her friends and their cramped apartment and their dreams of changing the classical music world one performance at a time. LA was too rigid, too polished, too concerned with image over substance. They wanted perfectly polished classical performers who could play exactly what was written without deviation or personal interpretation, and that simply wasn't who Layla was at her core.

So when Reena had called her three weeks ago, practically vibrating with excitement through the phone, to say that the DuPonts wanted to hire them again for their annual Christmas bash, Layla immediately booked her flight back to the East Coast. A flight that had been packed with pissed-off passengers dealing with delayed connections and crying children, everyone sniffling and coughing in the recycled air. The one major downside to winter travel—all the germs floating around in enclosed spaces, just waiting to knock you flat.

After roughly three hours of restless sleep on her lumpy old mattress, Layla was up and out on the streets with her violin, desperate to reconnect with the city through her music. She'd wanted to busk more than she'd wanted anything in months, needing to feel that direct connection with strangers who chose to stop and listen. The day had flown by in a blur of generous tips, a few cups of hot chocolate from her favorite street vendor, who remembered her order after nearly a year away, and a sizable crowd that had gathered by the end of the afternoon to hear her play.

But that's when she'd realized, with growing horror, she was going to be catastrophically late. She'd been too lost in the pure joy of performing; too caught up in the moment to properly monitor the time ticking away on her phone.

The twenty minutes she'd thought she'd had dwindled down to fifteen, then ten, then five, until she was running a full five minutes over her scheduled arrival time. They weren't due to begin performing for another half hour, but that precious time was meant for tuning their instruments, getting properly set up, and running through any last-minute changes to their set list. Puck was going to be absolutely livid, and not just because of her tardiness.

The bigger problem was that she hadn't had time to change into the elegant black gown that was expected for such a high-society event. Instead, she'd be playing Christmas carols to New York's elite dressed in black pinstripe slacks that hugged her legs perfectly, paired with a matching waistcoat that gave her a distinctly androgynous edge, and a crisp white high-collar shirt. Her sleeves were rolled up past her elbows in a deliberately casual way, and she had enough bangles and leather cuffs strapped to her wrists to stock a small boutique. Instead of the simple black flats that would have been appropriate, she was wearing her favorite black Doc Martens that had carried her through countless street performances.

Her hair was also a complete disaster from a formal event perspective. The sleek, professional bun that was expected was nowhere to be seen. Instead, Layla's natural dark curls were in full rebellious effect, bouncing with every step, and there was absolutely nothing she could do about it at this point. Nor could she do anything about the purple highlights she'd impulsively added during a moment of LA-induced boredom—streaks of violet that caught the light and definitely screamed "artist" rather than "refined classical musician."

At least her makeup was absolutely on point, she thought with some satisfaction. Silver eyeshadow that shimmered subtly in the light was paired with dark eyeliner that made her eyes pop dramatically. It was festive without being over the top, artistic without being unprofessional.

"Layla, where the fuck have you been? And why aren't you dressed properly?" Puck hissed as she skidded to a halt in front of her three friends, slightly out of breath from her mad dash through the city streets. They were in the same opulent building as last year, though she'd noticed the decorations were completely different during her frantic sprint past the main entrance. Not that she'd had time for a proper look as she'd sailed past the double doors and down the familiar service corridor.

"Alright, keep your knickers on," she replied with forced cheerfulness, trying to catch her breath. "I got a bit waylaid by the busking, so this is my outfit for tonight. Take it or leave it."

Reena snickered behind her hand, clearly finding the whole situation amusing, while Simon let a little "Oh shit" slip out as he took in her unconventional ensemble. Puck, however, went visibly red with a combination of stress and frustration.

"You absolutely cannot go out there dressed like that," he said, his voice rising to a near whisper-shout. "This is a black-tie event, Layla!"

"I am wearing black," she protested with a stubborn tilt of her chin, gesturing to her outfit. She knew he was absolutely right about the dress code, but Layla had a stubborn streak longer than the Brooklyn Bridge and twice as immovable. "Look, I'm here, I'm ready to play, and we're going to blow them away just like we did last year. No one's going to give a shit what I'm wearing once they hear the music."

Clenching his fists and muttering something that sounded like a prayer to the universe for patience, Puck picked up his cello case and led them out to the area designated for their performance.

"We're not on for the full night this time," he whispered urgently in Layla's ear as they got their instruments situated and ready. "Here's the set list—try to stick to it, yeah?"

"Can I interpret a bit? Add my own flair to things?" she asked hopefully, already knowing what his answer would be.

Puck scoffed, but there was resignation rather than anger in his voice now. "Why not? We're already breaking every rule in the book with you looking like that. If we're going to get fired or blacklisted from every decent gig in the city, we might as well do it in style."

Layla flashed him her most charming smile—the one that had gotten her out of trouble countless times before. "That's the spirit, Puck. Alright, let's get this show on the road and remind these people what real music sounds like."

Ignoring the raised eyebrows and barely concealed looks of shock from the elegantly dressed guests, Layla lifted her violin to her shoulder and began to play. She melted into an easy, familiar rhythm as she effortlessly glided her bow across the strings, eliciting the most wonderful melody that seemed to float through the air like magic. Yes, she might look completely out of place amongst all the diamonds and Dior gowns, like a punk rock fairy who'd wandered into the wrong party, but Layla knew her worth when it came to making music. She was so confident in her abilities, she decided to completely ignore the set list and launch into her own unique version of "Carol of the Bells".

Her interpretation was upbeat and fresh, infused with a modern energy that transformed the traditional carol into something entirely new while still honoring its classical roots. The melody danced and soared, incorporating jazz influences and contemporary rhythms that made the familiar tune feel alive and exciting. Puck, Simon, and Reena, despite their initial concerns about her appearance, once again followed her musical lead effortlessly, their instruments weaving together in perfect harmony as they had countless times before.

Layla came out of her music-induced trance to the sound of enthusiastic applause—loud, genuine applause that filled the ballroom with warmth. She couldn't help but smile broadly and send a triumphant wink over her shoulder to Puck, who rolled his eyes playfully but couldn't hide his own grin of satisfaction. The audience was clearly captivated, and wanting to ride this wave of success, they launched seamlessly into the next song on their list.

Similar to the previous year, Layla found herself people watching between songs, her eyes scanning the crowd of New York's social elite. No dramatic marriage proposals this time, thankfully, though she did spot a few heated conversations being conducted in hushed tones behind champagne flutes. She had specifically looked for Whitley throughout the evening, curious to see how she was doing after their late-night conversation the year before, but didn't catch sight of her until it was almost time for their performance to end.

The last song of the night was a jaunty, uplifting rendition of "We Wish You a Merry Christmas" that had several guests swaying along to the rhythm. The quartet received another enthusiastic round of applause as they took their bows and began the familiar ritual of carefully packing away their precious instruments.

Layla gently bumped Simon's arm as she secured her violin in its case. "So why aren't we playing for the full evening this time? Last year we were here until nearly midnight."

He shrugged, adjusting his tie, which had gotten slightly askew during their performance. "They've got some kind of special choir performing later, apparently. Mrs. DuPont said we were welcome to stay and watch if we wanted to."

"Are you planning to stick around?" Layla asked, genuinely curious about what kind of choir could follow their act.

Reena poked her head over Simon's shoulder, her eyes already bright with anticipation of their post-gig tradition. "Nah, we're off to Pink Pearl as usual. Want to come celebrate another successful performance?"

Layla was just about to answer in the affirmative, already looking forward to their usual decompression session at their favorite dive bar, when she caught sight of Whitley across the crowded room. The blonde woman gave her a brilliant, genuinely delighted smile and waved her over with obvious enthusiasm.

"I think I'll stick around and see what this mysterious choir is all about," Layla said, making a split-second decision that surprised even her. "See you all later. Don't get too drunk without me."

8

Reunions & Revelations

Carrying her violin case, Layla made her way through the throng of tipsy guests, dodging conversations about stock portfolios and vacation homes in the Hamptons.

"Well, look who it is," she said with a grin as she approached. "Whitley DuPont, in all her glory."

She wasn't sure if her deliberately laid-back greeting would be seen as rude in this formal setting, but Layla had never been one for excessive formalities, especially not with someone who'd already experienced her lack of filter.

Whitley's smile was radiant and completely genuine. "Layla I-don't-know-your-last-name, violinist extraordinaire. You played absolutely beautifully tonight. That version of 'Carol of the Bells' was inspired."

Giving a courteous bow of her head in acknowledgment of the compliment, Layla took a moment to really look at Whitley. She was just as stunning as she'd been the previous year, if not more so. Her blonde hair was swept up into an elegant updo with sparkly jeweled clips that caught the light and probably cost more than Layla's yearly rent. The ball gown was forest green this time instead of the emerald velvet from last year, but it hugged Whitley's curves in all the right places, creating a silhouette that was both sophisticated and undeniably alluring.

"Thank you kindly. We had an absolute blast up there," Layla replied, then studied Whitley's face more carefully. "You look well. Really well, actually. Much better than when I last saw you."

She didn't want to outright ask if Whitley had gone back to her manipulative ex-boyfriend, but she was genuinely curious about how the past year had treated her.

Whitley clearly caught on to the unspoken question, her eyes twinkling with amusement. "I am doing very well, thank you for asking. Much better than last year, obviously." She gestured to a tall man standing nearby, engaged in conversation with another couple. "I'm here with my date tonight, Steven."

Huh. Well, that didn't make Layla feel particularly great, but then again, seeing a beautiful woman with a man always left her feeling vaguely disappointed, even when she had no claim or expectation of anything different. Such was the life of a lesbian in a predominantly straight world.

"So, the 'tit' is long gone then?" Layla asked with characteristic bluntness, using their shared code name for Anthony.

Whitley snorted with laughter into her champagne glass, nearly choking on the expensive bubbles, which made Layla rather pleased with herself for breaking through that polished social veneer.

"Yes, he's completely gone. Ancient history." Whitley's expression grew more serious for a moment. "Oh, the choir is about to start their performance. I'm very much looking forward to hearing your professional opinion on them."

"Okaaayy," Layla replied, drawing out the word with curiosity. Sure, she was a musician, but that didn't automatically make her an expert on all things musical, especially not choral arrangements. Turning to face the makeshift stage area, Layla's mouth dropped open in complete shock when she saw the choir members step up to their positions. "Is...is that Jas?"

"Mmm-hmm." Whitley was practically beaming at her, clearly delighted by Layla's reaction.

Several more familiar faces stood out from the group, and Layla realized with growing amazement that she recognized the entire choir—every single member was one of the homeless kids from that midnight mass she'd taken Whitley to see the previous year.

"What? How is this even possible?"

"I told Jas to contact me, remember? I gave her my card that night at the church." Whitley's voice was warm with pride and satisfaction. "She was incredibly skeptical at first, understandably so, but eventually she and the rest of the kids learned to trust me and what the foundation could offer them. They've been a part of the DuPont Foundation for Gifted Musicians since February."

"Whit, that's absolutely amazing." The nickname slipped out naturally, and even though they'd known each other for just a handful of hours total, Layla felt a genuine bond with this woman. Despite their vastly different backgrounds, it felt like they'd been friends for years. "I can't believe you actually made it happen."

"They work incredibly hard and expect nothing but perfection from themselves," Whitley continued, her voice filled with maternal pride. "They've amazed all of us with their dedication and talent. What you're about to hear is the result of months of professional training, proper nutrition, stable housing, and unwavering determination."

"Is that what you went to speak to them about that night? After we watched them perform at the church?"

Whitley nodded, her eyes never leaving the group of young performers. "They were already great that night, raw and talented, but I knew they could be absolutely amazing with the right support and opportunities. I had the means to help, so it seemed like the obvious thing to do."

"That's really fucking incredible of you, Whitley. Seriously." Layla shook her head in wonder. "They look so different. Healthy. Happy."

"Regular meals and safe housing do wonders for a person's entire outlook on life," Whitley said simply, as if transforming the lives of dozens of homeless children was just another Tuesday for her.

Layla fell into respectful silence as the choir began their performance, and within the first few notes, she was completely captivated. They weren't just good—they were absolutely perfect, their voices blending in harmonies that seemed to come straight from heaven. Every single member looked confident and joyful, completely transformed from the wary, defensive kids she'd watched in that cold church a year ago. They drew the entire ballroom into their performance, creating a magical atmosphere that had even the most jaded socialites wiping away tears.

"I'm completely speechless," Layla whispered, genuinely moved by what she was witnessing.

"Whit, sweetie, I've been looking everywhere for you." A deep, slightly slurred voice cut through Layla's quiet contemplation like a knife. She flicked her eyes to the side, immediately annoyed by whoever thought it was acceptable to speak at such a volume when there were people performing.

The man who approached was tall, probably a good six feet, and handsome in that generic frat boy way that screamed privilege and entitlement. His hair was perfectly styled with what was probably expensive product, and his smile revealed teeth so white they could probably be seen from space. Layla couldn't help but wrinkle her nose in distaste as he slid a possessive arm around Whitley's waist without asking permission.

Right, so this was Steven then. Charming.

"I was just talking to a friend," Whitley whispered back, clearly trying to maintain appropriate volume levels during the performance. Steven, however, obviously didn't get the memo about basic concert etiquette because he continued to speak at full volume.

"Well, are you ready to get out of here yet? We've done all the necessary social rounds, haven't we? Time to head back to my place and have a party of our own, if you know what I mean." His tone was suggestive and presumptuous in a way that made Layla's skin crawl.

She could smell the alcohol on his breath from where she stood, and she could also see Whitley's face turning red with embarrassment. Rolling her eyes at his complete lack of social awareness, she turned towards him with her most intimidating glare.

"Oi, want to keep it down a bit? Some of us are actually trying to listen to these incredibly talented kids perform."

Steven flicked his bloodshot eyes to Layla, giving her a slow, dismissive once-over that lingered inappropriately on her unconventional outfit. "Sorry, who are you exactly?"

"I'm the person who's going to knee you in the nuts if you keep speaking so loudly and disrespectfully," Layla replied with deadly calm. "Those kids up there are putting on the performance of their lives, and you're being extremely rude by talking over them like they don't matter."

Not wanting to hear his inevitable snotty retort or witness Whitley's reaction to the confrontation, Layla took a deliberate step away from them and moved closer to the choir. She could hear a few moments of heated whispering behind her, followed by the sound of expensive shoes clicking away across the marble floor.

The choir finished their set to thunderous applause, and Layla spent the next hour chatting with Jas and several of the other kids, hearing about their incredible journey from the streets to this moment. Their stories were inspiring and heartbreaking in equal measure, and she found herself genuinely moved by their resilience and determination.

It was just past midnight when she found herself following the exact same routine as the previous year, minus the getting-locked-in part. She'd learned her lesson about checking exit routes. Still, she headed for the familiar emergency exit and pushed outside into the snowy alleyway, expecting to find nothing but empty darkness.

Instead, there was a very elegant woman casually leaning against a sleek black town car, waiting with a knowing smile on her face.

"Whitley." Layla chuckled, genuinely delighted by the surprise. "We really need to stop meeting in dingy back alleys like this. People will start to talk."

"Ah, but this time I'm not hurling Christmas decorations at brick walls in a fit of rage," Whitley replied with self-deprecating humor.

Layla stepped closer, noting Whitley looked much more relaxed than she had inside. "Shame, really. It was quite entertaining to watch last time. Anyway, what's going on? Everything alright?"

Rubbing her arms to ward off the December cold, Whitley stepped to one side and gestured gracefully towards the car door. "I was wondering if you'd like to get some hot chocolate. For old times' sake."

A warmth blossomed in Layla's chest that had nothing to do with the promise of a heated car. She knew better than to get excited over a woman who was apparently dating men, but she couldn't help the little surge of happiness that crept in with Whitley's invitation. There was something about this woman that drew her in, made her want to know more.

"I'm absolutely game," she replied with genuine enthusiasm. "I might actually order hot chocolate for myself this time instead of that tragic excuse for tea. No way I can stomach that dishwater again."

"I think that's a very wise decision." Whitley chuckled, stepping aside to allow Layla to pass and get into the luxuriously toasty car. "You can leave your violin in here if you want. Ryan will look after it."

"Absolutely, ma'am. Your instrument will be completely safe," the driver assured her with professional courtesy.

Layla smiled gratefully at Ryan before turning back to Whitley with a mischievous grin. "So, no 'tit number two' joining us tonight?"

Whitley burst out laughing, the sound filling the car with genuine joy. "Oh, God, no. Steven is definitely no more. It seems I'm absolutely doomed to date—"

"Complete and utter douchebags," Layla finished with a knowing smile, delighted to see Whitley continue laughing.

"Yes, exactly. Which is precisely why I told Steven to take a very long walk off a very short pier and thought it would be much nicer to spend time catching up with you instead. I'd much rather spend an hour with good company than go home to an empty apartment."

Layla grinned, feeling that familiar warmth spreading through her chest. "Well, I'm flattered that I beat out sitting at home alone. That's quite the compliment."

"I didn't mean it like that!" Whitley gasped, looking mortified at the implication.

Layla made exaggerated finger guns, her eyes twinkling with mischief. "Gotcha! I'm just taking the piss. Now come on, let's go get that hot chocolate and you can tell me all about your year of dating disasters."

9

Penthouses & Pussycats

Whitley sighed a deep, relieved breath as the car pulled away from the glittering lights of the DuPont Building, leaving behind another successful gala and, more importantly, another boyfriend officially dumped. Maybe she should be feeling upset about the end of yet another relationship, but the feeling of sadness or regret never materialized, no matter how long she waited for it to hit her.

Really, if she were being completely honest with herself, she'd known early on that Steven wasn't the one for her—wasn't even close to being the one. He was a pompous ass with an overinflated sense of his own importance, but after persistently asking her out for three solid months, wearing down her resistance with expensive flowers and constant attention, he'd finally managed to break through her defenses.

However, that didn't mean she was going to make the same devastating mistake she'd made with Anthony. No more holding on to toxic men for the sake of appearances, or because having someone by her side made her feel less lonely in social situations...which, in hindsight, was false anyway. Looking back with the clarity that distance provided, there had been plenty of times over the past year when she'd felt profoundly alone, even with a man by her side, surrounded by people at parties and events but feeling utterly disconnected from everyone around her.

Layla's unexpected presence tonight had definitely helped her move on pretty swiftly from the evening's romantic disappointment. Not that the party itself or the music had been in any way a letdown—it might have been her family's best Christmas gala yet, with record attendance and donations that would fund their foundation programs for months to come. But of course, Steven's boorish behavior and complete lack of social awareness had put a significant damper on what should have been a triumphant evening.

"So, not to be Captain Obvious here, but this definitely isn't the way to that charming little diner we went to last year," Layla said with amusement as she stared out the window at the increasingly upscale neighborhood they were driving through.

New York City really was breathtakingly beautiful in the snow, Whitley thought as she followed Layla's gaze. The white blanket transformed even the grittiest corners of the city into something magical, softening harsh edges and making everything look like a scene from a Christmas card.

"It isn't the same route, you're absolutely right. I should have asked first, but I thought we'd be much more comfortable if we shared an adult hot chocolate at my place instead of sitting in a crowded diner."

"Oh, fancy," Layla replied with obvious delight. "Sounds absolutely brilliant to me."

Whitley smiled at Layla's characteristically easygoing attitude and the way she seemed to roll with whatever life threw at her without complaint or drama. Considering that ninety percent of the time she was surrounded by stressed-out colleagues who treated every minor inconvenience like a major crisis, it was incredibly refreshing to soak in Layla's calm, adaptable energy.

The car pulled smoothly into the underground parking garage of Whitley's building, the heated space a welcome relief from the bitter December cold. Ryan maneuvered the vehicle expertly into Whitley's designated spot, her name painted in elegant script on the concrete wall. He was out of his seat the second the car came to a complete stop, moving around to open and hold the door for both women with the practiced efficiency of someone who'd been doing this job for years.

Eager to escape the lingering chill and get into the warmth of her apartment, Whitley jogged over to her private elevator as carefully as her heels would allow. She had the exclusive access that came with owning the penthouse. She pressed her thumb to the biometric scanner and waited for the familiar mechanical click that granted her entry to her sanctuary.

"This is some really fancy shit." Layla chuckled, her eyes wide with wonder as she took in the marble-lined elevator lobby and high-tech security features. "A nice step forwards in our friendship, DuPont. Although I think you'll be woefully disappointed when we eventually get to the stage of you seeing my place. I'm pretty sure my entire apartment could fit inside this elevator."

Tittering with genuine amusement, Whitley playfully pushed Layla into the elevator, enjoying the other woman's unfiltered reactions to her world. "Just wait until you see the view from upstairs."

They remained in comfortable silence as the elevator ascended smoothly to the top floor, the only sound being the quiet hum of expensive machinery. Whitley felt her body begin to relax for the first time all evening, and even though it was way past midnight and she should be exhausted, she found herself wide awake and energized. She was genuinely eager to spend some quality time with Layla, who, over the course of the past year, she'd come to miss in ways that surprised her.

Now and then, as Whitley went about her daily business—sitting in board meetings, reviewing foundation applications, attending social events—the bubbly violinist would pop into her mind completely randomly. She'd wondered if Layla had taken the job offer that Whitley had quietly arranged through her Hollywood connections. If she'd enjoyed the glitz and glamor of LA as much as the gritty authenticity of New York. If she would make an appearance at the party this evening, and what it would be like to see her again after all this time.

Layla let out a low, appreciative whistle when they stepped out of the elevator and into Whitley's sprawling open-plan penthouse. The space was pure luxury, Whitley knew that, without any false modesty. Every piece of furniture, every carefully chosen artwork, and every architectural detail had been selected to create the perfect blend of elegance and comfort. But more than just a showcase of wealth, it was her true sanctuary—the one place in the world where she could let go of all the expectations and responsibilities that came with being a DuPont. A place she spent as much time as possible in, hence the astronomical amount of money she'd invested in making it absolutely perfect.

"It's nice," Layla said with deliberate understatement, though her expression betrayed her genuine awe. "Not sure it beats that greasy diner, though."

Grinning at Layla's attempt to play it cool, Whitley immediately slipped off her expensive coat and peeled her aching feet out of the torturous high heels that had been slowly killing her all evening.

"Oh, God, that's so much better," she breathed with relief, wiggling her toes against the heated marble floor. "Do you mind if I quickly change out of this dress? I'm absolutely done with formal wear for the night."

"Go nuts," Layla called over her shoulder as she headed straight for the floor-to-ceiling windows that offered a panoramic view of Manhattan's glittering skyline. "Bloody hell," she mumbled under her breath, the awe in her voice causing a pleasant pang of something warm and indefinable to twist in Whitley's chest.

Shaking her head to dislodge whatever that feeling was—probably just pride in her home and pleasure at Layla's obvious appreciation—Whitley headed into her spacious bedroom and carefully slipped out of the designer gown. She desperately wanted a hot shower to wash away the evening's stress and the lingering scent of Steven's cologne, but it seemed impolite to leave Layla alone in the living room for that long.

Instead, she quickly changed into her most comfortable sweatpants and her favorite cashmere sweater, the kind of luxurious loungewear that cost more than most people's monthly rent but felt like being wrapped in a cloud. Feeling infinitely more like herself, Whitley padded back out to the kitchen area and headed straight for the stove.

"So, hot chocolate?" she called out, already reaching for her favorite saucepan.

Layla tore her gaze away from the spectacular view, but oddly, she didn't immediately answer. Instead, she just stood there and stared at Whitley with an expression that was difficult to read. Whitley waited patiently, assuming her guest was probably just overwhelmed by the change in scenery and the late hour.

She must be absolutely exhausted after performing all evening.

"Layla? Hot chocolate?" she repeated gently.

"Right, yes!" Layla finally answered, seeming to snap out of whatever trance she'd been in. "Alcohol and chocolate: the perfect combination for a night like this." She looked a little flushed, her cheeks pinker than they'd been moments before.

"Are you sure you're feeling alright? You must be completely exhausted," Whitley said with concern, studying Layla's face for signs of fatigue. "I feel terrible for dragging you all the way up here when I'm sure you'd much rather be tucked into your own bed getting some well-deserved sleep."

"I'm all good here, honestly," Layla assured her with a smile that seemed to chase away whatever momentary confusion had clouded her features. "I'm completely used to late nights—comes with the territory of being a musician. I'm just taking it all in, you know?" She gave an expansive flourish of her hands to demonstrate exactly what she was taking in. "It's absolutely gorgeous, Whitley. If this place were mine, I'd never bloody leave."

Warming the milk in her favorite saucepan, Whitley pulled two large ceramic mugs from the cupboard. They were the kind that were perfect for cradling in cold hands on winter nights. She might be an absolutely terrible cook who could barely manage to make toast without burning it, but she had perfected the art of making rich, decadent hot chocolate that could rival any fancy café in the city.

A series of loud banging sounds from the direction of the guest room alerted her to the imminent arrival of her feline roommate, and Whitley couldn't help but smile in anticipation of Layla's reaction.

Layla cleared her throat nervously. "Um...do you happen to own a mountain lion by any chance?"

"No, just a very large and extremely spoiled house cat." Whitley laughed, watching as an enormous Maine Coon cat sauntered into the room with the regal bearing of royalty. "Meet Milkshake. She's the true ruler of *Chez DuPont*, and she knows it."

"Christ, almighty, I could saddle her up and ride her around the living room like a pony," Layla said in amazement, staring at the massive feline who was easily the size of a small dog.

"That's definitely not something I'd advise trying," Whitley warned with amusement. "She's got quite the attitude and can be more than a little temperamental when the mood strikes her."

Stirring rich, dark chocolate into the warming milk, Whitley inhaled the sweet, comforting aroma that always reminded her of childhood winters and simpler times. "Here, grab it while it's hot," she called out, gesturing toward the steaming mugs. "I'll leave you to pour your own booze—help yourself to whatever looks appealing."

She was particularly partial to Irish cream in her hot chocolate and poured a generous glug of the smooth liqueur into her mug before adding the perfectly heated chocolate mixture. Sliding a mug across the marble counter to Layla, she watched with interest as her guest surveyed the impressive variety of high-end liquor Whitley kept stocked in her well-appointed bar area. She smiled with approval when Layla chose the same Irish cream she'd selected.

"Shall we make ourselves comfortable and sit?" Whitley suggested, already heading toward her plush sectional sofa.

Whitley sank gratefully into the soft cushions of her couch while Layla hopped around on one foot, trying unsuccessfully to remove her heavy boots without putting down her drink and risking spilling it on the expensive upholstery.

"I should have done this the moment I walked in. Sorry about the chaos," Layla apologized, still struggling with her laces.

The woman was pure, delightful chaos, and Whitley found her completely and utterly endearing in ways that surprised her.

"So," she said once Layla had finally managed to get settled, looking far more comfortable than Whitley would have expected a near stranger to be in her formal living space. Layla had curled her legs underneath her body and was hugging one of Whitley's expensive throw pillows like it was an old friend. "Tell me about your year. Actually, no—start earlier than that. Tell me about your childhood, your family, how you became the person you are."

"Starting with the really big, personal questions right out of the gate, huh?" Layla said with a grin. "Alright then, buckle up for the full biography. My name is Layla Carol Simmons. Thirty years old, though I've been told I don't look it. Originally from the absolute middle of nowhere in the UK—a tiny village where bugger all ever happens and everyone knows everyone else's business. My mum and dad are Roger and Beverly Simmons, both proper working-class folks who've never put on airs about anything. They own a modest semi-detached house with a little garden where Mum grows the most incredible roses you've ever seen. We had a dog growing up called Butter—a golden retriever who was dumber than a box of rocks but had the biggest heart in the world."

10

Tipples & Tales

Whitley settled back into the cushions, genuinely fascinated by this glimpse into a world so different from her own privileged upbringing.

"I started playing the violin when I was seven years old," Layla continued, her voice taking on a nostalgic quality. "Not because I desperately wanted to or showed any particular musical inclination, but because my parents desperately needed me to have some kind of structured hobby to channel my energy. I was somewhat of a handful growing up, if you can believe that."

Whitley rolled her lips together to suppress a laugh. "Mmm, I can absolutely believe that."

"Oi, enough commentary from the peanut gallery," Layla protested with mock indignation. "I thought you wanted to learn about my fascinating life story."

"My sincere apologies, Layla Carol Simmons. Please continue with your tale," Whitley said with exaggerated formality.

"Thank you very much. Right, where was I?" Layla paused dramatically, clearly enjoying having Whitley's full attention. "Right, so I had this violin basically shoved into my hands to give me something constructive to do other than drive my poor mum completely bonkers with my endless energy. Turns out I was a bit of a natural savant when it came to making music. Mr. Woodberry, my primary school music teacher, took me under his wing and started giving me private lessons after school. He was convinced I had real potential and suggested that my parents look into sending me to one of those fancy specialized music schools in London."

"But you didn't want to go?" Whitley guessed.

"God, no. I absolutely vetoed that idea immediately," Layla said with a shudder. "I didn't want to get trapped in some posh institution with a bunch of stuck-up little jackasses who'd look down on me for not speaking properly. You've heard how I talk—I don't exactly scream 'sophisticated classical musician', and even at that young age, I knew it would be absolutely awful. Plus, I had a brilliant group of friends in my village, and I couldn't bear the thought of leaving them behind."

Whitley shifted position to mirror Layla's relaxed posture, tucking her own legs beneath her. "What did your parents think about your decision?"

"They were absolutely wonderful about it, actually. They never pushed me or tried to force their own ambitions on me," Layla said with obvious affection. "When I told them I was perfectly happy continuing to play violin with Mr. Woodberry and didn't want to go away to school, they respected my choice completely. I did little concerts at the local town hall every Christmas, and that was enough for everyone."

"Ah," Whitley interrupted with understanding. "That explains why you're so incredibly talented at playing Christmas carols."

"Spot on, guv'nor," Layla said with an exaggerated cockney accent that made Whitley giggle. "I absolutely loved those Christmas performances. When it came time to finish secondary school, I told Mum and Dad that I wanted to get a regular job during the week and spend my weekends busking on street corners. They were completely supportive as long as I was happy and following my passion, which I definitely was for quite a while. Had a few girlfriends along the way over the years, but nobody particularly serious or worth talking about, really."

Whitley had suspected Layla might be queer based on various subtle cues, but she hadn't wanted to make assumptions or pry into personal matters. "So there's no special girlfriend waiting for you?"

"Nope, completely free and single at the moment," Layla confirmed with a casual shrug.

Swirling the remnants of her drink around the bottom of her mug, Whitley sighed contentedly. "Me too, obviously. Single again, but I definitely want to know more about your adventures. What made you decide to leave your village and try London?"

"Not much more to the story, really," Layla said modestly. "I eventually got restless and ended up busking in London for a few years, then somehow found my way here to New York. But enough about my boring life—can I ask you a question now?"

Whitley shrugged agreeably. "Of course, fire away."

"Why do you consistently date such complete and utter arseholes?" Layla asked with characteristic bluntness.

"Like, seriously, Steven tonight was just a blonde, slightly more obnoxious version of Anthony from last year. Have you got some kind of inexplicable weak spot for entitled frat boy douchebags?"

Placing her empty mug carefully on the glass coffee table, Whitley studied Layla's face with genuine curiosity. "I've honestly never met anyone who can be so incredibly forward and direct without coming across as rude or offensive. It's actually quite remarkable."

Layla scratched her head sheepishly. "I would apologize for being so blunt, but I honestly can't help it. It's just how I'm wired."

"Please don't apologize—I actually kind of love it," Whitley said with surprising honesty. "So many people in my world constantly placate and tell polite half-truths to avoid any potential conflict. It's incredibly refreshing to have someone just say exactly what they're thinking without all the social dancing. And to answer your very direct question: most of the men I meet are either in the same business circles as me or come from similar wealthy backgrounds. They're essentially products of their privileged environment, which more often than not turns them into the Anthonys and Stevens of the world."

"So why not search for romance in a completely different pond?" Layla suggested. "Date outside your usual social circles—find someone who brings something different to the table."

"Is that what you do when you're dating?"

"I certainly don't date other musicians, if that's what you're asking."

That was genuinely interesting. "Why not? Wouldn't you have more in common with someone who shares your passion?"

"Two reasons, really," Layla explained, counting on her fingers. "One, because we're all dramatic arseholes who take ourselves far too seriously, and two, because I actually want variety and different perspectives in my relationships. I absolutely love music—it's my entire life and identity—but I also like learning about completely different things from my partners. I want to be able to discover new worlds and ideas with my girlfriend. If all we ever had in common was music, I'd probably get bored pretty quickly."

Whitley scoffed with self-deprecating humor. "Well, you'd get pretty damn bored talking about finance and investment portfolios, that's for sure."

"Is that actually what you do for work?" Layla asked with genuine curiosity.

Stretching her legs out in front of her, Whitley was more than surprised when Layla immediately grabbed hold of her feet and placed them comfortably on her own knees. She couldn't help the involuntary moan of pleasure that escaped her throat as soon as Layla's strong fingers pressed expertly into the arch of her left foot, working out the tension from hours in expensive torture devices masquerading as shoes.

"Oh, God, that feels absolutely amazing," she breathed.

"Yeah, high heels are a complete bitch," Layla said matter-of-factly, continuing her impromptu foot massage. "So, you were saying about your career?"

"I'm in finance, yes—investments, portfolio management, that sort of thing," Whitley managed to say despite the distraction of Layla's talented hands. "I suppose I'm guilty of exactly the same thing you actively avoid. All my boyfriends have been in the same or very similar professional sectors as me, so our conversations and shared interests inevitably revolve around work and money."

"Well, now that you've identified the root of the problem, I fully expect to see you with some completely fresh blood by next Christmas," Layla said with authority.

"Ah, so we're already planning our next annual reunion, are we, Layla Carol Simmons?"

"It's become our tradition, hasn't it, Whitley DuPont?" Layla grinned. "Next year, it'll be my turn to ask all the probing personal questions about your life!"

"How about we extend tonight's conversation with one more drink?" Whitley suggested, not quite ready for their time together to end. "Something stronger this time, minus the hot chocolate. I can have Ryan drive you home whenever you're ready."

"Ah, twist my arm, why don't you," Layla said with exaggerated reluctance. "Plus, I have to admit that Milkshake over there has been eyeing me like I'm her next potential meal. I'm genuinely a little worried about what might happen if I try to move too suddenly."

Happy that Layla wasn't ready to leave just yet, Whitley carefully extracted her feet and scampered over to her well-stocked, rolling beverage cart, selecting a bottle of top-shelf bourbon.

"Here, this should keep you nice and warm," she said, pouring them each a generous glass of the amber liquid.

"Or send me straight to sleep—one or the other," Layla replied with a wink that sent that strange, twisty feeling racing through Whitley's chest again.

"So tell me honestly—how was LA?" Whitley asked, settling back onto the couch.

"Now how could you *possibly* know that I've been in LA, Whitley DuPont?" Layla asked with mock suspicion, though her eyes were twinkling with amusement.

"A little birdie might have mentioned it," Whitley replied evasively.

Layla slapped her thigh and barked out a delighted laugh, her dark curls bouncing as she moved her head. Whitley found herself oddly mesmerized by the way the light caught the purple highlights in Layla's hair.

"I bloody knew it was you!" Layla exclaimed triumphantly. "There was no way some random film executive from LA just happened to offer me a dream job out of nowhere. You didn't have to do that, you know."

Snapping herself out of whatever trance she'd fallen into while watching Layla's animated expressions, Whitley took a sip of her bourbon to steady herself. "You were incredibly kind to me that night when I was at my absolute lowest point. Not many people would have done what you did—taking a complete stranger under your wing like that. Plus, you're genuinely gifted as a violinist, and I just wanted to lend a helping hand if I could."

"Well, I truly appreciate it," Layla said with sincere gratitude. "It definitely helped me build up my savings account, which is always nice for a perpetually broke musician."

"But you didn't want to stay in LA permanently?"

"No, not really," Layla said thoughtfully. "LA is undeniably cool for a little while, and the work was steady and well-paying, but I'm definitely much more of an East Coast person at heart, I reckon."

Hopping up from the couch to pour herself another drink, Whitley glanced back toward Layla to ask if she wanted a refill. She definitely wasn't prepared to catch her guest openly staring at her ass with an expression of obvious appreciation. She also wasn't prepared for the sharp ping of excitement that thrummed through her entire body in response, sending heat racing through her veins in a way that was both thrilling and completely unexpected.

Silk Sheets & Morning Confessions

Layla was not in her own bed. She'd know by the familiar knot in her back if that were the case, the result of a mattress that had seen better days and springs that had given up the fight years ago. Plus, there was no draft around her neck from the poorly sealed window in her shared apartment that let in every bit of New York's winter chill. Instead, there was the luxurious feel of silk against her skin and a comfort she'd never experienced before, like being wrapped in a cloud of expensive softness.

Rolling over, she made it to the edge of the expansive mattress that seemed to go on forever. Not a morning person by any stretch of the imagination, Layla rose like the dead, stumbling towards the closest door with the grace of a newborn giraffe. Her mind was foggy with sleep and the lingering effects of last night's bourbon, and her hair was undoubtedly massive. She hadn't tied it up before falling asleep, so the likelihood that it now resembled a bird's nest was astronomically high.

The penthouse was quiet except for the distant sounds of the city far below, muffled by expensive soundproofing that made the space feel like a sanctuary floating above the chaos of Manhattan. Following the rich, enticing smell of coffee that beckoned to her like a siren song, she finally came across proof of life in the gleaming kitchen area.

Whitley sat at the breakfast bar in the same comfortable sweatpants and cashmere sweater she'd had on the night before, looking effortlessly elegant even in loungewear. Her blonde hair was slightly mussed from sleep, and she wore a pair of reading glasses that made her look both intellectual and incredibly attractive as she scrolled through what appeared to be financial reports on her tablet.

Right! You crashed at Whitley's last night, and she's still hot as hell even first thing in the morning. She's also staring at you like you're some kind of fascinating creature.

Looking down at herself, Layla winced with embarrassment. She hadn't put her jeans back on after their late-night conversation had turned into an impromptu sleepover. Standing there in just her crumpled white shirt that barely covered her thighs, her bare legs on full display, she sent a silent thank you to whatever gods might be listening that she'd at least had the foresight to shave prior to leaving her apartment yesterday morning.

"Tea?" Whitley's voice was slightly huskier than normal, roughened by sleep in a way that sent an unexpected thrum of excitement through Layla's little gay heart. Women were just absolutely the best, especially this woman, who somehow managed to look like a goddess even at what had to be an ungodly hour of the morning.

"Yes, please. Desperately," Layla replied, suddenly very aware of her state of undress and the way Whitley's eyes seemed to linger on her exposed legs. "Um, I'll just go put some trousers on first. Probably should have done that before wandering around your fancy apartment half-naked."

Swiveling on her heels with as much dignity as she could muster, she race-walked in the direction she'd come from, hoping her sleep-addled brain could remember which of the multiple bedrooms she'd crashed in. The penthouse was enormous, with what seemed like endless hallways and doors leading to rooms she hadn't even seen. Mercifully, there was only one door standing open, and the pile of her clothes scattered across the pristine hardwood floor confirmed she was in the right place.

Grumbling at how absolutely stupid she'd been to strut out there wearing nothing but a shirt like some kind of walk-of-shame cliché, Layla shook her head at her lack of morning awareness. She shouldn't have stayed the night at all, really. But then again, she hadn't exactly been in much of a state to traverse the city safely. One drink had turned into several, and Layla had already been completely knackered from her long day of travel and performing. The alcohol had expedited her need for sleep tenfold, making her eyelids heavy and her limbs loose and relaxed.

That was why she'd agreed to stay when Whitley had offered, she told herself firmly. It had nothing whatsoever to do with the fact she'd wanted to be close to Whitley for as long as possible, knowing the likelihood of them seeing each other again anytime soon was frustratingly low. Their annual gala meetups were fleeting moments of connection in otherwise separate lives. Whitley came from a completely different world—one of privilege and responsibility that Layla had no intention of frequenting on a regular basis.

Knowing her time in this luxurious penthouse was almost up, she didn't feel too weird about smoothing her hand over the silk sheets one last time, memorizing the incredible softness against her palm. She'd probably dream about that bed for weeks to come, comparing every future bed to this standard of absolute comfort.

With a final check in the full-length mirror to make sure she was decent and presentable, Layla rejoined Whitley at the kitchen breakfast bar, trying to ignore the way her heart skipped when the other woman looked up and smiled.

"Did you sleep okay?" Whitley asked, pushing her reading glasses up to perch them on top of her head in a gesture that was both casual and incredibly sexy.

Layla's mouth went completely dry at the sight. Everything about this woman was a turn-on, from her effortless elegance to her genuine kindness and the way she looked in those perfectly fitted sweatpants.

Why were lesbians cursed with constantly catching feelings for straight women? Maybe it was the universe's way of balancing out the fact that women were just so inherently awesome. That's what Layla reasoned, anyway, though it didn't make the situation any less frustrating.

"Sound as a pound," she replied automatically, then caught Whitley's blank, confused stare and quickly translated. "I slept great—absolutely fantastic. Those sheets are completely ridiculous, like sleeping on a cloud made of silk and dreams. Do you ever just get the urge to slide across them naked just for the pure sensory experience?"

"Um, I can't say that particular thought has ever crossed my mind," Whitley chuckled, a slight blush coloring her cheeks at the mental image Layla had just planted.

Layla took a grateful sip of her tea, which was, predictably, absolutely perfect. "You should try it sometime. It would be fun. I guarantee."

"I feel a little strange seeing you here like this," Whitley said suddenly, her voice soft and contemplative.

"Shit, I can go—" Layla started, immediately moving to stand up, assuming she'd overstayed her welcome.

Whitley frantically waved her hand, nearly knocking over her coffee mug in her haste to stop Layla from leaving. "No, no, I didn't mean it like that at all! I'm just so used to seeing you for a couple of hours once a year and then not seeing you again until the next Christmas. This feels different, more...intimate, I suppose."

"We've only actually met once before last night," Layla pointed out, settling back onto her stool.

Whitley shrugged, a small smile playing at the corners of her mouth. "It seems like much longer, though, wouldn't you agree? Like we've known each other for years instead of just a few chance encounters."

Layla placed her now empty teacup down on the marble countertop with a soft clink. "Yeah, that is pretty weird when you think about it. Like, we've spent what, maybe three hours together total prior to last night, and yet it feels like we've been friends forever. Does that sound super corny and ridiculous?"

Whitley laughed, the sound warm and genuine. "Maybe a little corny, but I completely get it. There's something about you that feels familiar, comfortable."

The strangled, gurgling sound of Layla's empty stomach suddenly cut through the peaceful morning atmosphere, echoing embarrassingly loudly in the quiet kitchen and leaving her wide-eyed and more than a little flushed with mortification.

"Jesus, sorry about that. I guess I should probably get out of your hair and go find some food somewhere," she said, already mentally calculating whether she had enough cash for a decent breakfast at the diner.

But Whitley was up and moving across to her massive, restaurant-quality refrigerator before Layla had even finished her sentence. "Absolutely not, that's nonsense. I've got plenty of food here. What do you want? Eggs and bacon? That's a proper British thing, right?"

"It is, but you really don't have to go to any trouble for me," Layla protested, though her stomach chose that moment to growl again, betraying her hunger.

"Let me cook for you, please," Whitley replied, her eyes genuinely pleading in a way that made Layla's heart do strange fluttering things in her chest.

That thrumming sensation of attraction was back again, stronger than ever, and Layla had to fight hard to keep it locked down and under control. Whitley was absolutely her dream woman in terms of looks alone, never mind the fact she was also incredibly kind and caring, and somehow put up with Layla's tendency towards blunt, unfiltered commentary.

"You have a dangerous habit of twisting my arm, Whitley DuPont," she said with a grin. "Alright, I'd absolutely love some breakfast. Thank you."

Whitley sent her a dazzling smile that could have powered half of Manhattan, and immediately set about gathering ingredients from her well-stocked kitchen.

Needing more caffeine to fully wake up and process this surreal domestic scene, Layla poured fresh tea for herself and coffee for Whitley, then settled back down to do the only thing she could reasonably do in this situation: watch Whitley move around her kitchen as subtly as possible while trying not to be too obvious about her appreciation of the view.

"I'll warn you right now, my cooking skills aren't exactly great," Whitley said animatedly as she pulled out pans and utensils. "But it should at least be edible, hopefully."

It was the happiest and most relaxed Layla had seen her since they'd first met, and the sight of Whitley so comfortable and carefree in her own space was absolutely captivating.

"I've survived Puck's attempts at cooking many times over the years, and I'm still breathing," Layla assured her. "You honestly can't be as potentially lethal as he is in the kitchen."

"Puck's the cello player, right?" Whitley asked, cracking eggs into a bowl with careful precision.

"Yup, and my absolute best mate in the world."

"So you're close friends with everyone in the quartet then?"

"I should bloody well hope so." Layla laughed. "We all share a shoebox-sized apartment together. If we didn't get along, it would be completely unbearable."

Seeing the grease in the pan starting to smoke ominously, Layla quickly hopped off her stool and scooted around to where Whitley stood, apparently unaware she was mere seconds away from starting an actual pan fire that would probably set off every smoke alarm in the building.

Reaching around Whitley's body, Layla flipped off the burner and carefully guided the smoking pan off the hot stove. It would have been a perfectly simple rescue maneuver if Whitley's hand hadn't still been gripping the pan handle, because Layla suddenly found herself genuinely struggling to let go of the other woman's warm hand.

"Easy there, Whit," she said, her voice slightly breathless from their unexpected proximity. "It's way too cold outside to be standing around waiting for the fire department to come and put out your fancy apartment."

"What? What did I do wrong?" Whitley asked, looking genuinely confused and slightly panicked.

Gently grabbing Whitley by the hips, Layla swept her over to the breakfast bar and bumped her legs against the closest stool, trying to ignore how perfectly Whitley's body fit against her own. "You put the pan on too-high heat, that's all. Nothing catastrophic. Now sit yourself down and let the professional take over."

Taking up the mantle of head chef, Layla whipped up two plates of perfectly cooked eggs and bacon, with fried bread—the kind of hearty breakfast that could cure any hangover and fuel a person for hours.

"Voilà, breakfast of champions," she announced with a flourish.

"I honestly can't believe I managed to mess up something so simple." Whitley sighed, looking genuinely disappointed in herself.

Taking the seat right next to her, close enough their knees almost touched, Layla shoveled in a forkful of perfectly runny eggs.

"I'm guessing you're pretty used to having chef-prepared meals delivered to your door, right?"

Whitley's rising blush answered the question more clearly than words ever could. "I also order takeout quite a lot," she mumbled, clearly embarrassed by her lack of culinary skills.

"So would I if I could afford it on a regular basis," Layla said matter-of-factly. "There's absolutely nothing wrong with that, Whit. Not everyone was born to be a culinary genius like myself."

The self-deprecating brag worked perfectly at pulling Whitley out of her momentary melancholy. The small smile and shake of her head let Layla know she'd succeeded in lightening the mood.

"You really do make excellent eggs," Whitley admitted. "What am I going to do for another whole year without you popping over to make me breakfast and save me from kitchen disasters?"

"Eh, it'll just make next year's reunion all the more exciting and anticipated," Layla replied, though the thought of not seeing Whitley for another twelve months made her chest tighten with unexpected sadness.

Placing her fork down carefully, Whitley turned slightly to face Layla more directly. "Speaking of next year, I want to organize a special fundraising event. Hopefully, we can incorporate it into the DuPont Christmas Gala so I don't have to survive separately planning and hosting two major events in December."

"Sounds cool," Layla replied, though she would be lying if she said she was one hundred percent focused on the conversation. Her attention kept drifting to Whitley's lips, which seemed to grow softer and more kissable the more she looked at them.

"So would you?" Whitley asked expectantly.

Oops. Layla had definitely missed something important while staring at Whitley's mouth like a lovesick teenager. Shit. "Hmm, sure, yeah. What exactly are we talking about?"

She received a paper napkin thrown directly at her face in retaliation. "Focus, Simmons."

Layla scrubbed her face with the napkin, grinning sheepishly. "I'm totally focused now. You're lucky I'm communicating in complete sentences after such a late night and early morning."

"Noted for future reference," Whitley said with amusement. "Now, I asked if you and your group would be willing to work with Jas's choir on a collaborative performance. We'd make it into a full concert experience."

"Yeah, absolutely, of course we would," Layla replied enthusiastically. "That sounds amazing. Will the funds raised go to your music foundation?"

Whitley shook her head, her expression growing more serious and passionate. "No, actually. I want to use this opportunity to highlight the other charity I run for abused women and children. I thought using the gala's platform would be a perfect way to shine a light on both foundations and the important work they do."

"We are absolutely there for that cause," Layla said firmly. "You don't even have to pay us for the performance."

Whitley immediately went to protest, but Layla cut her off with a raised hand. "It's completely non-negotiable, Whit. This is too important."

"You drive a hard bargain, Layla," Whitley said with admiration. "Fine, I'll agree to your terms, but only if you say you'll attend the family party with me as my date."

12

Collaborations & Ringlets

Layla furrowed her brows in confusion, trying to process what Whitley had just said. "Isn't that what we were just talking about? The gala and the concert?"

"Nope, not at all," Whitley said, with a mysterious smile that made Layla's heart skip in ways she was trying very hard to ignore. "Yes, we have the DuPont Gala every year, and that's a huge public event with hundreds of guests, photographers, and all the social obligations that come with it. But that isn't 'the family party' I'm referring to. We also have a much more intimate private soirée with only our closest friends and family members—maybe thirty people in total."

"Um, I'm neither of those things." Layla laughed, though the idea of being considered either sent a warm flutter through her chest that she definitely shouldn't be feeling about a straight woman.

Whitley scoffed dismissively, waving her hand as if Layla's objection was completely ridiculous. "I think you are, or at least you will be, a close friend. I can feel it—there's something special about our connection."

Layla narrowed her eyes playfully, studying Whitley's face for any signs of deception or a hidden agenda, though she suspected there were none. "Will you be attending this exclusive family party on the arm of another well-dressed douchebag who'll embarrass you in front of your relatives?"

"Absolutely not," Whitley replied with conviction that surprised them both. "I'll be going with you, on *your* arm. We'll go together as friends, completely man-free for the evening. Although you may have to run interference with a few persistent suitors who don't understand the word 'no. '"

Layla kind of liked the idea of that more than she should have, even though she knew Whitley was talking about going as friends and nothing more. And even though her rational brain kept reminding her this was just a platonic arrangement, she couldn't help but see it as a sort of date in her hopeful imagination.

A platonic date with a gorgeous straight woman. Remember that, you disaster lesbian!

"I'm pretty scrappy when I need to be," Layla said with a grin that was probably a little too enthusiastic. "I'll take 'em all on if you want me to, Whitley. Consider me your personal bodyguard for the evening."

"Perfect." Whitley clapped her hands together with obvious delight. "So, you'll do the benefit concert collaboration and attend the private family party with me as my date—I mean, as my friend?"

Sticking out her hand in an exaggerated businesslike gesture, Layla waited for Whitley to shake it and seal their deal. "It's absolutely a deal. But does this mean we'll actually see each other throughout the year while we're planning everything? I mean, I presume you'll want to be involved in the creative process."

Layla didn't like the sudden flash of unease and something that looked almost like sadness that crossed Whitley's beautiful features.

"Actually, I won't be able to be directly involved," Whitley said, her voice taking on a more formal, distant tone. "I'm scheduled to be on a flight to London the day after tomorrow for an extended business trip. It's highly unlikely I'll be back until this same time next year."

Flinging her head back dramatically, Layla laughed with a mixture of amusement and frustration at the cosmic joke that their timing seemed to be. "See!" she cried, gesturing wildly. "It's totally our thing! We're destined to be ships passing in the night."

Whitley laughed along, though there was a note of genuine regret in her voice. "Hopefully that pattern won't continue forever. I'd like to actually spend more time getting to know you properly."

The buzzing sound of a phone vibrating against leather cut through their conversation, coming from somewhere in the living room area. "It's not mine," Whitley said, checking her own device.

Searching around the plush couch where they'd spent most of the previous evening, Layla found her cell phone wedged down between the expensive cushions like a piece of lost treasure.

"It's just Puck checking in on me, making sure I didn't get murdered or kidnapped," she said, glancing at the screen. "I probably need to head home soon. We're planning to do some busking later this afternoon, and I need to shower and change into something warmer."

"Oh, okay then. Well..." Whitley hovered uncertainly between the kitchen and living room, clearly not wanting their time together to end but not knowing how to prolong it. "I guess this is it for now?"

Layla had an overwhelming, almost irresistible urge to slip her arms around Whitley's slender waist and pull her in close, to feel that perfect body pressed against hers and maybe, just maybe, find out what those soft lips tasted like. But she hadn't completely lost her mind just yet, so she settled for opening her arms wide and giving Whitley the choice to enter into what would have to be a strictly platonic hug—one that Layla would definitely not enjoy beyond the acceptable bounds of friendship, no matter how incredible Whitley felt in her arms.

The sensation of Whitley's body sliding in close, fitting perfectly against her own curves, was something Layla could only describe as pure magic. The way Whitley melted into the embrace, her arms wrapping around Layla's shoulders and her face nestling into the crook of her neck, sent shivers of electricity racing through every nerve ending. Layla was in serious trouble here, and maybe it really was for the best that they only ran into each other once a year. Any more frequent contact and Layla might do something stupid like fall completely in love with a woman who would never see her as anything more than a friend.

"Have a fantastic time in London," Layla said softly, breathing in the intoxicating scent of Whitley's expensive perfume. "Say hello to the royals for me when you see them at whatever fancy events you'll be attending."

"You know them personally, do you?" Whitley replied with a grin, pulling back just enough to look into Layla's eyes.

"Oh, we're absolute besties," Layla said with mock seriousness. "The King and I have tea every Tuesday."

"Then I'll be sure to pass on your warmest regards and tell him you're doing well."

The hug ended far too soon, and Layla knew she had to take a physical step back before she did something that would ruin their friendship forever. "Do you want my phone number, by the way? You know, for the collaboration and planning purposes?"

"Oh my God," Whitley said, looking genuinely horrified at her oversight. She immediately moved to a small side table in the living room and pulled out an elegant leather-bound notepad. "I absolutely cannot believe I almost let you disappear from my life again without getting your contact information. What kind of friend does that make me?"

Oh, how Layla desperately wished Whitley wouldn't let her go at all, in any sense of the phrase.

"My sister, Aubrey, will be in charge of all the foundation business while I'm away in London," Whitley explained as she carefully wrote down Layla's number in what was probably the most beautiful handwriting Layla had ever seen. "I'll make sure to tell her to call you as soon as possible to set up a proper meeting with you and the quartet. Maybe I can even join the planning sessions over Zoom or video call, depending on the time difference."

"Whatever works best for your schedule," Layla said, trying to keep her voice light and casual, even though the thought of not seeing Whitley for another year made her chest ache. She grabbed her coat from where she'd draped it over a chair and slipped on her boots, the familiar weight of her everyday clothes feeling strange after a night in silk sheets. "I should probably get going."

"Ryan is already waiting for you in the parking garage," Whitley said, ever the thoughtful hostess. "I texted him a few minutes ago."

"You know I could just take a regular cab, right?" Layla protested. "I'm perfectly capable of getting myself home."

"Absolutely not, that's nonsense," Whitley said firmly. "It's freezing outside, and the streets are still icy from last night's snow. We also left your violin in Ryan's capable hands, so you would need to meet him at the car anyway. Plus, it's entirely my fault that you're not already at home, still tucked in your own bed where you should be on a Sunday morning."

"How do you figure that?" Layla asked with amusement as she made her way towards the elevator.

"I plied you with expensive liquor when you were already exhausted from traveling and performing," Whitley said, following her to the door. "I'm completely responsible for your current state of homelessness."

Passing the large hallway mirror near the elevator, Layla caught sight of her reflection and grimaced at what she saw. Her hair was absolutely freaking huge, a wild mass of curls that had expanded to roughly twice its normal size overnight. Although, the purple highlights still looked pretty badass, so there was that small consolation.

"Christ, you could have told me I looked like a scarecrow," she said, trying unsuccessfully to tame the unruly mass with her fingers.

Giggling with genuine affection, Whitley stepped up directly behind her, both of them looking at Layla's reflection in the ornate mirror. "You look totally cute, honestly. Your hair is beautiful—is it naturally that curly?"

"Oh yeah, it's got a bloody mind of its own," Layla replied, hyperaware of Whitley's proximity and the way their eyes met in the mirror. "Always has, since I was a kid."

Layla held her breath as Whitley slowly brought her hand up and casually curled one of Layla's wild ringlets around her finger, the gentle touch sending sparks of electricity shooting straight down her spine. The moment felt charged with something indefinable; something that made the air between them crackle with possibility.

As if Whitley suddenly became aware of what she was doing and how intimate the gesture was, her hand quickly disappeared and she took a step back, breaking the spell that had settled over them.

"Take care of yourself, Layla," she said softly, her voice seeming to carry notes of regret and longing that Layla probably imagined. "I'll speak to you soon, I hope."

"Yeah," Layla replied, her voice barely above a whisper as she tried to process the emotions swirling through her chest. "See you around, Whitley."

The elevator doors closed between them, and Layla was left staring at her own reflection, wondering if she'd imagined the entire moment or if there really had been something more than friendship in Whitley's touch.

Either way, she was in deep trouble, and the next year was going to feel like an eternity.

13

Farewells & Queer Panic

After an exhausting afternoon of packing suitcases and dealing with what could only be described as pining—yes, that was exactly what it felt like to Whitley; an almost adolescent pining over Layla that made her feel ridiculous and confused in equal measure—Whitley finally relaxed in the plush leather back seat of her family's car. Ryan was as silent as ever behind the wheel, which she didn't mind in the slightest. Her brain was already giving her a relentless one-way conversation she couldn't seem to turn off, analyzing every moment of the previous night and this morning with obsessive detail.

A night of farewells lay ahead of her, including the traditional DuPont family dinner before any major trip, but more importantly, she'd have a few precious hours to grab some alone time with her sister to chat about whatever the hell was going on in her thoroughly confused mind. She needed perspective, needed someone she trusted to help her make sense of these unexpected feelings that had blindsided her completely.

Whitley wouldn't even attempt to feign ignorance about what was happening to her. She was attracted to Layla—genuinely, powerfully attracted in a way that made her stomach flutter and her pulse quicken. It was what she'd finally admitted to herself during the long hours of folding clothes and staring out her penthouse windows. As soon as Layla had disappeared into that elevator, Whitley had felt a profound sense of loss settle over her like a heavy blanket; a forlorn ache she'd never experienced before in her life.

The feeling was utterly crazy when she really thought about it. She was completely used to people coming in and out of her life on a regular basis—it was simply par for the course in her world of business and high society. Colleagues transferred to different cities, casual acquaintances moved into different social circles, boyfriends came and went with predictable regularity. They all flowed through her life like water, and she'd never felt anything remotely like this hollow, yearning sensation that Layla's absence had left behind.

Layla was a beautiful mess of dark curls, infectious charisma, and a completely unfiltered mouth that said exactly what it was thinking, and Whitley found herself entirely enchanted by every single aspect of her personality. But the rational part of her mind kept insisting that they barely knew each other beyond a few conversations and shared moments. As they'd discussed that very morning, they'd spent maybe a handful of hours together total, so how could Whitley possibly be feeling this intensely about someone who was essentially still a stranger?

And why, in all her thirty-plus years of life, had she never found herself attracted to women before this moment? She'd met countless beautiful, intelligent, accomplished women through her work and social circles, but not even one had ever sparked even the faintest flutter of romantic interest. She'd always assumed she was completely, unquestionably straight, never even considering any other possibility.

The most confusing part was that she still found men physically attractive—she could still appreciate a handsome face and a well-built body when she saw one. So what did that mean about her sexuality? Was it just Layla, specifically, who had awakened something new in her, or would other women suddenly become irresistible now that some internal door had been opened? This was exactly why she desperately needed some time with Aubrey. Her brilliant, no-nonsense sister would help her straighten things out, no pun intended.

Half an hour outside the bustling chaos of the city, Whitley felt her shoulders begin to relax and her breathing slow to a more normal pace. She genuinely loved the energy and excitement of New York City, thrived on its constant motion and endless possibilities, but time at her parents' secluded estate in the countryside always helped her recharge and refocus her scattered thoughts. Right now she definitely needed to not only work through what she was already thinking of as "the Layla situation" but also mentally prepare herself for her extended stay in London.

God, she genuinely wished she'd had the foresight to schedule this trip for after Christmas. But at the time she'd made these plans months ago, she'd had no idea that Layla would be back in New York, had no reason to think their paths would cross again so soon. Things with Steven had been mediocre at best, nothing remotely worth writing home about, and it honestly hadn't bothered Whitley one bit that she'd be spending nearly a year away from him. That complete lack of concern about leaving him behind should have spelled the definitive end of their relationship months ago, but as with all her other boyfriends, she'd avoided having the difficult conversation when she should have.

But Steven was neither here nor there now; he was officially ancient history, relegated to the growing pile of failed relationships that littered her romantic past. Instead, the real problem was that Whitley would now be spending another entire year away from Layla, separated by an ocean and countless time zones. Which, logically speaking, shouldn't be an issue at all given that they barely knew each other, and yet it felt like a massive, insurmountable problem. The twisty, anxious feeling in Whitley's stomach only intensified as she thought about not seeing Layla's expressive face, not hearing her infectious laugh, not experiencing her unfiltered honesty for twelve more long months.

It had briefly crossed her mind to reschedule her departure or to find some excuse to delay the trip by a few weeks or even months. But too many people were counting on her presence in London—not just the staff and consultants who had been working for months to set everything up for her arrival, but more importantly, the vulnerable women and children the new foundation branch would be designed to help. The London office of the DuPont business empire wanted to mirror the successful charitable foundations Whitley had established in the United States, and of course she wanted to be directly involved in getting such an important project off the ground.

She was genuinely excited about the work she'd be doing, passionate about expanding their reach, and helping even more people in need; however, the selfish, newly awakened part of her desperately wanted more time at home, getting to know Layla properly, working closely with her on next year's collaborative concert project, exploring whatever this connection between them might become.

"We're here, ma'am," Ryan announced as the car crunched to a stop on the circular gravel driveway.

Whitley rolled her eyes with familiar exasperation. "Ryan, how many times do I need to ask you to call me Whitley instead of ma'am? We've known each other for years."

"Probably a few more times, ma'am," he replied with a small, knowing smile that crinkled the corners of his eyes.

Despite her mild frustration with his stubborn formality, Whitley found herself smiling back as she waited for him to come around and open her door with his usual impeccable manners.

The December air was just as brutally cold as it had been in the city, but out here in the countryside it somehow felt fresher and healthier, almost cleansing in its purity. Looking up at the sprawling mansion that had been her childhood home, with its elegant stone facade and countless windows glowing warmly against the darkening sky, Whitley sighed with deep contentment. No matter how many years had passed since she'd lived under this roof, she always felt as if she were truly coming home whenever she visited her parents.

Her mother had done a superb job, as she did every year, decorating the exterior for the Christmas season with meticulous attention to detail. Two gorgeous, perfectly shaped pine trees stood like festive sentries on either side of the massive double oak doors, their branches heavy with fresh snow. Gentle white lights twinkled throughout their needles, bouncing cheerfully off the carefully arranged Christmas baubles and handcrafted ornaments that had been collected over decades of family holidays. The doors themselves were adorned with two ornate wreaths positioned symmetrically, which Whitley knew from years of watching her mother work, were made entirely by hand using materials gathered from their own extensive grounds.

"Thank you, Ryan," she said warmly as she stepped out into the crisp evening air. "I'll be staying here overnight, so you can head home to your family. Please give my best regards to Lisa and tell her I hope she's feeling better."

Ryan tipped his chauffeur's cap with old-fashioned courtesy. "I certainly will, and thank you for asking about her. See you bright and early tomorrow morning for the airport run."

Eager to escape the biting cold and immerse herself in the warmth of family, Whitley hurried up the stone steps toward the imposing front entrance. The door swung open before she'd even reached for the handle, as if her mother had been watching for her arrival from one of the front windows.

"Sweetheart!" Lucienne DuPont greeted her eldest daughter with a dazzling smile that could have lit up the entire foyer. Despite being in her sixties, she remained strikingly beautiful, with silver hair styled in an elegant chignon and carried herself with a natural grace that seemed passed down like an heirloom.

"Hi, Mom," Whitley replied, allowing herself to be swept into one of her mother's signature embraces—warm, enveloping, and scented with the expensive French perfume she'd worn for as long as Whitley could remember.

"Everyone is already here and accounted for," Lucienne said, stepping back to study her daughter's face with the keen eye of a mother who could always tell when something was troubling her children. "Aubrey and William are in the den, probably cheating at whatever card game they've invented this time. Your father is in the kitchen, attempting to cook dinner despite my repeated offers to handle the meal myself. I did try my best to talk him out of it, but you know exactly what he's like—stubborn as a mule when he gets an idea in his head. But don't worry too much about the potential culinary disaster. If the food turns out to be completely inedible, I have a Plan B ready to deploy."

Whitley chuckled, picturing her father's determined expression as he battled with pots and pans in the kitchen. "I'm sure whatever he makes will be perfectly fine, Mom. How long do we have until dinner? I need to steal Aubrey away for a quick piece of business."

Lucienne's expression immediately shifted to one of maternal disapproval, her eyebrows rising in the way that had struck fear into the hearts of all three DuPont children throughout their youth. "Business discussions? Tonight? Whitley, this is supposed to be your farewell dinner—a family celebration before you disappear to London for months. Can't whatever it is wait until after the holidays?"

"No, unfortunately it really can't wait," Whitley said, trying to project more confidence than she felt. "But I promise you, as soon as we've had our conversation, that will be absolutely it for work talk. No more business for the rest of the evening, I swear."

She could see her mother wasn't particularly happy about this development, but Lucienne had learned over the years when to pick her battles with her strong-willed children. "Fine, but you have exactly thirty minutes and then we're having proper family time with no distractions."

"Thanks, Mom, you're the best," Whitley called over her shoulder, already racing off toward the den where she could hear the familiar sounds of her siblings' competitive banter.

Aubrey and William were sitting cross-legged on the Persian rug in front of the fireplace, playing what appeared to be an intense game of cards when Whitley burst into the room. Her sister was clearly winning based on the deep scowl plastered across William's normally cheerful face, and there was a small pile of what looked like chocolate coins beside Aubrey's knee.

"Aubs, I need to steal you for a moment," Whitley announced without preamble.

"Hang on just a second, I'm about to beat his ass again," Aubrey replied, not looking up from her cards and clearly savoring her victory.

"Now, please," Whitley said, and her tone must have sounded desperate enough because both Aubrey and William's heads snapped up to look at her with immediate concern.

"Is everything okay?" William asked, his competitive irritation instantly replaced by brotherly worry.

Whitley looked back and forth between her siblings, suddenly realizing that William was just as good at giving advice and emotional support as Aubrey. Two heads were definitely better than one when it came to sorting out complicated personal situations, right?

"I honestly don't know," she answered truthfully, her voice small and uncertain in a way that was completely unlike her usual confident demeanor.

14

Toaster Ovens & London Plans

T he playing cards were immediately abandoned on the floor as William and Aubrey scrambled to their feet with the kind of coordinated urgency that only twins could manage.

"Is it some kind of legal issue?" Aubrey asked, her mind immediately jumping to the various business complications that could arise in their world of high finance and corporate responsibility.

"No, nothing like that," Whitley replied, shaking her head.

"Health problems?" William added, his voice tight with concern as he studied his sister's face for any signs of physical distress.

"No, I'm perfectly healthy."

"Oh, for God's sake, just tell us what's wrong because I'm genuinely on the verge of a full-blown panic attack here," Aubrey shot back with characteristic directness.

Grabbing both by the wrists, Whitley practically dragged them over to the comfortable leather couch that dominated one side of the room. They sat in expectant silence as she began pacing back and forth in front of the crackling fireplace, her nervous energy making it impossible to sit still.

"I broke up with Steven last night," she finally announced, as if that explained everything.

"Thank God, he was a complete tool," Aubrey said immediately, her relief evident.

"Agreed," William supplied with a satisfied nod. "That guy was a walking red flag."

But Whitley continued her agitated pacing, clearly not finished with her revelation. "I've met someone else. I think. Maybe. I'm not entirely sure what's happening."

"That was fast work, sis." William laughed, settling back into the cushions. "So what's the problem? Is he married or something equally complicated?"

"Um..." Whitley stopped pacing and turned to face them both, her hands twisting together nervously. "It's a her. She...she's a woman."

Aubrey and William exchanged one of their "twin" looks, using the kind of silent communication they'd perfected over thirty years of shared existence.

"Okay," Aubrey replied calmly, as though Whitley had just announced she was thinking of changing her hair color. "Do we know her?"

"Layla," Whitley said simply, the name carrying more weight and emotion than a single word should be able to hold.

"The violinist from the Christmas parties?" William asked, his eyebrows rising with interest and recognition.

After the previous year's dramatic breakup with Anthony, Whitley had told her siblings about her unexpected evening with Layla—the midnight church visit, the late-night diner conversation, the way a complete stranger had somehow managed to help her process one of the worst nights of her life. They'd been genuinely grateful she'd had someone kind and trustworthy to talk to during such a vulnerable moment. It was partly the reason they'd specifically asked their mother to rehire the same quartet for this year's gala.

"Yes, the violinist," Whitley confirmed, her voice barely above a whisper.

Aubrey looked confused, trying to piece together the timeline. "Did you see her last night after the party ended?"

"Obviously she saw her, genius," William scoffed, earning himself a sharp elbow to the ribs. "We hired her quartet to perform again."

Aubrey then punched William in the arm with more force than was necessary. "I meant after the official party ended, asshole. Like, did they spend time together privately?"

Not in the mood to referee one of their typical sibling squabbles, Whitley clapped her hands sharply to refocus the twins' attention on her crisis. "Yes, I saw her during the party performance, and then after I broke up with Steven, I waited for her to finish packing up her violin and asked her back to my place for—"

"Jesus Christ, Whitley!" Aubrey interrupted with delighted laughter. "You slept with her? On the same night you dumped Steven? That's some serious rebound action!"

"No!" Whitley practically shouted, her cheeks flaming red with embarrassment. "No, I absolutely did not sleep with her! I asked her back for hot chocolate, just like we did the year before. But I didn't want to go sit in some crowded diner wearing my formal gown again, so I invited her to my apartment instead."

"I take it she said yes to your invitation?" William asked with a knowing smile.

"She did, and it was absolutely lovely," Whitley said, her voice taking on a dreamy quality as she remembered the easy conversation and comfortable intimacy of the evening. "She's...well, she's like no one I've ever met before in my entire life. I started getting these feelings while we were talking—these butterflies and warm sensations that I couldn't quite identify. I don't know how to explain it properly, but I think...no, I know I'm attracted to her."

Standing up from the couch, Aubrey took Whitley gently by the arm and guided her to sit down between her and William. "Is she the first woman you've ever felt an attraction to?"

"Yes, absolutely the first. What does that mean about me?"

"You owe Layla a toaster oven," William quipped with barely contained laughter.

"I...what?" Whitley was thoroughly confused by this non sequitur.

"Yeah, it's supposedly a lesbian thing," he continued, his shoulders already shaking with suppressed mirth. "If they successfully convert a straight woman, they receive a toaster oven as a reward."

"Ignore him completely," Aubrey scoffed, shooting her twin brother a withering look. "He's being an idiot."

Whitley turned to her sister with genuine concern. "Do I really have to buy her a toaster oven? Is that actually a thing?"

William's shoulders shook harder as he lost the battle against his laughter. Aubrey sighed deeply, shaking her head at her brother's immaturity.

"Forget about the ridiculous toaster oven joke. What exactly are you struggling with here?"

Was she actually struggling, or was she just nervous about these new feelings? "I...I honestly don't know what I'm supposed to do with all of this."

Getting himself back under control, William placed a reassuring hand on Whitley's shoulder. "You don't have to do anything right now, Whit. Maybe just take some time to let it all sink in and see how you feel. You've got Layla's phone number, right?"

Whitley nodded, remembering the careful way she'd written down those precious digits.

"So maybe start by developing a genuine friendship with her," William continued thoughtfully. "You've known each other for a relatively small amount of time when you add it all up. Maybe see if your feelings go beyond just physical attraction."

"William's absolutely right," Aubrey agreed. "I know this feels like a huge revelation, but that doesn't mean you have to act on it immediately."

Whitley gnawed at her bottom lip, a nervous habit from childhood. "But what if she meets someone while I'm away in London? What if I lose my chance?"

"What if *you* meet someone while you're there?" William countered logically. "It could actually be a good thing—test the waters, see if you're attracted to other women too."

Screwing up her nose in distaste, Whitley shook her head emphatically. "I don't want to do that at all."

"But you *do* have to go to London, Whit," William supplied gently. "The foundation work is too important."

"I know, and I genuinely want to go to London. I'm excited about the project and helping more people," she said with a sigh. "I just wish it wasn't happening tomorrow."

Aubrey stood and made her way to the small beverage cart in the corner, selecting a bottle of their father's best bourbon. "I think this situation is worth waiting for, Whitley," she began, pouring three generous glasses. "You don't come to us very often about your love life."

"Never, actually. She never comes to us about relationships," William interrupted with emphasis.

Whitley scoffed indignantly. "What are you talking about? I always come to you guys when I have problems."

"No, you come to us *after* you've already left the guy and need help processing the aftermath," Aubrey stated matter-of-factly as she handed out the bourbon. "But never before—never while you're still figuring out your feelings. This is honestly the first time you've felt something real and meaningful, I'd imagine."

"And it's probably even harder to process because the person happens to be a woman," William added thoughtfully.

Whitley sipped her drink, savoring the burn of expensive alcohol. "But shouldn't I have had some kind of inkling by now? I mean, shouldn't there have been signs or hints throughout my life that I might be attracted to women?"

William smiled gently at his sister's confusion. "We're definitely no experts on this subject, Whit, but I'm guessing it doesn't necessarily work like that for everyone."

"You're not bothered by the possibility of me being interested in a woman?" she asked quietly, needing to hear their acceptance out loud.

Aubrey cackled with genuine delight. "Fuck no, I think it's absolutely awesome!"

"Yeah, no more dickhead frat boys for us to worry about." William laughed, raising his glass in a mock toast.

Even though she'd known deep down they wouldn't care about her sexuality, a small but significant weight lifted from her shoulders when she heard them say it explicitly.

"Should I tell Layla how I feel?"

"The night before you jet off to another country for an entire year?" Aubrey said, the rhetorical nature of the question blatantly obvious.

"I think that kind of conversation deserves more than just a few hours, don't you?" William added, posing another rhetorical question.

"Yes, of course, you're both right," Whitley stated with growing clarity. "Which brings me to the other reason I needed to talk to you both tonight."

Whitley explained her vision for the following year—the ambitious plan to combine both of her foundations in a collaborative fundraising event that would showcase the choir and the quartet while also raising money for abused women and children. She outlined her ideas for making it a centerpiece of the Christmas gala, creating something that would blow the socks off New York's elite while serving multiple charitable purposes.

"This could actually work really well," Aubrey muttered, her business mind already turning over the logistics. "I'll get to work closely with Layla on the planning. I can subtly scope her out—see what kind of person she really is."

"Yeah, we need to make sure she's good enough for our sister," William supplied, exerting his protective brotherly instincts.

"I absolutely *do not* want you interrogating the poor woman," Whitley said firmly. "She doesn't even know I like her in that way. She's going to think we're all completely insane if you start with the 'what-are-your-intentions-with-my-sister' routine."

"William won't do anything stupid," Aubrey said, shooting daggers at her brother with her eyes. "But it would be genuinely good for me to get to know her better as a person. Plus, it gives you a solid foundation on which to build a real friendship. You'll have every legitimate reason to call and text throughout the year, maybe even video chat. Let things develop organically."

William nodded in agreement. "And then when you're back home next year, if you still feel the same way about her, you can have that important conversation."

"It's definitely better than seeing her only once a year and spending the other eleven months wondering 'what if,'" Aubrey added. "You've clearly connected on a meaningful level."

Their conversation came to an abrupt end as Lucienne entered the room with perfect timing. "Kids, dinner is finally ready, and miraculously, it actually looks edible," she announced. The note of genuine surprise in her voice made all three siblings smile. Lucas DuPont was many wonderful things, but a competent cook wasn't one of them.

The three siblings exchanged a look that silently communicated their conversation wasn't over, just postponed. But for now, Whitley had to focus on saying goodbye to her family and try to put thoughts of Layla to the back of her mind. She'd have plenty of long, lonely hours on the plane and in London to mull everything over.

One thing was crystal clear, though: what she was feeling toward the violinist was completely new and different. Not just in the sense it was Whitley's first same-sex attraction, but because her feelings were already deeper and more telling than any of her previous relationships had ever been. Aubrey and William were right—she needed time to work through these emotions properly. If there could ever be a real chance that Layla might want to go out with her, she needed to make sure she was ready to give it her all. They both deserved nothing less than complete honesty and commitment.

What was another few months in the grand scheme of things, really?

15

Beer & Business Propositions

A week after Layla last saw Whitley, standing in that hallway mirror with Layla's curls wrapped around her elegant fingers and unspoken words hanging in the air between them, she received the call she'd been both expecting and hoping for. Not that she wasn't anticipating it based on their conversation, but a part of her had wondered if the offer to collaborate with the prestigious DuPont Foundation would actually materialize into something concrete, or if it would disappear like so many other promising opportunities that had seemed too good to be true.

Aubrey DuPont was all business at the beginning of their phone conversation, her voice crisp and professional in a way that immediately reminded Layla of Whitley's own authoritative tone during their more serious moments. Aubrey laid out the preliminary plan for the fundraising concert with impressive detail and discussed payment arrangements, to which Layla refused once more with the same firm conviction she'd shown Whitley. Aubrey had laughed with genuine amusement and said Whitley had already warned her not to bother offering any cash because she knew Layla would turn it down in a heartbeat without even considering it.

They'd made a plan to meet in person to discuss the finer details, and here it was—the day Layla had been looking forward to with a mixture of excitement and nervous anticipation. Not only because the fundraiser was going to be epic and potentially career-changing, but because it also meant she'd get the opportunity to meet the people closest to Whitley and to see her world through the eyes of those who knew her best.

Whitley had also begun a message thread with Layla a few days ago, much to her utter delight, and the constant buzzing of her phone made her roommates tease her mercilessly. GIFs and memes made up the majority of their texts; silly back-and-forth exchanges that felt surprisingly natural despite the ocean between them. But there were also photos of London's snow-covered streets and landmarks, and occasionally pictures of Whitley herself, looking windswept and beautiful against the backdrop of the city, which Layla secretly loved and *definitely* saved to her phone like some kind of lovesick teenager.

In return, Layla sent videos of her busking sessions with Puck and the gang, capturing the energy of street performances and the generous tips from holiday shoppers. Their communication was easy and comfortable, flowing as naturally as their in-person conversations had, making the distance between them feel somehow more manageable.

Comfort, however, wasn't exactly what came to mind as Layla pushed through the heavy glass door of one of New York's most exclusive restaurants. The kind of place where a single appetizer probably cost more than she spent on groceries in a week.

The interior was all marble and crystal, with soft lighting that made everything look expensive and intimidating. Layla couldn't help wondering if Aubrey was one of those wealthy people who liked to flaunt their money and make others feel small by choosing venues that screamed exclusivity. She hadn't sounded like that type during their phone conversation, but you never really knew with rich people—they could be surprisingly unpredictable in their displays of privilege.

"May I help you?" a woman dressed in an impeccable black uniform asked, her tone polite but cool as she regarded Layla with mild but barely concealed irritation. She clearly thought Layla didn't belong in this rarefied atmosphere, and honestly, looking down at her outfit of ripped skinny jeans and an oversized knitted jumper that had seen better days, Layla could completely understand why the hostess had reached that conclusion.

"I'm here to meet Aubrey DuPont," Layla replied with more confidence than she felt, straightening her shoulders and meeting the woman's gaze directly.

The look of surprise that flashed across the hostess's carefully composed face was deeply satisfying to witness. Layla could practically see the wheels turning as the woman tried to decide if she was in the presence of some kind of undercover celebrity or eccentric artist. After all, only genuinely important people met with members of the DuPont family at establishments like this.

"Right this way, please," the hostess said, her tone immediately shifting to one of deferential respect.

Briefly stomping her boots on the entrance mat to dislodge the snow and slush she'd picked up from the pavement, Layla followed the woman through the elegantly appointed dining room towards the back of the restaurant. She immediately met the intelligent eyes of Aubrey DuPont, who was seated at a corner table that offered both privacy and an excellent view of the room.

They hadn't been formally introduced, but Aubrey looked similar enough to Whitley—the same bone structure, the same confident bearing, the same golden hair—for Layla to make the connection instantly.

"Aubrey," she said warmly, holding out her hand as the hostess showed her to the table with a flourish.

Aubrey stood gracefully and shook her hand with a firm grip that spoke of confidence and strength. "Miss Simmons, so lovely to finally meet you in person."

Oops, had she already made some kind of social mistake by being too casual?

"Oh, are we doing the formal second-name thing? My bad if I got that wrong."

Aubrey grinned, and the expression transformed her face in a way that made her look much more approachable and genuinely friendly. "No, no, absolutely not. I'm sorry,

I'm just used to using formal titles in business settings out of habit. Please, feel completely free to call me Aubrey."

"Same here, but make it Layla," she replied, settling into the plush chair across from Whitley's sister.

"May I get you something to drink, ma'am?" the hostess asked, her attention focused entirely on Layla now she'd been identified as someone worthy of respect.

Christ, Layla had completely forgotten the hostess was still hovering nearby, waiting to take their order. "I'll take a beer, thanks. Whatever you've got on tap is fine."

"A beer?" The hostess's voice carried a note of definite judgment, as if Layla had just requested something completely inappropriate for the refined atmosphere.

"Do you not sell beer here?" Layla asked with genuine confusion, never understanding why upscale restaurants looked down on certain perfectly legitimate beverages. There were loads of fantastic craft beers in the world, and not everyone wanted to drink wine with their lunch, for fuck's sake.

"I'll have one too, actually," Aubrey said smoothly, smiling at the now-blushing hostess with the kind of gracious authority that came from years of navigating social situations.

"Of course, absolutely. Brian will be your server today, and he'll be with you both shortly," the hostess replied, her professional composure restored.

Layla watched her retreat towards the bar area before turning back to Aubrey. "You didn't have to do that, you know. If you actually wanted wine or champagne or whatever, it's totally cool with me."

Aubrey carefully realigned the already perfectly situated silverware before answering in a small gesture that reminded Layla of Whitley's own tendency towards precise movements. "I like beer a lot, actually, especially with lunch. Wine makes me sleepy in the afternoon."

Layla shrugged, appreciating the honesty. "So, should we get straight to business then?"

"Whitley mentioned you were a straight shooter who didn't like to waste time on small talk."

"I prefer getting the business stuff out of the way first," Layla explained. "Then we can actually relax and enjoy ourselves without any agenda hanging over our heads."

"That makes perfect sense. Are you nervous about this meeting?"

Layla studied Aubrey for a long moment, sensing there seemed to be more layers to this lunch than a simple business discussion about a fundraising concert.

Something in Aubrey's expression suggested additional motives that hadn't been explicitly stated.

"I really want this collaboration to work out well for everyone involved, so I guess I am a little nervous about making a good impression."

"Please don't be anxious about anything," Aubrey said reassuringly. "Whitley is more than confident you'll pull this entire project off brilliantly."

"Me specifically? What do you mean by that? I thought I was just playing violin as part of the quartet, right?"

Taking a thoughtful sip of her water, Aubrey made a small humming sound. "Maybe that's all it will be, maybe not. It really depends on how this lunch conversation goes."

Layla really disliked word games and dancing around important topics. "Can we cut the shit here?" she asked bluntly, noting how Aubrey's eyebrows rose a fraction at her directness. "Look, this is obviously a meeting with some kind of agenda, but I'm not one of your usual corporate suits who needs to be handled with kid gloves. We both know there's more going on here than planning a simple concert. Just tell me exactly what you expect from me, and I'll give you a straight yes or no answer. Playing games and being mysterious isn't necessary."

"Well, okay then," Aubrey said with obvious approval of Layla's no-nonsense approach. "I want you to come on board as a part-time instructor at the Foundation for Gifted Musicians. Part-time specifically, so you still have plenty of freedom to live your life however you want—busking, performing, whatever makes you happy. But I think you'd be a tremendous asset to our program. We have plenty of traditionally trained classical teachers with impeccable credentials, but from what I've seen and heard of your work, you would bring a completely fresh perspective our students desperately need."

"You've only actually seen me perform twice," Layla pointed out reasonably.

"I have access to the internet, Layla," Aubrey replied with a knowing smile. "In fact, I'd like your entire quartet to consider getting on board with teaching positions. You're all incredibly talented and would bring something unique to our program."

Well, this was definitely interesting, and completely unexpected. Layla let the silence settle between them while she processed this surprising offer, taking her time to consider the implications. After their drinks were delivered by an attentive server, she stretched the quiet moment even further by taking several thoughtful swallows of beer, which tasted nice but not particularly exceptional.

"Are you asking me to do this as some kind of favor to Whitley?" she asked directly. "Because it wouldn't be the first time she's quietly arranged job opportunities for me."

"No, absolutely not," Aubrey replied firmly. "Whitley doesn't know anything about this teaching offer. She has more than enough on her plate with the London project, and I make my own decisions about foundation staffing. The salary is negotiable, but I think you'll find it respectable."

"I'll need to discuss this with the others before I can give you a definitive answer," Layla said practically. "I can't speak for them or make commitments on their behalf."

"Of course, that's completely reasonable and exactly what I'd expect."

"There is one thing that's absolutely non-negotiable for me, though," Layla began, her tone becoming more serious.

Aubrey gestured for her to continue, clearly interested in hearing her conditions.

"No one interferes with my lessons or tries to dictate my teaching methods. I'll teach the music I love, using my own approach and style. I won't be micromanaged or forced into some rigid classical framework that sucks all the joy out of learning."

"Deal," Aubrey said immediately, extending her hand across the table.

Layla laughed with surprise at how quickly that had been resolved. "Right, well that was much easier than I expected. I'll talk to the others later today and get back to you with their decisions. You'll probably want to meet with them individually too, but as for me personally, I'll absolutely do it."

Aubrey's offer wasn't exactly the career path Layla had originally envisioned for herself, but it was surely a step in the right direction towards something more stable and meaningful. Teaching kids to play classical music with a modern twist was going to be incredibly fun, and it would be a way to bring younger generations to appreciate the genre without all the stuffy pretension that usually surrounded it.

Sitting back in her comfortable chair, Layla noticed Aubrey was watching her with an expression of thoughtful assessment.

"You're very go-with-the-flow, aren't you?"

Layla shrugged casually. "I suppose I am. I'm not particularly scared of taking chances or trying new things. Life's too short to spend it playing it safe, and so far, that philosophy has worked out pretty well for me."

"I can see what she likes about you," Aubrey said quietly, something meaningful flickering in her gaze.

There was definitely something in Aubrey's tone and expression that made Layla pause and really look at her. "I like her too," she replied honestly.

"Mmm, I can see that as well," Aubrey murmured with a knowing smile.

What exactly was all that supposed to mean? Layla felt like there were entire conversations happening beneath the surface that she wasn't quite catching.

"I'd love for you to join my brother and me for drinks this evening," Aubrey continued, smoothly changing the subject. "We can toast your new job and celebrate the fundraiser collaboration. William works on the finance side of things, just like Whitley does. He'll be the head bean counter keeping track of all the budget details for this project."

Yup, there was definitely something more complex going on here than simple business networking. There was no obvious reason why Layla needed to meet Whitley's brother over drinks, especially not on the same day as this lunch meeting. The whole thing felt orchestrated, like some kind of informal interview or evaluation process.

"Sure, I'd be happy to meet him," Layla replied. "Should I invite the others if they end up being interested in the teaching positions?"

"Maybe we can arrange that for another evening," Aubrey said diplomatically. "Tonight, I'd prefer if it was just the three of us, if that's okay with you."

"Alright, but I get to pick the venue," Layla said with a mischievous grin.

Aubrey laughed, clearly intrigued by this condition. "Deal. Where did you have in mind?"

"Pink Pearl. 8:00 p.m. sharp."

"We'll be there," Aubrey agreed, though Layla could see curiosity and perhaps a hint of apprehension in her expression.

16

Trifle & Club Confessions

"**S**o it's a resounding yes from everyone, then?" Layla looked around at each of her three roommates and best friends, waiting for their final confirmation.

"Fuck yes, it is," Simon said emphatically, his excitement obvious. "Paid teaching positions within the DuPont empire? They're actually one of the few genuinely good organizations left in this world, from everything I've heard."

"Plus, we get to teach music our own way while still having time to busk and perform if we want to," Reena added enthusiastically. "It's like the perfect balance of stability and creative freedom."

"Puck?" Layla prompted, looking at her best friend who had been uncharacteristically quiet during their discussion.

"Count me in completely," he said with a decisive nod. "I think we could do a tremendous amount of good working with those kids. Plus it gets our foot in the door with some major industry names and connections. And we could afford to buy the fancy ramen with the weird flavors. Wouldn't that be nice!"

Layla clapped her hands together with satisfaction. "Brilliant! I'll tell Aubrey the good news this evening."

Simon raised his hand in the air, invoking the system they'd established years ago when four opinionated people trying to give their thoughts simultaneously inevitably led to chaos and bickering.

"Yes, Simon, you have the floor."

"Why exactly are you having drinks with Whitley's siblings if you only just had lunch with the sister today? Seems like a lot of DuPont family time in one day."

"I honestly don't know their specific motivation," Layla replied with a shrug. "But I don't mind spending time with them. I'm taking them to the Pearl, so it should be interesting."

Puck grinned with the wolfish expression that usually meant he was about to say something that would embarrass her. "I can see right through you, Simmons." He chuckled knowingly.

"Shut it, Puck," Layla shot back, already knowing where this conversation was heading.

"What? What are we missing here?" Reena asked with growing excitement, sensing drama.

"Our dear Layla wants to impress Whitley's siblings so she has a better shot at winning over their sister," Puck announced with obvious delight at his own perceptiveness.

Damn Puck and his ability to read her like an open book! "That's not it at all," she protested weakly.

"Oh, yes, I'm absolutely right about this." Puck cackled with satisfaction. "I can see it written all over your face."

"I thought Whitley was straight, though?" Reena asked with confusion.

"We're not here to dissect my nonexistent love life," Layla said firmly. "We're here to discuss the job offer, which we've already done."

"And we have discussed it thoroughly," Puck retorted with a shit-eating grin that made Layla want to throw something at his head. "Now we're in friend mode and we want to know what's really going on with you and this mysterious heiress."

"Nothing is going on between us. Nothing at all."

Simon shook his head in disbelief. "Then why won't you tell us where you disappeared to after the gala? Is it because you were with Whitley?"

God, they could be relentless when they sensed a secret, like bloodhounds on the trail of something juicy. So Layla had been deliberately secretive about staying at Whitley's penthouse that night. So what? It was her prerogative to keep some things private, right? It didn't necessarily mean anything significant.

"I don't have to report my whereabouts to you lot!" she protested.

Reena bobbed her head knowingly. "Of course you don't have to tell us anything. But...did you sleep with her?"

"No!" Layla practically shouted.

"But you *did* stay at her place overnight, right?" Puck was like a dog with a bone when he got onto something interesting.

Huffing with exasperation, Layla glared at all three of them with as much intimidation as she could muster. "Fine! Yes, I stayed at Whitley's apartment. Nothing romantic happened between us. We're friends, that's all. She's straight as far as I know, and probably always will be. Maybe I have a tiny, insignificant crush on her, but I'm a big girl and I know nothing can realistically come of it. That doesn't mean I can't get to know her and her family better. It would be nice for her brother and sister to actually like me, if only for the fact we're planning on working together professionally for the next year. Now, will you please leave me the fuck alone about it?"

She stood up abruptly and went to storm off towards her bedroom, but Puck's voice stopped her in her tracks.

"You should make them a trifle," he called out thoughtfully. "They won't have a bloody clue what it is, but you can always tell things about a person, or people, if they like a trifle."

Layla halted, turning back towards the kitchen area. She was famous among their friend group for her trifles, a skill she'd learned from her grandmother back in England.

"You really reckon that's a good idea?"

Puck jumped up from the couch and headed towards their tiny kitchenette with purpose. "If you want to make a memorable impression on them, absolutely. We've got everything you need, I think."

"Parker will let you stick it in the club's refrigerator until they're ready to take it home," Simon added helpfully.

"Or just ask for a couple of spoons and let them eat it right there in the club," Reena remarked as she joined Puck in rummaging through their cabinets. "It's not the weirdest thing that's ever happened in that place, trust me."

Puck placed a packet of colorful Jello on the counter with a triumphant flourish. "It's *definitely* not the strangest thing to happen at Pink Pearl, and you know they'll fall completely in love with you the moment it hits their taste buds. You know...because you'll be working together closely—not because you want to do unspeakable things to their sister and become part of the DuPont family empire."

Layla chose to ignore that last provocative remark entirely. "Fine, you've convinced me. I'll make them a proper trifle."

With the glass dessert bowl carefully balanced in her hands, Layla entered Pink Pearl four hours later, the familiar sounds of thumping bass and laughter washing over her like a warm embrace. Parker waved her over to the bar without even raising an eyebrow at the sight of the large glass bowl filled to the brim with layers of cream, custard, and sponge fingers. It really *wasn't* the weirdest thing that had ever happened in this establishment, though explaining that fact to Aubrey and William might prove to be a different matter entirely.

The DuPont siblings were already positioned at the bar, both of them staring at Layla like she might be some kind of fascinating but potentially unhinged individual. They looked somewhat out of place in their expensive business attire among the eclectic crowd of artists, musicians, and various other characters that made Pink Pearl their regular hangout.

"I brought you dessert," Layla announced cheerfully, as though this were the most normal thing in the world.

"To a nightclub?" Aubrey asked, though a genuine smile was gracing her lips with obvious amusement.

"Yeah, absolutely."

"I'm William, by the way," the tall, handsome man beside Aubrey said, extending his hand with the same confident bearing that seemed to be a genetic trait within the DuPont family.

"Layla. Here, take this heavy thing," she said, carefully transferring the substantial glass dish to him and signaling Parker behind the bar. "Can we get some proper spoons over here?"

"Sure thing, love. But save me some of that gorgeous creation, yeah?" Parker replied with her usual flirtatious grin.

"I'll make you your own personal one," Layla promised.

"What exactly is happening here?" Aubrey laughed, looking around at the club's atmosphere with fascination.

"We're sharing a dessert and celebrating," Layla answered matter-of-factly. "It's my specialty—been making them since I was knee-high to a grasshopper."

William looked from Aubrey to Layla, his eyes studying her with the same assessing expression his sister had worn earlier in the day during their lunch meeting.

"Yeah, I get it now," he said with dawning understanding.

"Right?" Aubrey said, nodding emphatically as though some important piece of a puzzle had just clicked into place.

Layla didn't know exactly what they were talking about, but she had a strong suspicion it had something to do with Whitley and whatever conversations had been happening about Layla within the family.

"So? Do you want to try it or just stare at it all night?"

Parker handed over three spoons with a flourish. The music blared around them at a volume that made normal conversation nearly impossible, while people danced with abandon and couples made out in dark corners.

"What exactly is it?" William asked with squinted eyes.

"Jello, ladyfingers, which, I know is hilarious coming from a lesbian, but they're just sponge cakes. Canned fruit cocktail, custard, cream, and chocolate shavings on top. I may have put a splash of sherry in it too, because that's traditional."

Shaking their heads in what was probably disbelief at finding themselves eating homemade dessert in a queer nightclub, Aubrey and William took the offered cutlery and sunk their spoons into Layla's carefully constructed trifle.

Shoving a generous spoonful into her mouth, Layla hummed with satisfaction. It really was a good one, if she did say so herself. She watched with growing amusement as the twins' expressions changed from skepticism to surprise to genuine delight, both immediately going back for seconds.

"This is incredible," Aubrey said after swallowing. "I honestly can't believe you brought us homemade dessert to a nightclub, but I'm so glad you did."

"You said this was supposed to be a celebration," Layla replied with a shrug. "Celebrations near Christmas must involve trifle. It's basically a law where I come from."

Wiping his mouth with a cocktail napkin, William dug his spoon in for another large bite. "Yeah, but like, we're literally in a club! With strobe lights and everything!"

Layla grinned widely, feeling completely in her element. "Trifle is allowed wherever and whenever people need something sweet in their lives. Now, since we've got the dessert sorted, do you want to dance?"

Delayed Flights & Winter Wonderlands

Whitley frantically applied lipstick with shaking hands as the town car sped through the familiar streets of Manhattan, the city lights blurring past her window in streaks of gold and white. She was supposed to have been home two days ago, but a last-minute setback with paperwork and final approvals had delayed her return from London, leaving her scrambling to make it to tonight's event on time.

Twelve long months. She'd somehow survived an entire year away from her family, living in a country that stubbornly favored tea over coffee and where the weather was even more unpredictable than New York's.

It had been a fantastic experience working with the London office, challenging and rewarding her in ways she hadn't expected. They'd managed to set up the new foundation branch with minimal bureaucratic issues and maximum impact for the women and children they served. She was over the moon with what they had accomplished.

Terri Clark, the woman she'd hired to run the London operation, was going to be a wonderful leader and administrator. She was compassionate, hardworking, and full of the kind of infectious enthusiasm that made everyone around her want to do better. Whitley felt completely confident in her choice and had no worries whatsoever about stepping away from the day-to-day operations to return home.

Now she had to refocus her attention on her life in New York. There were plenty of important things waiting for her attention at home. She had business matters that had been piling up during her absence. But first, there was tonight's fundraiser to attend, the culmination of a year's worth of planning and preparation. By all accounts from her family and friends, it was going to be huge, and potentially the most successful event the foundation had ever organized.

Although Whitley had done her absolute best to stay informed about the planning process and keep abreast of all the comings and goings from across the Atlantic, she honestly knew very little about the actual detailed plan for this evening's entertainment. There were two main reasons for this frustrating lack of information.

Firstly, whenever she'd managed to catch Aubrey on the phone or video calls, her sister had simply told her not to worry about the specifics, that everything was under control, and she should just focus on her work in London. Aubrey had been maddeningly secretive about the details, insisting it would be better as a surprise.

Secondly, and perhaps more significantly, whenever she'd spoken to Layla during their regular calls and video chats, they'd inevitably ended up chatting about a myriad of other topics entirely—Layla's teaching experiences, funny stories from her busking adventures, Whitley's observations about British culture, random thoughts about music and life—conversations that usually finished with both of them laughing uncontrollably about something completely unrelated to event planning.

Whitley sighed deeply as she thought about Layla, her chest tightening with a familiar mixture of longing and nervous anticipation. If anything, she was more enamored with the violinist than ever before. After they'd started texting regularly last year, everything had just sort of naturally slotted into place. It hadn't taken much time for her to realize her attraction went far beyond the purely physical, though that was certainly still a significant factor.

The more they'd messaged and called throughout the year, the closer she'd felt to Layla on every level. They'd shared stories about their childhoods, their dreams, their fears, their daily frustrations, and small victories. Layla had a way of making even the most mundane details of life seem interesting and worth discussing, and Whitley found herself looking forward to their conversations more than anything else in her week.

There had been a few occasions when Layla had mentioned women she'd met—casual dates, brief flirtations, nothing serious, but enough to make Whitley's stomach clench with jealousy.

During those conversations, Whitley had thought she might actually cry from sheer frustration at being thousands of miles away and unable to do anything about her feelings. But she hadn't allowed herself to break down. Instead, she'd forced herself to be supportive and listen as Layla spoke about these other women, offering advice and encouragement where she could, even when it felt like swallowing glass.

Thankfully, none of these women had stayed in Layla's life for very long. Apparently, none of them could match Layla's energy or appreciate her unique blend of chaos and creativity. But these brief mentions of Layla's dating life had only solidified Whitley's determination and her plan for when she finally returned to New York.

There was no more time to waste on hesitation or fear. She had to tell Layla *exactly* how she felt and desperately hope her feelings were reciprocated. Aubrey seemed to think they were, based on her observations during the year of working closely with Layla, but then again, Aubrey herself had become pretty smitten with the violinist. By all accounts, the entire DuPont family had fallen under Layla's spell.

After the now legendary incident with a homemade trifle served in a nightclub, both Aubrey and William had been completely obsessed with Layla's unconventional charm. They'd called Whitley the very next day, laughing their way through a detailed recounting of Layla's dessert-giving escapade and her complete comfort with the unusual situation. William had told Whitley he completely understood why she was attracted to Layla, describing her as "a chaotic rainbow of a person" and declaring he was absolutely all for them dating.

After that memorable evening, Aubrey had made a deliberate point of introducing Layla and her quartet friends to Whitley's parents during several lunch meetings and social gatherings. The senior DuPonts had been completely charmed by Layla's directness, her talent, and her sincere dedication to the students she was teaching.

Whitley's parents didn't yet know she was harboring romantic feelings for Layla—that conversation was still to come—but after hearing all of their glowing stories about her throughout the year, Whitley was honestly more afraid they wouldn't think *she* was good enough for Layla when the truth finally came out.

And then there were the students at the music foundation, who, according to Aubrey, were absolutely devoted to their new teachers. Aubrey was convinced at least half of the young musicians were in love with either Layla or Puck, attributing their popularity to their charming British accents that apparently sent the teenage students "a bit gaga," as Aubrey had put it.

As lovely as it was that her family had gotten to know Layla so well over the past year, Whitley couldn't help but feel somewhat cheated by the situation. She was the one who desperately wanted to spend real, substantial time with Layla, face to face. She just wanted to be in the same room and share the same air. Video chatting and texting, wonderful as they were, simply didn't count as real time together in her mind.

Giving her carefully styled hair one last nervous fluff in the car's mirror, she reasoned tonight was going to be the start of something entirely new in her life. They were finally in the same city for the foreseeable future, with no ocean separating them and no time zone complications. It was the perfect opportunity to discover if Layla might want to take their relationship out of the friend zone and into something deeper and more meaningful.

A sharp frisson of nerves ran up her spine like an electric current. She'd tried countless times to rehearse what she would say to Layla, practicing different approaches and word choices, but nothing ever came out sounding right when she spoke the words aloud. In the end, she'd decided to trust that the right words would flow naturally when the moment presented itself.

A long line of elegant town cars and stretch limousines waited patiently in the December cold to access the fundraiser's designated drop-off point. It was officially a red-carpet event, complete with photographers and entertainment reporters, but Whitley had absolutely no desire to walk that gauntlet of flashing cameras and shouted questions.

"I'll hop out here, Ryan," she said, gathering her evening bag and wrapping her coat more tightly around herself.

"Are you sure, ma'am? It's quite cold, and you'll have to walk several blocks."

"Yes, I'm certain. There's no need for you to sit in this traffic jam for another hour."

"Very well. Have a wonderful evening, and welcome back to New York. It's truly nice to have you home again."

She gave him a genuinely warm smile, touched by his kindness. "It's incredibly good to be back, Ryan. Thank you for everything."

As usual, December had left New York City totally frozen, with a bitter wind that cut through even the most expensive winter coats. Whitley elegantly stepped from the warm car and immediately bustled toward the side entrance of the hotel, her heels clicking rapidly on the icy sidewalk.

Bruno, the DuPont family's longtime head of security, spotted her approach and quickly opened the heavy door, allowing her to slip inside quickly and quietly without attracting any unwanted attention.

"Thanks so much, Bruno. Make sure you keep warm out there tonight—it's brutal."

"Yes, ma'am. Good to have you back."

Walking briskly down the carpeted corridor, Whitley did her best to avoid the busy servers and event staff who were rushing back and forth with last-minute preparations. Maybe she should have just braved the red-carpet gauntlet after all—at least then she wouldn't be getting in everyone's way as they tried to do their jobs.

"There you are!" Aubrey's voice rang out across the hallway, filled with relief and excitement.

Rushing forward with her arms outstretched, Whitley scooped her sister up and held her tight, breathing in the familiar scent of her perfume. "Oh, God, you look absolutely beautiful, Aubs."

"You too, sis. It's so good to see you in person again, Whit. I've missed you."

They were quickly joined by an enthusiastic William, who squeezed both of his sisters tightly in a group embrace that nearly lifted them off their feet.

"Hey there, world traveler. Welcome back to the colonies."

"Where are Mom and Dad?" Whitley asked, looking around the bustling corridor.

Aubrey nodded toward the main event hall, where the sounds of a gathering crowd could be heard. "They're in there already, greeting guests and making sure everything's running smoothly. The show's about to start. You really did cut it pretty close getting here. We were starting to worry."

Whitley rolled her eyes with familiar exasperation. "Blame the unpredictable London weather and delayed flights. But I'm here now, so let's go see what magic you've all created."

Following her siblings through the ornate double doors into the main hall, Whitley audibly gasped at the sight that greeted her. The entire space had been completely transformed into what could only be described as a winter wonderland, but unlike anything she'd ever seen before.

"It's Winter in Wonderland," William whispered in her ear, his voice filled with pride. "Like Alice in Wonderland, but with a completely different twist."

Different was definitely the correct word, and if Layla hadn't been the main creative contributor to this incredible visual spectacle, Whitley would gladly eat her expensive ball gown. The esthetic was unlike anything she'd ever experienced.

"Steampunk Winter in Wonderland," she murmured to herself in amazement, taking in every incredible detail. "It's absolutely brilliant."

Not only was the room decorated in this fantastical style, with gears and clockwork mechanisms integrated into winter scenes, but she could see that each performer was dressed in different variations of Alice in Wonderland characters, all with Christmas-inspired steampunk twists that were both whimsical and sophisticated.

Making her way toward her parents, who were already seated in the front section of the transformed ballroom, Whitley did her best to spot Layla among the performers preparing backstage. Her heart was racing with anticipation at the thought of seeing her again after so many months apart.

Top Hats & Oven Gloves

"Sweetheart," Lucienne whispered as Whitley approached, immediately pulling her into a seated hug that smelled of expensive perfume and maternal warmth. "Welcome home, darling. We've missed you so much."

"Sorry I'm running so late," she replied breathlessly, leaning past her mother to give her father's hand a quick, affectionate squeeze. "The flight delays were unavoidable."

The lights began to lower dramatically, and suddenly the choir appeared on stage, beginning to sing a low, hauntingly quiet version of "Silent Night" that sent shivers down Whitley's spine. The stage scenery was spectacular, depicting a strange and magical world that seemed to exist somewhere between dreams and reality. It was completely hypnotizing—a sensory marvel that made the audience collectively hold their breath.

Then Whitley heard it—the first delicate stroke of a bow gliding across violin strings—a sound she'd recognize anywhere in the world. She'd know Layla's distinctive playing style even mixed in with a crowded orchestra. The lights dipped to almost total darkness before suddenly erupting into a dazzling show of technical mastery and artistic brilliance.

The choir raised their voices in perfect harmony, singing the familiar carol in a completely new and previously unheard arrangement that made it almost unrecognizable, yet somehow more familiar and meaningful than ever before. Whitley's eyes immediately snapped to center stage as Layla danced her way into the spotlight, playing her violin with fluid grace and obvious joy.

Her appearance was utterly breathtaking. Layla's wild dark hair was streaked with dramatic silver highlights that caught the stage lights like starlight. She wore ripped black skinny jeans that hugged her legs perfectly, paired with tall black boots that added to her commanding presence. A billowing white shirt dipped tantalizingly low, revealing just a peek of black lace that teased the audience's imagination. The ice-blue tailcoat she wore was clearly custom-made, featuring big brass buckles and ornate buttons that gleamed under the lights.

But the piece Whitley loved most was the magnificent top hat perched at a jaunty angle, complete with brass goggles that gave Layla the appearance of a beautiful, musical Mad Hatter.

"Isn't she absolutely amazing?" William whispered in her ear, but Whitley couldn't answer, her focus completely unwavering, as she watched Layla command the stage.

Layla twirled and dipped as she played, her body moving in perfect synchronization with the music flowing from her instrument. She was completely immersed in the performance, and Whitley found herself completely lost in watching her. How was it possible for someone to make such complex yet incredibly sweet sounds while moving with such athletic grace and precision? The only violin performances Whitley had experienced in the past were those of the LA Philharmonic Orchestra, where the musicians sat rigidly in their chairs and barely moved beyond the necessary bow movements.

Ninety minutes of pure musical artistry later, Whitley felt emotionally and physically wrung out, as if she'd been on an intense journey herself. Layla, Puck, Simon, Reena, and the entire choir had taken the audience on a magical winter adventure through sound and movement, completely entrancing everyone in the room. The audience was now on its feet, giving thunderous applause that seemed to shake the very foundations of the building.

They'd begun this standing ovation nearly ten minutes ago, and the crowd showed absolutely no signs of stopping their enthusiastic appreciation. The energy in the room was electric, charged with the kind of excitement that only came from witnessing something truly special and transformative.

With a final, graceful bow that made her coattails swirl dramatically, Layla handed off her precious violin to a stagehand and replaced it with a wireless microphone. "Thank you, thank you all so much!" she called out, her voice carrying easily over the continued applause.

Several more minutes of enthusiastic clapping, whistling, and cheering ensued, the sound building to an almost deafening crescendo.

"Alright, shut it!" Layla shouted with characteristic directness, causing Whitley to burst out laughing along with the rest of her family. The brash command did exactly what it was intended to do—the audience finally fell into expectant silence, though smiles remained on every face.

"Tonight is about much more than just a spectacular show celebrating the upcoming festive season, even though it was fucking epic!" The crowd laughed, appreciating her unfiltered commentary. "Tonight is fundamentally about raising money for the DuPont Foundation, which works tirelessly to help battered women and children find safety, hope, and new beginnings. So, with that critically important mission in mind, let's not pretend that you're all not totally loaded and perfectly capable of digging deep into those designer pockets."

This time, the crowd's applause was in acknowledgement of Layla's bluntness regarding their wealth and social status. A welcome honesty for a group expecting the typical platitudes. Some audience members were already reaching inside jacket pockets and expensive purses for their checkbooks, clearly moved by both the performance and the cause.

"I'd like to invite the entire DuPont family up onto the stage," Layla gestured grandly toward their section, "because without their vision, generosity, and unwavering commitment to helping others, none of this would be possible, and the world would be a significantly shittier place. So please, give it up for Lucienne, Lucas, Aubrey, William, and the absolutely delectable Whitley DuPont!"

Delectable. The word bounced around Whitley's head like a pinball, sending warm shivers through her entire body as she followed her family toward the stage. The crowd was clapping thunderously again, their enthusiasm infectious and overwhelming. Expecting her experienced parents to take the lead as they always did at public events, she was more than a little surprised when the microphone got handed directly to her instead.

"This is your baby, sweetie," Lucienne whispered in her ear with obvious pride. "You conceived this collaboration, so you should be the one to speak about it."

Okay, it looked like she needed to pull a coherent speech out of her jet-lagged, emotionally overwhelmed butt.

Taking the microphone with slightly trembling hands, she looked out at the sea of expectant faces. "Good evening, everyone. I have to apologize—I don't have any prepared remarks because I literally just flew in from London a few hours ago."

"Wing it!" Layla called out from the other side of the stage, her voice carrying clearly across the space and earning another round of laughter from the audience.

Giving Layla a grateful smile she hoped conveyed even a fraction of what she was feeling, Whitley took a steadying breath. "I'm going to keep this short and sweet, because honestly, after that incredible performance, anything I say will be anticlimactic. As Layla so eloquently pointed out, you're all incredibly wealthy and successful people. So please, I'm asking you to donate as generously as you possibly can tonight. The work we do with battered women and children isn't just important, it's genuinely life-altering and lifesaving."

She paused, looking out at the attentive faces in the audience. "As for tonight's phenomenally spectacular show, I honestly can't take any of the credit for what you've just witnessed. That belongs entirely to my brilliant siblings, Aubrey and William." Whitley turned to gesture toward them, offering a round of applause which the crowd enthusiastically matched. "They've worked tirelessly for an entire year to make this vision a reality."

"Lastly, we absolutely must give another tremendous round of applause to the most talented musicians I have ever had the privilege of not only seeing perform live, but of knowing personally as friends," she continued, her voice growing stronger with emotion.

A wave of thunderous sound echoed around the hall once more. Layla immediately grabbed Puck by the hand, who in turn grabbed Reena's, who was already holding on to Simon's. It created a beautiful domino effect as the entire choir and quartet lined up, holding hands, across the stage and took one final, synchronized bow that brought tears to many eyes in the audience.

Whitley smiled brilliantly at the captivated crowd, everyone in awe of witnessing such stunning talent. "Because we've combined tonight's fundraiser with our annual Christmas gala, I'd like to invite everyone to head out to the bar area so our wonderful event coordinators can transform this space for the next phase of our evening. We'll be back in here in approximately thirty minutes for dinner, dancing, and more entertainment. So please, go enjoy some drinks, mingle, and we'll see you all very soon. Thank you so much for being here tonight."

As the room began to empty with the buzz of excited conversation, Whitley finally had her first real chance to speak privately with Layla after an entire year of separation.

"Look who's finally back in town," Layla said with a radiant grin, sliding up next to her in all her steampunk wonderland glory, the top hat still perched perfectly on her head.

"You look fantastic!" The words tumbled out before Whitley could stop them, but she didn't care anymore about playing it cool. "And hello to you too!" She laughed, feeling giddy with relief and joy.

Layla cocked her head with amusement, the top hat somehow staying perfectly in place despite the movement. "Are we going to hug, or are we just going to stand here grinning at each other like idiots?"

After a full year of separation, Whitley couldn't wait even one more second. She stepped into Layla's open arms and held on tightly, breathing in the familiar scent of her perfume mixed with the faint smell of stage makeup and performance adrenaline. They stayed wrapped in each other's embrace until someone nearby pointedly cleared their throat.

Whitley wanted to pout at the interruption, but she forced herself to step back reluctantly. She still needed to gauge whether Layla had missed her in the same intense, yearning way that Whitley had missed her every single day.

"We need to let the events team do their jobs and set up for dinner," Lucas said diplomatically, gently coaxing them out of the performance space and toward the bar area where the rest of the guests were gathering.

"Hang on, I've got presents for everyone!" Layla shouted suddenly, breaking away from the group and dashing toward a side room where the performers had left their personal belongings.

The DuPont family exchanged amused glances at her infectious enthusiasm. "She really didn't need to get us anything," Lucienne said with obvious affection. "She's already given us so much."

Puck, who'd been packing up his cello nearby, shrugged with a knowing smile. "She felt like she absolutely had to do something special. We've all had such a blast working on this fundraiser project together."

"It's been the most fun any of us have had in years," William called out from his position at the bar, where a line was already forming, as guests eagerly sought festive drinks.

"Guys, over here!" Everyone turned toward Layla's voice. She had returned with a large gift bag placed at her feet and was practically vibrating with excitement.

"Aubrey, can you grab your brother?" Lucienne called to her youngest daughter, who was already making her way back from the bar area.

Whitley was the first to arrive at Layla's impromptu gift-giving station because she simply couldn't resist the magnetic pull of being close to her again. She watched with growing delight as Layla handed out small, carefully wrapped packages to each member of her family, laughing and chatting as they opened their presents with obvious enthusiasm and curiosity.

Her father was especially delighted when he unwrapped a set of novelty oven gloves that read in bold letters: "Many Have Eaten, Few Have Died." The joke was particularly perfect given his notorious reputation as a well-meaning but dangerous cook.

Feeling a small stab of disappointment that Layla seemed to have forgotten about her in the gift-giving excitement, Whitley kept a carefully neutral smile on her face as the rest of her family laughed and joked together over their thoughtful presents.

Just as she was about to slip away quietly and head back toward the bar to give them space, Layla suddenly tugged on her arm, leading her away from the group and into the relative privacy of the corridor.

"I got this especially for you," Layla said softly, holding out a small wrapped box with an expression that seemed almost nervous.

Whitley looked down at the carefully wrapped package in her hands. "What's this for?"

"It's your present, obviously."

"But I didn't do anything to deserve a gift." She laughed, though her heart was racing with anticipation.

"You did more than you know. Besides, I don't need an excuse to buy you something special," Layla replied, then quickly added, "but you should probably temper your enthusiasm a bit. It's really not much, just something small I thought you'd like."

With trembling hands, Whitley carefully unwrapped the gift, her breath catching when she saw what was inside. "I love it," she whispered, holding up the personalized ceramic mug that clearly stated it was the property of Whitley DuPont. On the opposite side were two delicately hand-painted candy canes that looked like they'd been crafted by a professional artist.

"I have a matching one back at my apartment," Layla explained, her voice soft and almost shy. "I thought I could keep it at your fancy penthouse, you know, for our annual hot chocolate sessions after the gala evenings. Make it a proper tradition."

Rolling her lips together to steady herself, Whitley took a deep, soothing breath before lifting her gaze to directly meet Layla's. The moment felt charged with possibility, holding a year's worth of unspoken feelings and carefully contained longing.

"Would you go out with me?" The words came out in a rush, bypassing all her careful planning and rehearsed speeches.

19

Dates & Personalized Mugs

Keep cool, just keep cool, Layla internally chanted as her heart hammered against her ribs like it was trying to escape her chest entirely.

"Okay, just for transparency's sake," Layla began, her voice slightly breathless as she tried to process what had just happened between them in this quiet corridor. "Are you asking me to go grab a hot chocolate somewhere, therefore fulfilling our yearly tradition like we always do? Or are you asking me out on an actual date, one that is decidedly not platonic and could potentially end with us both naked and tangled up in your silk sheets?"

Whitley's face immediately flamed a brilliant shade of red, which was both incredibly cute and genuinely encouraging for Layla's hopes. "Um...both, actually," she replied, her voice barely above a whisper.

"And you're absolutely sure about it? The second part, I mean?" Layla pressed, needing to be completely certain before she allowed herself to get carried away by hope and desire. As far as she was concerned, Whitley had never shown any romantic or sexual interest in another woman before now. Sure, they may have shared a few confusing looks and lingering pauses over the past couple of years—moments that could potentially be misconstrued as sapphic longing—but Layla knew from bitter experience it wasn't always easy to accurately read the signals from straight women who might just be naturally affectionate or curious.

"Very sure," Whitley said with growing confidence, her voice stronger now. "I've honestly thought about little else for over a year, Layla. You've been on my mind constantly."

Whoa! That was definitely not the response Layla had been expecting. "Then yes, absolutely yes. To both parts of your question."

This might genuinely be the best night of Layla's entire life, and that was saying something considering she'd just performed in front of hundreds of New York's elite and helped raise a fortune for charity.

Whitley smiled at her with such genuine warmth and affection that Layla felt it resonate through her to her very soul, like a tuning fork struck against her heart.

"Shall we stay at the party for a little while longer, make the necessary social appearances, and then head back to my place? I had Aubrey stock the refrigerator with whipped cream."

Layla couldn't help herself—she wanted to giggle as Whitley's eyes went wide with what looked like sudden panic at her own words.

"Cream, huh?" Layla replied with deliberate suggestiveness, enjoying the way Whitley's blush deepened.

"No, I mean, well, yes, there's cream, but it's for the hot chocolate," Whitley stammered adorably. "Not for...I wasn't suggesting..."

Stifling her amusement at Whitley's flustered state, Layla gently caught her arm in a reassuring gesture. "I know exactly what you meant, love. I was only teasing you. Come on, let's go back inside and mingle with all these obscenely wealthy people who hopefully have very deep pockets."

The ballroom was already filled to capacity with elegantly dressed guests chatting animatedly, couples dancing to the live band, and small groups singing along to familiar holiday songs as they stepped through the ornate double doors. In truth, Layla wanted to be *absolutely* anywhere but at this gala right now. Ideally, she'd prefer to be snuggled up in Whitley's luxurious penthouse with very little clothing on either of them—that would definitely be her best-case scenario for how this evening could progress.

But those sorts of activities would have to wait, and not just because she wanted to squeeze as much money as possible out of the wealthy people filling this room for the foundation's important work. More significantly, Whitley might not be emotionally ready for physical intimacy yet. If it had taken her an entire year to finally work up the courage to ask Layla out on a date, she might need some time to get comfortable with the reality of woman parts smushing together.

Grabbing two crystal flutes of expensive Champagne from a passing server's tray, Layla raised her glass towards

Whitley in a celebratory gesture and took a healthy, fortifying swig of the bubbling liquid. Spotting Aubrey, William, Puck, Simon, and Reena gathered near the dance floor, she motioned for Whitley to follow her through the crowd.

They danced and laughed together through several upbeat songs, the music providing a perfect soundtrack for their group's celebratory mood. Everyone deserved to have some genuine fun after months of hard work preparing for this event, but Layla found her need to be alone with Whitley only grew stronger as the minutes ticked by. Every accidental brush of their hands, every shared glance, every moment of standing close together on the crowded dance floor only intensified her desire to have a real conversation about what was happening between them.

"Can we have that hot chocolate now?" Whitley whispered directly into her ear halfway through a slow, romantic Michael Bublé ballad, her breath warm against Layla's skin and sending shivers down her spine.

Nodding eagerly, Layla made quick work of saying goodnight to their friends and family members. If she wasn't completely mistaken, the knowing grins on Aubrey and William's faces said quite a lot about their awareness of the situation. Were they already privy to Whitley's romantic feelings? Had she confided in her siblings about her attraction?

It took considerably longer to extract themselves from Lucienne and Lucas, who were both a bit tipsy from the evening's Champagne and overly affectionate in the way that made Layla's heart ache with homesickness. As much as she genuinely enjoyed living in New York and building her career here, not having her own family close by was difficult at times. Lucienne and Lucas had welcomed her into their family circle over the past year with open arms, and their warmth had eased her homesickness considerably.

"Good evening, Ryan," Layla called out cheerfully, her breath forming white clouds in the frigid December air as they hurried through the steadily falling snow towards the waiting car.

"Good evening, Layla. I love your costume tonight," Ryan replied with genuine enthusiasm as he held the car door open for them. "Very creative and perfectly executed."

Shit, she still had the elaborate top hat perched on her head. Whipping it off with a laugh, she ducked into the blissfully heated vehicle with a sigh of relief. "Thanks, man. I was definitely going for the whole Mad Hatter in Winter Wonderland vibe."

"Well, you completely sold me on the concept." He laughed warmly. "Where shall we head tonight?"

"Home, please, Ryan," Whitley said softly, settling into the plush leather seat beside Layla.

They settled into the comfortable silence of the car's interior and grew quiet, the only sounds being the gentle hum of the engine and the soft jazz music playing through the sound system. Layla desperately wanted to say something meaningful, anything that might bridge the sudden awkwardness that had descended between them, but her mind was racing with too many thoughts and emotions to form coherent sentences.

She'd fantasized about this exact moment, never truly believing it could actually happen in real life. Well, technically speaking, they weren't officially on their first date yet—this car ride was still part of their established friendship routine. But the air between them felt fundamentally different now, charged with new possibilities and unspoken desires.

Was Whitley expecting them to simply have their traditional hot chocolate and conversation as they always did? Layla honestly wasn't sure she could manage to act normally, not with so many urgent questions running rampant through her mind and her body humming with awareness of the woman sitting so close beside her.

Layla's internal musings and nervous energy lasted throughout the entire car ride. She noticed a slight tremor in Whitley's hand as she reached for the elevator biometric scanner, clearly feeling just as nervous and uncertain as Layla was about what came next.

Taking a step forward so her front was pressed snugly against Whitley's back, Layla placed her hand gently on Whitley's hip in what she hoped was a comforting gesture.

"It's okay, love. Nothing has to happen tonight that you're not ready for. We can just talk about the idea of dating...explore what that might mean for us."

Straightening up and turning around, Whitley found herself encircled in Layla's arms, their faces now just inches apart. "What if I want something to happen between us?" she asked quietly, her voice filled with a mixture of hope and uncertainty.

"Let's go inside first," Layla replied, her mouth suddenly completely devoid of moisture. "We should probably have this conversation somewhere more private than your parking garage."

After a charged ride up to the penthouse, Whitley slipped away to change out of her formal gown while Layla positioned herself by the floor-to-ceiling windows, ostensibly admiring the spectacular view of the city spread out below. This time, though, she wasn't really thinking about the glittering lights or how impressive the penthouse was. No, her mind was entirely focused on the woman currently removing her clothes in another room, and every part of her wanted to abandon propriety and go find Whitley to show her exactly what she did to Layla's body and heart.

"I'll make us some hot chocolate," Whitley announced from behind Layla, her voice slightly breathless.

Closing her eyes and taking several deep, calming breaths, Layla slowly turned around. Whitley had changed into her comfortable sweatpants and that perfectly fitted cashmere jumper, and she looked absolutely edible in the soft lighting of the living room.

"That sounds perfect. Do you need any help in the kitchen?" Layla offered, though she wasn't sure she trusted herself to be in close quarters with Whitley right now.

"No, thank you. Just make yourself comfortable and I'll have it ready in a few minutes."

Layla wished desperately that she had brought a change of clothes with her. Everything about her costume suddenly felt too tight, too constricting. Her skin felt hot and oversensitive. If she were being honest with herself, it wasn't really the clothing that was the problem—it was the company and the charged atmosphere between them.

Let Whitley lead this. Give her the time and space she needs to figure out what she wants.

The rich, comforting smell of melting chocolate gradually brought Layla back to the present moment. Whitley approached with a warm smile, carefully placing a steaming mug on the glass coffee table. Layla couldn't help but grin when she noticed Whitley was using the personalized mug she'd given her as a gift.

"Damn, I really wish I'd thought to bring my matching mug tonight," she said with regret. "We would have been perfectly coordinated."

Whitley shrugged casually, though there was something meaningful in her expression. "You can bring it over the next time you come visit. Hot chocolate nights don't have to be limited to once a year anymore, you know."

"So you really *do* want to date me?" The question burst out of Layla before she could stop herself, and she immediately rolled her eyes at her own chronic impatience and impulsiveness. It was a lifelong condition she'd suffered from since...well, forever, really.

Whitley's smile was radiant and amused. "I'm honestly impressed it took you this long to ask directly. I was sure you would have cracked and demanded answers during the car ride."

"I'm growing and maturing as an adult. What can I say?" Layla replied with an exaggerated wink that made Whitley bite her lower lip in response.

"Hmm, I'm sure you are," Whitley murmured, and the way she said it sent heat racing through Layla's veins.

20

Hot Chocolate & Heated Moments

Tension thicker than custard descended over the room like a heavy blanket. Jesus, Layla was having intense feelings in some very inconvenient places. Her clit pulsated to the rhythm of her rapidly beating heart, and the sight of Whitley biting that perfect lower lip was almost too much for her to handle. She was only human, after all, and there were limits to her self-control.

"Okay, I need you not to do that again, Whit," she said, her voice slightly strained with the effort of maintaining composure.

"Do what?" Whitley asked, looking genuinely confused by the request. "I don't understand what I did wrong."

"Biting your lip like that. It's officially banned until I know it's okay for me to kiss you, which hopefully happens after our first proper date. If that's still what you want, of course?"

Whitley's eyes widened with surprise and something that looked like pleased realization. "Biting my lip...turns you on?"

Layla let out a bark of laughter at the innocent way Whitley asked the question. "Whit, absolutely everything you do turns me on. The way you move, the way you talk, the way you look at me...it's all incredibly sexy."

"How...how long have you actually liked me?" Whitley asked quietly, as though she was afraid of the answer.

"Um...since the moment we first met," Layla replied honestly, watching carefully for Whitley's reaction. She saw her swallow hard and noticed the way her pupils dilated slightly. Those were definitely good signs. "But as far as I knew, you were completely straight, and I'm far enough along my rainbow journey to have already learned my lesson about getting involved with straight women. No offense intended."

"None taken at all," Whitley assured her quickly.

"So I guess what I'm trying to say is that I just want to make absolutely sure this is really about you and me as individuals, and not about—"

"Experimenting," Whitley finished for her, understanding immediately where Layla's concerns were coming from.

"Exactly." Layla was self-aware enough to know that no matter how intensely attracted to Whitley she was, she couldn't allow herself to be someone's sexual experiment or temporary curiosity. Their friendship was worth far more than that, and more importantly, Layla knew she was worth more than that. A casual friends-with-benefits arrangement definitely wouldn't be enough for her heart to handle.

Shifting closer on the couch, Whitley placed her trembling hand on Layla's thigh, the warmth of her palm seeping through the fabric of her costume. "I didn't want that kind of casual arrangement either, which is exactly why I've taken this entire year to really figure out my feelings and what they mean. It's true that I've never been attracted to a woman before in my life. But then you came along, and something deep inside me stirred to life. I couldn't even begin to explain what was happening to me at first."

Layla felt her breath catch as Whitley continued, her voice growing stronger and more confident.

"But then it gradually became crystal clear that I found you attractive. Incredibly sexy, actually. And yes, it momentarily shocked me to realize I was capable of feeling this way about another woman. I spoke to Aubrey and William about it, and they suggested I should take the time while I was in London to really explore these new feelings."

"With other women?" The question came out sharper than Layla had intended, and she could feel a spike of jealousy at the very thought.

"Yes, that was their suggestion," Whitley admitted. "But I didn't pursue anyone else, because all I could think about was you. Every day, every conversation, every moment...it all came back to you."

Layla tried desperately to keep the satisfied smirk off her face, but she failed completely. "I can't say that news upsets me in the slightest."

"Yes, that triumphant grin entirely gives away your feelings." Whitley chuckled, seeming more relaxed now.

"Our friendship means absolutely everything to me, Layla. This past year of getting to know each other better through calls and messages has been wonderful and meaningful. But it's not enough anymore. I've actually felt jealous of my own family members, for goodness' sake."

"Why would you be jealous of them?" Layla asked, genuinely curious.

Waving her hands in the air in frustration, Whitley shook her head with obvious exasperation. "Because they got to spend real time with you, face to face, while I was stuck thousands of miles away only able to talk to you through a screen."

Throwing caution completely to the wind, Layla reached up and gently cupped Whitley's face in both hands, her thumbs brushing softly across those perfect cheekbones. "I've loved every single second of getting to know you better too, Whit. Trust me when I say I know exactly how you feel about the distance and the longing."

She loved the way Whitley immediately leaned into her touch, like a cat seeking warmth and affection. Was this the right moment to lean in for their first real kiss?

"So you'll actually date me then?" Whitley asked, her eyes shining with hope and vulnerability. Did she really think Layla would say anything other than an enthusiastic yes?

"When do we start? I want us to have our first official date as soon as possible," Layla replied eagerly.

"How about right now?" Whitley moved a little closer, closing some of the distance between them on the couch. "I think this evening already constitutes our first date, don't you?"

Unable to resist the magnetic pull any longer, Layla closed the remaining distance between them. Whitley's lips were every bit as soft as she had imagined during countless daydreams, and they tasted like rich chocolate and Champagne—absolutely the best combination ever. She breathed Whitley in, allowing her intoxicating scent to infiltrate every square inch of her heightened senses.

Opening her mouth slightly, Layla dipped just the tip of her tongue into the seam of Whitley's lips. The low, breathy groan she managed to tease out of her was absolutely electrifying. Layla's nerve endings were firing in all directions, and her entire body vibrated with anticipation and desire.

Whitley responded by sucking gently on Layla's tongue, her hands fisting in the fabric of Layla's shirt to pull her even closer. If they weren't careful, this moment was going to end up progressing much further than either of them was truly ready for. Layla desperately wanted to make love to Whitley—there was no question about that—but she wanted them to have a proper discussion about physical intimacy first.

Nipping gently at Whitley's bottom lip, she reluctantly pulled back, disconnecting their mouths despite every instinct screaming at her to continue. Whitley's immediate grumble of displeasure made her laugh softly.

"Why have we stopped kissing?" Whitley asked with obvious frustration, already leaning forward to try to recapture Layla's lips.

"Because we need to talk more about what we both want from this," Layla replied, though it took considerable willpower to maintain the distance between them.

"Why do we need to talk right now?" Whitley protested, continuing to lean forward in pursuit of more kisses.

Laughing at her persistence, Layla gently took Whitley's shoulders and pushed her back against the couch cushions. "Because we've literally only just decided to try dating five minutes ago. Sleeping together is a completely different conversation and decision!"

"We were just kissing, not having sex, Layla," Whitley pointed out reasonably.

"We were roughly ten seconds away from ripping each other's clothes off, Whit!" Layla countered. "I could feel how quickly things were escalating."

Whitley blushed deeply but didn't attempt to deny the accuracy of that assessment. "What if I want to sleep with you tonight?" she asked quietly.

Bloody hell, she wasn't making this easy at all. "Whitley, I would love nothing more than to ravage you until sunrise and show you exactly how incredible it can be between two women. But we need to slow down just a bit. This...this means far more to me than a single night of passion."

"You're absolutely right, and I'm sorry for pushing," Whitley said, sitting back and smoothing down her jumper in an attempt to regain some composure. The gesture was endearing and slightly awkward.

"Please don't apologize for wanting me," Layla said firmly. "Kissing you is honestly a dream come true. All my Christmas wishes made into reality."

"Such a charmer." Whitley giggled, the sound like music to Layla's ears. "But just so you know, I'm not scared to do this, Layla. I genuinely want to go out with you and explore what we could be together, because I have this strong feeling it's going to be something pretty extraordinary."

"I feel exactly the same way. So let's have a proper first date and see where it takes us."

Suddenly jumping up from the couch, Whitley ran out of the room without explanation, leaving Layla sitting there completely confused and wondering if she'd somehow said something wrong.

"There!" Whitley shouted from somewhere in the hallway, her voice getting progressively louder as she returned to the living room. "I've ordered dinner from that amazing Italian place downtown. It should be here in about thirty minutes. We can have a romantic meal together over a bottle of good wine while the snow falls outside. All the classic requirements for a perfect first date. I'm going to get dressed up properly for the occasion. You just sit right there looking absolutely delicious, and I'll be back soon to pour us some wine."

No sooner had Whitley finished her enthusiastic explanation than she disappeared again, leaving Layla sitting alone with a lazy, satisfied grin spreading across her face. Whitley really, truly wanted this relationship to work.

Standing up and stretching, Layla retook her position by the windows, watching the city lights twinkle below. She could see her reflection in the glass, which made her laugh out loud. She looked crazy in her steampunk costume, like she'd just escaped from a theatrical production. Her hair was completely out of control, a wild mass of curls with silver streaks, but there really wasn't much she could do about it at this point.

Plus, Whitley should probably get accustomed to Layla's weird and wonderful fashion sense sooner rather than later. Looking at her reflection more critically, she found herself really liking the dramatic silver streaks woven through her dark mane.

"Hmm, maybe I should keep them permanently," she mused to herself, her voice soft as she watched the snow fall harder outside. The weather forecasters had warned of a significant snowstorm moving through the area, and they clearly weren't exaggerating. At this rate, New York would grind to a complete halt within a few short hours.

In the window's reflection, Layla saw Whitley's behemoth cat, Milkshake, saunter into the room. It took one look at Layla and immediately began cleaning its arse. There was at least one DuPont not entirely enamored with Layla, then.

The distinctive clicking of high heels on marble pulled Layla's attention away from the increasingly dramatic weather outside and the scowling cat. Turning around, her entire body went rigid at the sight that greeted her.

Layla had seen Whitley dressed up in gorgeous designer gowns and expensive jewelry many times, but this particular look was her favorite to date.

"I thought you said you were getting dressed?" she managed to say, her voice slightly hoarse.

"I did get dressed," Whitley replied with obvious feigned innocence.

Layla gritted her teeth, realizing Whitley was absolutely trying to kill her with desire. Yes, she had technically changed clothes in the sense that she was no longer wearing her comfortable sweatpants and jumper. But now she was wearing something infinitely more dangerous: a silk robe in deep emerald green that finished scandalously high on her thighs, teasing Layla with tantalizing glimpses of the smooth skin she desperately wanted to get her hands, mouth, and teeth on.

"Whit," she said, her voice carrying a warning tone.

"Layla," Whitley replied sweetly, pretending she had no idea what effect she was having.

"I thought we just had a conversation about taking things slow and not rushing into physical intimacy?"

"We *did* have that conversation," Whitley agreed with a mischievous smile. "And I think years of wanting you, plus one romantic meal and a glass of wine, is quite slow enough. Don't you agree?"

21

Mistakes & Morning Confessions

How was it even possible Whitley was waking up completely alone in her enormous bed? More importantly, and far more frustratingly, how had she managed to go to bed alone after what had seemed like such a promising evening?

They'd shared a delightful meal of exquisite Italian cuisine delivered from one of the city's most exclusive restaurants. They'd consumed an entire bottle of rich red wine while engaging in increasingly flirty conversation that had made Whitley's cheeks warm and her pulse quicken with anticipation. Everything had seemed to be progressing perfectly toward what she'd hoped would be a stellar, passionate ending to their first official date.

But then Layla had kissed her one last time with what felt like genuine desire, wished Whitley a polite good night, and disappeared into the guest bedroom without so much as a backward glance.

At first, Whitley had genuinely thought Layla was joking around, perhaps playing some kind of seductive game. But once the guest bedroom door had closed with a definitive click and hadn't opened again for the rest of the night, Whitley had stood there in the hallway completely aghast at how completely wrong she'd judged the situation and had misread all the signals.

Layla's passionate words throughout the evening had been in direct contradiction to her ultimate actions. She'd repeatedly said she wanted Whitley, had looked at her with obvious desire, and her kisses had certainly reflected genuine attraction and longing. But then, when it came to the crucial moment...absolutely nothing had happened.

Even after Whitley had spent the entire evening sitting provocatively in that silk robe with expensive lingerie underneath, and even after she'd made her interest abundantly clear through words and actions, Layla had simply walked away from her. Sure, they'd made out passionately over the course of the evening, sharing heated kisses that had left Whitley breathless and aching for more, but that was exactly where all the fun had stopped.

The harsh glare of morning sunlight reflecting brilliantly off the fresh snow outside lit up Whitley's spacious bedroom like a spotlight. Rolling her head to the side with a groan, she squinted at the digital clock on her nightstand. It was only 8:30 a.m.—far too early to be awake.

Her attention suddenly snapped to the distinct sound of a door opening and closing somewhere else in her apartment. Whitley was too disoriented and groggy to decipher exactly which door had made the noise, but her heart immediately began racing with panic. Shit, could Layla possibly be sneaking out without saying goodbye? Was she planning to disappear before they could have any kind of conversation about what had happened between them?

Straining her ears and holding her breath, Whitley waited in tense silence for any additional sounds. There! That was definitely the sound of someone knocking gently on her bedroom door. Relief flooded through her system as she realized Layla wasn't trying to escape.

Scrambling frantically from the tangled sheets of her bed, Whitley race-walked across the room and yanked the door open without taking even a second to think about her appearance or state of dress. If she'd paused for just one moment longer to consider her actions, Whitley might have realized that she was wearing absolutely nothing except a pair of delicate lace panties. Not a single other stitch of clothing covered her body.

Layla's eyes immediately grew wide as they automatically scanned Whitley's exposed form from head to toe. It took Whitley several beats to fully comprehend her mortifying mistake and realize exactly what Layla was seeing.

"Oh my God!" she gasped, immediately whipping her arms across her chest in a futile attempt at modesty. Using her foot to slam the door shut again, she pressed her back against it and hissed, "Fuck, fuck, fuck!"

Frantically scouring the floor of her bedroom, she finally located her discarded silk robe and wrapped it tightly around herself, pulling the belt snug and blowing out a deep, shaky breath as she tried to regain some semblance of composure.

The gentle knocking sound came again, more tentative this time. Willing the intense heat in her face to recede to a less obvious shade of red, she slowly made her way back to the door. Opening it just a crack, Whitley peered at Layla through the narrow sliver of space, hoping her embarrassment wasn't too painfully obvious.

"Hey there," Layla said softly, giving her a small, understanding smile and an awkward little wave. "Can we talk for a few minutes?"

Biting her lower lip nervously, Whitley opened the door a bit further while trying to sound completely unaffected by what had just happened. "What's up?" she asked, though she could still feel her face burning with mortification.

"I made a mistake last night," Layla said directly, her voice carrying a note of regret that immediately caught Whitley's attention.

"A mistake?" Whitley's heart sank as various horrible possibilities raced through her mind. Was Layla referring to kissing her? Was she already regretting admitting her attraction and asking for a relationship? Was she having second thoughts about everything they'd shared? Well, this conversation was certainly going horribly wrong already.

Layla took a deliberate step forward until she was positioned only inches away from Whitley, close enough she could smell her familiar perfume mixed with the lingering scent of wine from the night before.

"I shouldn't have left you alone last night, Whit. I wanted to give you space and time to make absolutely sure that being with me physically was truly what you wanted and were emotionally ready for. But you'd already told me clearly you were ready. So after spending hours tossing and turning uncomfortably in that guest bed, I finally realized that my hesitation was less about protecting you and more about me being the one with serious concerns."

"What kind of concerns?" Whitley asked, genuinely curious about what could have made Layla pull back when they'd both been so obviously ready to take things further.

"I was concerned that you'd rock my world so thoroughly and completely that when you inevitably decide to leave me, I'd be absolutely fucked, and not in the fun, pleasurable way," Layla admitted with characteristic bluntness.

This was certainly interesting, and not at all what Whitley had been expecting to hear. "And why exactly would I leave you?"

"Because you're this wonderful, accomplished philanthropist who only thinks of helping others and making the world a better place," Layla said, her voice taking on an almost self-deprecating tone. "Meanwhile, I'm a scattered, chaotic musician who's still trying to figure out how to make something meaningful of herself. I don't have a steady paycheck or any kind of financial security, and I live with three other people in an apartment the size of your closet. I'm too straightforward and blunt, and I usually end up putting my foot in my mouth at the worst possible moments. My sense of fashion has been questioned and criticized many times by people who matter, and I don't own a single ball gown or piece of designer clothing."

Layla paused, looking confused. "And you're smiling at me right now? Why are you smiling?"

Whitley couldn't help herself, because yes, Layla *was* a straight-shooting, wild-haired, chaotic force of nature who dressed however the hell she wanted without caring about anyone else's opinions. And Whitley loved every single aspect of that beautiful, authentic mess. She genuinely wanted Layla's particular brand of delightful chaos in her life.

"None of those things you just listed would ever make me want to leave you, Layla," she said firmly. "I'll tell you exactly what would make me walk away, though. Cheating. Dishonesty. Betrayal of trust."

"I would never, ever do any of those things to you," Layla replied immediately, her voice filled with conviction.

"Then please stop worrying about all the rest of it," Whitley said gently. "We've kissed and it was fucking wonderful—better than I ever imagined it could be. I'm ready to have sex with you. I want to be intimate with you. We're friends first and foremost, and that friendship is incredibly important to me, so please trust me when I tell you I wouldn't say these things to you lightly. Not if I thought it could negatively affect our friendship in any way."

"You have absolutely fantastic breasts," Layla said suddenly, her eyes dropping automatically to where Whitley's robe had shifted slightly.

Whitley giggled at the unexpected compliment and the perfect example of Layla's tendency to speak without filtering her thoughts. There was the foot-in-mouth bluntness she'd grown to love so much.

"Thank you very much. I'd love to reciprocate that compliment, but I haven't actually seen yours yet."

"Let's rectify that situation immediately," Layla said with growing confidence. "If you still want to, that is."

Instead of answering with words, Whitley slowly tugged at the silk ties of her robe, letting the fabric fall open as she took a deliberate step backward. She wanted to give Layla a view she'd remember for the rest of her life. She smirked with satisfaction as Layla's eyes immediately dropped to her newly exposed breasts, her pupils dilating with obvious desire.

"I'm going to make love to you now, Whit," Layla said, her voice dropping to a husky whisper that sent shivers down Whitley's spine. "If there's anything you don't like or that makes you uncomfortable, tell me immediately. No means stop, always. If there's anything specific you want me to do to you, tell me, and I'll do it gladly."

Whitley made a sound that was part eager agreement and part desperate whimper. "Do whatever you want to me, Layla, but for the love of God, please just touch me! I've been waiting for this for so long."

22

Big O's & Snow Day Discoveries

Whitley was lifted off the floor in one swift, powerful motion that made her gasp with surprise and delight. Even though she was only mere feet away from her king-sized bed, she instinctively wrapped her legs around Layla's waist, pressing their bodies together as intimately as possible. Their lips crashed against each other with desperate hunger, months of pent-up desire finally being released. Layla's strong hands grabbed her ass possessively, kneading her cheeks with passionate fervor that made Whitley's entire body come alive with sensation.

The insistent pulsing between her legs drove Whitley to roll her hips against Layla's body, seeking any kind of friction or relief. "I'm so incredibly turned on right now," she breathed against Layla's lips. "I've never felt anything like this before."

Layla took the final few steps toward Whitley's enormous bed with careful precision. She lowered Whitley gently onto the silk sheets without breaking the contact of their lips for even a moment. "Don't move a muscle," Layla commanded softly, giving her one last lingering kiss before standing back up. "I want to look at you properly."

Whitley watched with fascination as Layla began to strip off her clothes with deliberate slowness, revealing every inch of pale, freckled skin. She took in every detail greedily—the light constellation of freckles that dusted Layla's shoulders like stardust, the graceful curve of her neck, the sudden revelation of her perfect breasts with their dusky pink nipples already hardened with arousal.

"Now I can return that compliment," Whitley murmured, her voice thick with desire. "You have fantastic breasts, Layla. They're even more beautiful than I imagined."

"Do you want to touch them?" Layla asked, her voice carrying a note of hopeful invitation.

"Yes, desperately," Whitley replied honestly. She wanted to do so much more than just touch them. Her mouth was practically watering with the desire to latch onto Layla's nipples, to feel their weight in her palms as she massaged and explored every curve and sensitive spot.

"Can I take your knickers off?" Layla asked, her fingers already hovering at the waistband of Whitley's delicate lace panties.

Whitley nodded eagerly. "Yours too, please. I want to see all of you."

Layla smiled with obvious pleasure, slipping her thumbs under the waistband of her boy shorts. The fabric hit the floor, and Whitley gasped audibly at the sight before her. Layla was absolutely stunning in her complete nakedness—curvy and soft in all the right places, with smooth skin that seemed to glow in the morning light. The neat patch of dark curls between her legs immediately captured Whitley's attention, and the sight had remarkable effects on her body. She could feel wetness soaking through her panties as her arousal reached new heights. If she weren't already turned on to the point of complete distraction, she'd probably be embarrassed by her body's obvious response.

"Like what you see?" Layla asked with a knowing grin, clearly aware of the effect she was having.

"Very much indeed," Whitley managed to say. "Now, can we please get to the point where you put your gorgeous body on mine? I'm dying here."

Laughing at her impatience, Layla stepped forward and reached for the waistband of Whitley's underwear. "Just one more second, love."

The cool morning air immediately nipped at Whitley's most sensitive areas, making her shudder with a combination of cold and anticipation. Layla's calloused hands from years of violin playing stroked slowly up her legs, causing goosebumps to erupt across her skin in waves. When the tip of Layla's tongue suddenly skirted up the inside of her thigh, she sucked in a sharp breath in anticipation of what was coming next.

Whitley had thought about this moment countless times during her year in London. She'd wondered what it would feel like for Layla to touch her so intimately, to explore her body with those talented musician's hands. But all her private ruminations and fantasies had *absolutely* nothing on the incredible reality of the situation.

"Open your legs a little more for me, love," Layla requested softly, her breath warm against Whitley's sensitive skin.

Whitley's nostrils flared as she opened herself up further, completely vulnerable and exposed. Layla's eyes never left her center, drinking in the sight with obvious appreciation and desire. Whitley wanted to completely undo her lover, to drive her as crazy with want as she was feeling. Considering this was the first time she was attempting to seduce another woman, Whitley decided to rely entirely on her instincts and natural responses.

With one hand fisting the expensive silk sheets beneath her, her other hand snaked over her hip and dropped to her sex. She saw Layla's pupils dilate dramatically as she used two fingers to spread herself open, displaying her arousal and readiness.

"Layla, please," she whispered desperately. "I need you so much."

No more words were necessary or exchanged. Layla dipped her head and ran her tongue in one long, slow stroke up Whitley's slit. They both moaned in perfect unison at the first contact, the sound echoing through the quiet bedroom.

Oh God, it's finally happening. This is really happening!

Whitley felt her thighs begin to tremble with every expert stroke of Layla's tongue. She'd certainly had orgasms before with previous partners, but nothing even remotely close to the monster climax that was currently building its way through her entire body. The sensation started low in her belly and radiated outward until every single nerve ending vibrated with pure ecstasy.

The incredible experience only got better as Layla added two fingers to the mix, sliding them inside with perfect precision. Her thrusts started out slow and sure, allowing Whitley to adjust to the new sensations, but as Whitley's hips began to buck uncontrollably, those thrusts became faster and more urgent to match her desperate need.

"Oh!" It wasn't particularly original or eloquent, but that singular word was the only thing Whitley could manage to articulate as wave after wave of intense pleasure crashed down on her like a tsunami. The world around her went completely quiet, and her vision fogged over with the intensity of sensation. There was nothing in existence except this blissful, overwhelming silence and the incredible woman between her legs.

"I should have known you were a screamer." Layla's amused voice gradually crept through the silent euphoria that had enveloped Whitley's consciousness. Blinking slowly and trying to focus, Whitley realized she was gasping desperately for breath, and her throat felt raw and sore.

"W-what?" she managed to croak out, still disoriented from the intensity of her climax.

Layla's face appeared above her, and Whitley could see her own arousal glistening on Layla's mouth and chin. Had she really done that? Had her body produced all that evidence of pleasure?

"You just screamed loud enough to wake the entire building, love," Layla said with obvious pride and satisfaction. "And it's done absolute wonders for my ego, I have to say."

Covering her face with both hands in embarrassment, Whitley laughed breathlessly. "Sorry about that. I had no idea I was being so loud."

Her hands were gently peeled away from her face. Layla shifted position until her nose was rubbing affectionately against Whitley's, their faces inches apart.

"Never, *ever* apologize for making those beautiful sounds," she said firmly. "They were utterly perfect."

Whitley reached up and sucked gently on Layla's bottom lip, tasting herself there. "I'd very much like to see if I can get you to make similar noises," she said with growing confidence.

She breathed the words directly into Layla's mouth as her hands began to wander and explore. Yes, she definitely wanted to do some thorough investigating of her own. Rolling them over with more strength than she knew she possessed, Whitley positioned herself astride Layla's thighs, looking down at the beautiful woman spread beneath her.

"I honestly don't know where to start," she admitted, though it wasn't nerves that were the issue. The problem was that Layla's body was so incredibly beautiful, Whitley didn't know what to focus on first. She wanted to kiss every inch of skin, to touch and lick and explore everything. All of it. But mostly, she wanted to bring Layla the same earth-shattering pleasure she'd just experienced.

"My breasts are quite sensitive, so I really like them being played with," Layla offered helpfully. "Penetration alone doesn't really do much for me because I don't feel it as intensely, but when it's paired with tongue work on my clit it gets me seeing stars every time."

"Okay, good to know," Whitley replied, appreciating the clear direction. She was already trailing her fingertips up Layla's abdomen to cup her breasts in both hands. The low, appreciative moan Layla let slip had Whitley immediately snapping her eyes up to watch her face. Layla was pushing her chest out, offering herself more fully, her eyes closed and her tongue unconsciously darting out to lick her lips.

Bending down, Whitley experimentally flicked her tongue across the tip of Layla's left nipple. The sharp intake of breath she earned made her smile with satisfaction. Layla really *did* love having her breasts touched and teased. Swapping sides, she gave Layla's right nipple the exact same treatment, earning another breathy gasp of pleasure.

Feeling increasingly confident with each positive response, she gradually worked her way down Layla's body until she was positioned between her legs, face hovering over the patch of dark hair that had captured her attention and imagination from the moment she'd first seen it. Layla's distinctive scent filled her senses completely—musky and sweet and utterly intoxicating.

This was another thing she'd dreamed about frequently during those long, lonely nights in London. Once again, the reality blew all her expectations completely out of the water.

"Are you okay down there?" Layla asked breathlessly, clearly eager for more contact.

"I'm taking you in, memorizing every detail," Whitley replied honestly.

"Could you possibly take me in with your tongue?" Layla suggested with barely contained desperation.

Whitley chuckled at the request, then lowered her head to comply. The first taste of Layla's arousal made her pause in wonder. She was sweeter than Whitley's own taste, with a flavor that reminded her of smooth bourbon sitting on her tongue. She immediately needed another sample. This time, Whitley took a longer, more thorough swipe with her tongue.

"I really like this," she commented absently as she moved back for another exploratory lap, completely absorbed in this new experience.

"*You* like it?" Layla panted, her voice strained with need.

"Shh, I'm busy here," Whitley said with newfound authority, ignoring any potential protests as she got back to her important work. She experimented with sucking gently on Layla's swollen lips, then flicked her tongue directly against her clit until Layla cried out sharply. But Whitley didn't want the experience to be over too quickly, so she deliberately stopped and shifted her focus to Layla's entrance instead. She explored with her tongue, nuzzling her nose into the soft folds and breathing in that intoxicating scent. God, she could happily drown in everything that was Layla.

"F-fingers," Layla gasped desperately. "Jesus Christ, Whit, please put your fingers inside me. I need to feel you."

Refusing to let Layla's skin escape her mouth for even a moment, Whitley dragged her tongue back up to place it on Layla's clit. After several more moments of focused attention with her tongue, she carefully dipped her fingers inside and reveled in the incredible silky feeling of Layla's inner walls. She was so warm and wet, gripping Whitley's fingers with a surprising strength that made her own arousal spike again.

"Harder, please," Layla begged, her voice breaking with desperation. "I need you to really move. I'm so close."

Layla's pleading did something profound to Whitley's resolve and awakened something primal within her. She couldn't wait any longer to give her everything she needed. Pistoning her fingers with increasing intensity, she took Layla with deep, hard thrusts while maintaining the pressure of her tongue. Her eyes widened in amazement when she felt a sudden rush of liquid coat her fingers as Layla's body responded.

"Fuck, oh God, yes, right there! Don't stop, right there!" Layla screamed, her back arching off the bed.

Whitley only relented when Layla grabbed her wrist firmly, her entire body shaking as she howled her release into the room with abandon.

"I—I thought I was supposed to be the one with the talented fingers." Layla laughed breathlessly through deep, shuddering inhales as she tried to recover.

"I might not play the violin professionally," Whitley said with newfound confidence, "but I'm beginning to think I can play your body pretty damn well."

She didn't know where this sudden surge of sexual confidence was coming from, but she absolutely loved it. She loved being this close to Layla, loved making her body react and respond so intensely. Thank God it was turning into a snow day, because Whitley had so many more things she wanted to explore and discover.

23

Expectations & Family Dynamics

L ayla groaned audibly as she stretched out her aching back, feeling muscles she'd forgotten she had, protesting after their marathon session. Wow, when Whitley really got going, she absolutely went for it with single-minded determination and impressive stamina. They'd been tangled up in bed for the better part of an entire day, only emerging from the cocoon of silk sheets when absolutely necessary.

They'd stopped periodically to refuel with hastily prepared snacks and to watch through the huge windows as the snow continued to relentlessly bury the city in white. Everything outside was at a complete standstill—no traffic moving, no pedestrians braving the elements, just a winter wonderland that had effectively shut down all of Manhattan. And that situation was more than perfectly okay with both of them. The unexpected snow day had given Layla and Whitley precious, uninterrupted time to really explore each other thoroughly, in multiple positions and various rooms throughout the luxurious penthouse.

The part of Layla that had harbored lingering concerns about Whitley's emotional readiness for physical intimacy had completely buggered off somewhere around orgasm number five. It had become crystal clear that Whitley was a fully grown woman who knew her own mind and heart with absolute certainty. Layla couldn't keep second-guessing Whitley's decisions or treating her like she might break. She had to trust that Whitley would speak up immediately if they did anything she wasn't completely comfortable with.

But did that same confidence and certainty translate to their relationship outside the bedroom? Was Whitley truly ready to tell people about them, to make their connection public and official? Did she want something more substantial than just a few earth-shattering rolls in the hay, no matter how incredible those had been? Those were the complicated thoughts plaguing Layla as she unsuccessfully tried to untangle her sore, satisfied muscles.

"You look far too deep in serious thought for someone who has had multiple spectacular orgasms," Whitley observed from beside her, her voice still slightly hoarse from their activities. Layla turned her head and smiled at the sight that greeted her. Whitley's hair, which was usually perfectly styled and controlled, was now fanned out in a glorious mess across the expensive silk pillowcase.

"I suppose I *am* thinking too much," Layla admitted with a rueful smile.

Shifting gracefully into a sitting position despite her obvious fatigue, Whitley stretched her arms high above her head, inadvertently giving Layla a tantalizing view of her perfect breasts. Layla had studied them intimately and extensively over the past day, but she still couldn't get enough of the sight. They really were fabulous in every way.

Unable to resist the magnetic pull, Layla shot forward and captured Whitley's nipple between her lips, sucking gently on the sensitive bud.

"Again?" Whitley asked with a mixture of surprise and renewed arousal in her voice. "Already?"

Layla continued to lavish attention on the hardening nipple with her tongue and teeth. As much as she genuinely wanted to ravish Whitley again, right here and now, her earlier troubling thoughts caused her to reluctantly release the nipple with an audible pop and sit back up.

"Soon, definitely soon," she promised. "But can we talk seriously for a few minutes first?"

"That sounds ominous," Whitley replied, though her expression remained relaxed and her smile warm. She looked so devastatingly beautiful in the soft afternoon light filtering through the windows.

"Are we actually together now?" Layla asked directly, needing clarity above all else. "Like, officially a couple? Or is this something you want to keep on the down low, just between us for now?"

Whitley rolled onto her side, resting her head comfortably on Layla's chest and draping one arm across her waist. "What do you want from this?" she asked quietly, and there was an unmistakable nervousness in her voice that made Layla's heart clench.

Layla immediately curled her arm protectively around Whitley's body and pulled her closer, wanting to eliminate any doubt or insecurity. "I want this, Whit. Like, I really, truly want all of it. The relationship, the commitment, everything that comes with being together."

Whitley's deep sigh of relief echoed through the quiet room, instantly extinguishing all of Layla's anxiety in one fell swoop. The sound was music to her ears.

"Me too...all of it," Whitley said firmly. "But we need to be realistic about managing our expectations going forward."

Frowning with confusion, Layla tried to interpret exactly what Whitley meant by that somewhat foreboding statement.

"I honestly don't know what that means," she admitted. "Can you be more specific?"

"As much as I would love nothing more than to see you every single day, it's simply not going to be possible with our schedules," Whitley explained patiently. "Now that we're finally in the same city for longer than twenty-four hours at a time, you're going to see firsthand just how much I work. The foundation responsibilities, the business obligations, the social commitments—it's relentless. I don't want to disappoint you or make you feel neglected."

Layla shimmied her way down the bed until she was positioned face to face with Whitley, their noses almost touching. "I completely get it, and I understand the demands on your time. Honestly, I'm going to be incredibly busy too, especially over the coming weeks. The quartet has several major shows already lined up for the new year. We're taking the choir to perform at a couple of care homes to give the residents a special treat. Plus, I'll still be busking regularly because I love it and need the income."

"So how do we make this work if we're never going to see each other?" Whitley asked with genuine concern.

Layla smiled warmly and playfully nipped at Whitley's nose. "Babe, we've essentially been doing exactly this for at least a year already, just without the incredible sex component. We call each other, we text constantly, we FaceTime whenever possible. The foundation is already there."

"But what about the physical intimacy?" Whitley pressed, her voice taking on a slightly desperate edge. "I mean, we've literally just started having sex, and I really, really like it and want to do so much more of it." She punctuated her statement by running her tongue along

Layla's neck, sending instant heat shooting straight to her core.

"We make absolutely sure we meet at least once a week for dinner and extended sexy times," Layla replied with conviction. "Trust me when I say I don't want to go without this either. What we have is too good to sacrifice."

They stayed comfortably harbored in each other's arms in peaceful silence, skin against skin, heartbeats gradually synchronizing. It was the insistent buzzing of Whitley's phone on the nightstand that finally pulled them reluctantly back to the reality of the outside world.

"It's Mom," Whitley said after glancing at the screen. "She's checking up on our expected arrival time for tonight."

"Ah, right. It's the exclusive DuPont family party tonight." Layla remembered with a mixture of excitement and nervousness.

"It is indeed. You're still planning to come with me, right?" Whitley asked, though there was an underlying uncertainty in her voice.

"Am I attending as your talented violinist or as your girlfriend?" Layla asked pointedly, wanting to understand exactly what she was walking into.

"Can't you be both?" Whitley shot back with one of her characteristically quick retorts.

Layla loved Whitley's ability to match her directness head-on without flinching. It meant she wasn't intimidated by Layla's tendency towards bluntness and could hold her own in any conversation.

"Of course I can be both," Layla agreed with a grin. "But are you genuinely okay with coming out to your parents so soon after we've gotten together? That's a big step."

"Absolutely, without any hesitation," Whitley replied confidently. "They already love you as a person, and they only want me to be happy above all else. Plus, Aubrey and William already know about my feelings, so it's not like it'll be a complete shock to the family."

"Mmm, I did wonder about that," Layla mused. "They're about as subtle as a brick to the face when they're trying to be sneaky."

Whitley laughed delightedly at the assessment. "Whatever do you mean by that?"

Rolling her eyes dramatically, Layla scoffed. "Aubrey's questions during our business meetings were way too personal and obvious. She was clearly fishing for information about my feelings for you."

"Yet somehow you still didn't figure out how I felt about you?" Whitley pointed out with amusement. "She couldn't have done such a terrible job of being obvious."

Unable to come up with a worthy counterargument to that perfectly valid point, Layla settled for tickling Whitley mercilessly until she forgot all about being right.

"Mercy, please!" Whitley cackled breathlessly, squirming under Layla's relentless fingers. The phone buzzed again with another message, more insistent this time.

"You should probably reply to your mother before we have her busting down your front door with security," Layla suggested practically.

Still catching her breath from the tickle attack, Whitley quickly shot off a reassuring text message. "There, done. Crisis averted. Now can we please get back to—"

"Managing expectations?" Layla interrupted with a teasing grin.

Whitley visibly winced at hearing her own words repeated back to her. "It sounds terrible when you say it like that."

"It didn't sound particularly great the first time either," Layla admitted. "I was half expecting you to unceremoniously turf me out of bed and send me packing."

"Never in a million years," Whitley said firmly. "In fact, let's stay in this bed until the very last possible minute. I can get dressed quickly when we finally have to leave."

"Deal," Layla agreed enthusiastically. "But does that mean the serious talking portion of our afternoon is officially over?"

Whitley smoothly lifted herself up and maneuvered over until she was straddling Layla's hips, her hair falling like a curtain around their faces. "Yes, the talking is done. We're officially together now. You're my girlfriend, and I'm yours. We both acknowledge it might be challenging at times with our schedules, but we've successfully navigated long-distance before. I just wanted us to be completely clear about expectations and boundaries. I thought you'd appreciate the direct approach."

"I do appreciate it," Layla confirmed sincerely. "I need clear, honest communication even when it's difficult or uncomfortable."

"Aubrey and William are going to completely lose their minds when we tell them." Whitley grinned mischievously, skating her hands teasingly across the tops of Layla's breasts.

"No more serious talking," Layla declared, arching into the touch. "We'll deal with all the family dynamics and logistics later. For now, I think we can *definitely* squeeze in several more earth-shattering orgasms before we have to face the world, don't you think?"

"Oh, definitely," Whitley agreed with enthusiasm. "Absolutely definitely."

Announcements & Childhood Bedrooms

"We're really, really late." Layla laughed as they finally climbed into the back of Ryan's car, both still slightly breathless and glowing from their extended afternoon activities. So much for Whitley's confident assertion she could dress quickly when the time came.

"It's perfectly fine, nothing to worry about," Whitley replied with forced casualness, though her voice carried a note of uncertainty.

Layla raised a skeptical eyebrow at Whitley's phone, which was buzzing frantically with what appeared to be increasingly urgent messages. "You might want to tell your cell phone that everything's fine, because it seems to disagree."

"Mom just gets a little antsy when things don't go exactly according to her carefully planned schedule," Whitley explained with familiar exasperation.

"And how, exactly, are you planning to explain our poor timekeeping to your family?" Layla asked with amusement. "Because I don't think telling your parents I was eating you out on the dining room table is going to go over particularly well as an excuse."

Whitley immediately flushed a deep shade of red and shot a panicked glance towards Ryan in the front seat. He either didn't hear the comment or was professionally pretending not to, maintaining his focus on the snowy roads ahead. Either way, it suited everyone just fine.

"I'll just say I lost my purse and we had to search the entire apartment for it or something equally believable," Whitley said, clearly grasping for any reasonable explanation.

Snickering with delight, Layla shook her head knowingly. "Aubrey and William are going to see right through that flimsy story in about two seconds flat. Sorry, love, but you've got the freshly fucked glow happening in a major way right now."

"And you haven't got the same obvious glow?" Whitley challenged, though her tone was more amused than defensive.

"Oh, I absolutely have it too," Layla laughed without any shame, "but I have this mess of unruly curls that hides most of my face from scrutiny. I always look at least a little disheveled, so no one will notice the difference."

Whitley huffed with frustration at the unfairness of the situation. "Damn it all to hell."

The car smoothly pulled up to the DuPont family's impressive front entrance, the mansion looking like something out of a Christmas card with its elegant holiday decorations and warm lights glowing in every window. Layla immediately skipped out of the vehicle and ran around to the other side to open Whitley's door with a flourish, sending a conspiratorial wink towards a smirking Ryan as she passed him.

If she hadn't visited this magnificent estate several times over the past year, Layla probably would have been too distracted and intimidated by the sheer magnitude and grandeur of the property to focus on anything else. But that initial awe had passed quite a while ago, so now she could concentrate entirely on Whitley and making sure tonight went as smoothly as possible.

Although she knew Lucienne and Lucas fairly well by now and had developed genuine affection for both of them, tonight felt fundamentally different. She wasn't just the quirky, talented violinist they'd grown fond of—she was now their daughter's romantic partner, which carried entirely different implications and expectations. Neither she nor Whitley really knew how Whitley's parents would react to this significant development in their relationship.

"Ready for this?" Whitley asked the moment she climbed gracefully out of the car, her voice carrying a mixture of excitement and nervous energy.

"Let's do this thing," Layla replied with more confidence than she actually felt. The desire to check her clothing one last time made her fingers itch with nervous energy. She wasn't typically someone who gave much of a damn what people thought of her appearance or choices, most days. But Whitley was incredibly important to her, and this evening mattered more than she wanted to admit. She desperately wanted Whitley's parents to see her as more than just an eccentric musician with unconventional style. She wanted them to see her as a worthy partner for their daughter, and someone who could potentially be part of Whitley's future.

"You look absolutely wonderful," Whitley intimately whispered in her ear as they stood together at the imposing front door, waiting to be admitted. The fitted feminine tuxedo really did look pretty fucking awesome, if Layla did say so herself. It was a brilliant shade of red, with delicate silver snowflakes sewn into the waistcoat with obvious care and attention to detail. Whitley had completely surprised Layla with the custom outfit earlier in the evening, having somehow arranged for it to be delivered while they were otherwise occupied.

After convincing Ryan to make a quick detour to Layla's apartment to retrieve her treasured silver pocket watch—along with an overnight bag Reena had thoughtfully packed for her with typical efficiency—Layla's ensemble was finally complete. Her trusty black combat boots gave the formal look a bit of rebellious edge, taking away from what might otherwise have been an overly rigid, conventional appearance. She was absolutely up for a fancy night out when the occasion called for it, but it simply wasn't in Layla's nature to be suited and booted too perfectly.

"You look pretty amazing yourself," Layla replied sincerely, taking in Whitley's stunning appearance.

Whitley had chosen to leave her golden hair down, styled in loose waves that cascaded over one shoulder. Her dress was entirely silver with subtle red snowflakes embroidered throughout the fabric, and seemed to shimmer with every movement. The pattern was barely visible under normal lighting, but when the light caught the dress at just the right angle, the snowflakes became visible and made Whitley look like an ethereal snow queen from a fairytale.

"There you both are, finally!" Lucienne huffed with obvious relief when she opened the heavy front door, though her expression was more concerned than truly annoyed. Gentle classical music played from somewhere deeper in the house, creating an atmosphere of elegant sophistication. "Get in here immediately before you both freeze to death."

Being hauled into the warm house and instantly enveloped in one of Lucienne's characteristically crushing hugs, Layla tried her best to relax and settle her nerves. It wasn't particularly easy, though. The uncomfortable fact that she had thoroughly debauched Lucienne's beloved daughter many, many times throughout the day settled on her conscience like a heavy iron weight she couldn't seem to shake off.

They moved through the elegant foyer and stepped into the main living area to greet the rest of the assembled family and friends. Puck, Reena, and Simon were also in attendance, which immediately made Layla relax somewhat. Having familiar faces and allies in the room always helped ease her social anxiety. As they exchanged warm greetings and holiday wishes with everyone, though, that weight of guilt and nervousness only seemed to get heavier and more oppressive until Layla felt like she couldn't stand the deception anymore.

"Can we tell them now?" she whispered urgently to Whitley, unable to contain her discomfort any longer.

Whitley turned to look at her with surprise. "What, right now? This very moment?"

Layla nodded emphatically, her anxiety reaching a breaking point. "I feel like I'm actively lying to them by not saying anything, and it's giving me really weird, uncomfortable feelings that I can't shake."

Whitley's expression immediately softened with understanding and compassion. "You're really worried about what they'll say when they find out, aren't you?"

"Maybe," Layla muttered reluctantly, accepting the beautifully crafted cocktail that Lucas offered her with a grateful smile. She noticed Aubrey was eyeing them both with obvious curiosity before deliberately nudging William sharply in the ribs. He scowled at his twin sister before following her pointed line of sight directly to where Layla and Whitley stood close together. Layla could feel their combined quizzical stares penetrating straight through to her bones.

Why was she freaking out so intensely about this? The DuPont family knew her well by now, having spent considerable time with her over the past year. They genuinely liked and respected her as a person. There was no logical reason for this level of anxiety.

Whitley decisively tapped her crystal glass with the elegant ring on her right hand; the clear chime immediately drawing everyone's focus. "Can I have everyone's attention for just a moment, please?"

"Darling, can't whatever this is wait until after we've eaten dinner?" Lucienne asked with mild impatience, clearly eager to maintain her carefully planned evening schedule. "The chef has worked so hard on this meal."

"It will literally only take a few seconds, I promise. I'm quite sure we won't starve to death in that time."

"Well then, get on with it already," Aubrey heckled good-naturedly from across the room, her face full of barely contained amusement. Her expression led Layla to strongly suspect Aubrey knew exactly what announcement was about to happen.

"First of all, it's wonderful to see everyone here tonight," Whitley began, her voice growing stronger and more confident with each word. "I missed you all during my time in London, and we haven't had any proper opportunity to catch up since I returned home yesterday. Second, I have some rather significant news that I'd like to share with all of you."

"Please tell me you're not planning to move permanently to the UK," her father interjected with obvious concern, his brow furrowed with worry.

"No, absolutely not. I'm staying right here in New York," Whitley assured him quickly. "I wanted to formally introduce you all to someone very special in my life."

"Someone special?" Lucienne asked, her voice carrying notes of both excitement and subtle concern. "As in a new man you've met?" Her eyes automatically strayed to Layla with an odd, almost knowing expression.

"No, definitely not a new man," Whitley replied, taking a deep breath for courage. "Here goes nothing. Layla and I are dating. Romantically. We're together as a couple."

Lucienne immediately gripped her chest dramatically and breathed out with obvious relief. "Oh, thank goodness for that!"

Layla's eyebrows shot up so high they practically hit her hairline. She looked at Whitley with complete startlement, both clearly stunned by the reaction. Did

Lucienne's response mean she and Lucas had already suspected or known somehow? How the hell could that have happened?

"Um..." was all Whitley managed to articulate, which was considerably more coherent than anything Layla could produce in her shock.

Lucienne waved her hand dismissively, brushing away their obvious confusion with maternal authority. "My dear daughter, you really aren't very subtle about your feelings. It's a trait you inherited directly from your father, and Aubrey and William have it too. The sheer number of times you mentioned Layla's name during our calls, and the particular look that came into your eyes whenever you talked about her, were dead giveaways. Plus, I've known that Layla has been absolutely sweet on you since the very first night you two met."

Layla snorted with laughter despite her nervousness. "Completely busted, apparently."

"And you're both genuinely okay with this?" Whitley asked, still seeming somewhat stunned. "With us being together?"

Lucas laughed heartily, his face creasing with genuine joy. "Of course, we're more than okay with it! We love you both dearly, and if Layla is who makes you truly happy, then we couldn't possibly be more delighted by this news."

"Exactly what your father said," Lucienne agreed emphatically. "Now, can we please go eat this beautiful dinner before my stomach starts trying to digest itself from hunger?"

Whitley and Layla nodded in unison, still somewhat dazed by how smoothly the announcement had gone. The assembled crowd began moving towards the elegant dining room, leaving the two of them momentarily frozen in place as they processed what had just happened.

"That went remarkably well," Whitley commented, turning to look directly at Layla with obvious relief and happiness.

"Yeah, I'd definitely say that was a success," Layla agreed, feeling a massive weight lift from her shoulders.

"Are you feeling alright now?" Whitley asked with concern, studying Layla's face carefully.

Layla breathed out slowly and smiled with genuine contentment. "More than alright, actually. Let's go eat this fancy dinner, and then we can dance together properly. Tonight, I'll show you just how incredibly happy I am about all of this."

"Just so you know, we're staying here overnight," Whitley mentioned casually as they began walking towards the dining room.

Layla wiggled her eyebrows suggestively with obvious mischief. "Have you ever gotten naughty in your childhood bedroom before?"

Whitley immediately flushed that familiar shade of red. "No, never."

"Want to change that tonight?" Layla asked with a wicked grin.

Layla watched with satisfaction as Whitley unconsciously licked her lips in response. "You have absolutely no idea what you're in for," Whitley promised with heat in her voice.

Suppressing an excited squeal of anticipation, Layla found herself admiring the view of Whitley's perfect arse as she walked ahead towards the family gathering. They were going to have to completely re-evaluate those earlier conversations about managing expectations, because Layla was utterly, completely, and irrevocably gone for this woman.

25

Boardrooms & Executive Decisions

Time was absolutely standing still. Whitley was completely sure of it. She'd been trapped in this blasted boardroom for going on three torturous hours, watching the minutes crawl by on the clock mounted on the wall. Why did men always have to reduce every single discussion to some kind of ridiculous dick-measuring contest, turning simple business matters into elaborate displays of ego and dominance?

All they had to do was efficiently get through the quarterly financial reports and projections, review the numbers that were clearly laid out in front of them, and then they could all get on with their actual lives. But as usual, the conversation had inevitably steered completely off track and devolved into yet another pointless argument between two of the more stubborn board members, each determined to prove his superior business acumen to the room.

Whitley's mind inevitably drifted to Layla, as it had done during every spare minute for the past week. That was exactly how long it had been since they'd managed to spend any meaningful time together face to face, and the separation was driving her frustratingly crazy with longing.

If Whitley wasn't buried in work at the office, dealing with endless meetings and financial reports, she was attending some charity-related function or foundation event. When she miraculously did have a few hours of spare time, Layla was invariably either busking on street corners to earn money or rehearsing intensively with the quartet for their upcoming performances.

"So that's completely settled then," Ron Jenkins announced with his characteristic pompous authority. "Whitley will return to London for an extended assignment."

What? Snapping herself abruptly back into the present moment and the stuffy boardroom, Whitley stared in shock at Ron Jenkins, the arrogant man who had just casually decided her immediate future without any consultation whatsoever.

"I'm sorry, I completely zoned out for a moment," she admitted honestly, though her voice was already taking on a dangerous edge. "Why exactly are you saying that I'm going back to London?"

"There's been an official request from the DuPont headquarters across the pond," Jenkins explained with infuriating casualness. "They want a more permanent, high-level figure present to oversee operations and maintain continuity."

"And you've simply decided, without bothering to consult me at all, that I'm the one who should move to London to fulfill their request?" Whitley's voice was deceptively calm, but anyone who knew her well would recognize the warning signs of her building anger.

Jenkins shrugged dismissively, as if her concerns were completely irrelevant. "You went there before to help them set up the foundation branch. You already have experience with their operations and have also established relationships."

"No." The single word rang out clearly in the suddenly silent boardroom. Twelve sets of eyes immediately focused on her with varying degrees of surprise and concern. Whitley was always the ultimate team player, the one who never complained about assignments or travel demands. She had traveled more extensively than anyone else in the company and consistently worked twice as hard as her male colleagues. None of the men sitting around this conference table could honestly dispute that fact. She always agreed to whatever was asked of her, but enough was finally enough. It was past time for someone else to shoulder the heavy lifting and international responsibilities.

Just the mere idea of being separated from Layla again, of putting an ocean between them when their relationship was still so new and precious, made her chest tighten with anxiety and panic. It was already incredibly difficult being in the same city and not being able to spend quality time together due to their demanding schedules. There was absolutely no way she was leaving the country again after only just returning.

"Whitley," Jenkins began in that infuriatingly condescending tone he always used when he thought he was dealing with an unreasonable woman.

"I said no, and I meant it," she interrupted firmly, her voice gaining strength and authority with each word. "I do the bulk of international travel for this company, and it's time that pattern stopped immediately. I'm the designated heir to the DuPont business empire, Ron. My proper place is here in New York, at the helm alongside my father, learning the intricacies of running this organization."

Her eyes deliberately shifted to Lucas, who sat silently observing the confrontation with his characteristic calm demeanor. His small, almost imperceptible nod of approval reassured Whitley she was absolutely doing the right thing by standing her ground.

"But we all have families and personal commitments to consider," Ron protested weakly, clearly grasping for any argument that might sway her decision.

Whitley's anger spiked to dangerous levels at his hypocritical statement. "And how the hell am I supposed to start building a family of my own if I'm never in one place long enough to maintain meaningful relationships? Yes, Ron, you all have families. Well-established, *grown* families with children who are already adults."

"Whitley is absolutely right," Lucas interjected smoothly, his voice remaining calm and steady despite the obvious tension in the room. "She's carried an unfair burden of travel responsibilities for far too long. The London office didn't specifically request a board member for this assignment, so we should send someone from higher management who's eager for international experience."

Whitley continued to fume internally as she watched Ron's face. He was never the least bit shy about volunteering her for extensive travel assignments, and she wasn't naïve enough to miss his underlying motivations. It was clearly a calculated way for Ron to maintain his dominance and rule the corporate roost while she was conveniently out of the country. Misogyny, thy name was definitely Jenkins. He had never been happy when Lucas officially named and began training Whitley as his successor, and he'd been looking for ways to undermine her authority ever since.

"Craig made his strong interest in international travel opportunities very clear last month," Damian called out from the other end of the long conference table. "Why don't we send him instead?"

"I completely agree with that suggestion," Whitley added immediately. "Craig is solid, experienced, and diplomatic. The London team will have no problems working effectively with him."

"All those in favor of sending Craig instead of Whitley," Lucas called for an official vote.

Every hand in the room went up except for Ron's, his face flushed with obvious frustration at being outvoted so decisively.

"The majority rules, as always," Lucas announced with satisfaction. "Peggy, please arrange for Craig to meet with me first thing tomorrow morning to discuss the assignment details."

"I think we should call it a day, gentlemen," Whitley said firmly, standing up and gesturing for the others to follow suit. As the board members began gathering their papers and preparing to leave, her thoughts immediately turned to Layla and how *she* would handle a room full of pompous old men like these.

A genuine grin etched its way across her face as she pictured the scene. She could absolutely envision Layla in all her steampunk glory, standing confidently at the head of this very table. "Alright, fuck off out of the room then," she could practically hear Layla saying with characteristic bluntness before dropping casually into the head chair and putting her combat boots up on the expensive glass table.

The vivid mental image made Whitley miss Layla even more intensely than before.

One by one, the board members shuffled out of the room with their briefcases and wounded egos, until only she and Lucas remained. He stayed standing by his chair, watching his daughter with obvious pride and curiosity.

"That was quite an impressive protest, honey," he observed thoughtfully. "Very unlike your usual diplomatic approach."

Shit, was he upset with her for causing a scene? "Was I wrong to speak up so forcefully?" she asked, suddenly uncertain about her bold stance.

Lucas immediately shook his head with conviction. "It's about time you did, if you ask me. I've been waiting for this moment."

"Why did you never say anything before? Why didn't you encourage me to set boundaries sooner?"

Lucas settled back into his chair, his expression becoming more serious and paternal. "Because I genuinely believe you needed to reach that point of realization on your own, my darling daughter. Running the DuPont business machine isn't easy by any stretch of the imagination. It requires tremendous guts, unwavering determination, and incredibly hard work. But it also requires balance, and that's the hardest lesson to learn."

He paused, gathering his thoughts before continuing, "I can't tell you how many years it took me to truly understand that concept. My own father repeatedly told me to slow down and take proper breaks, to find time for the things that mattered beyond business. But being rather stubborn and convinced I knew better, his well-meaning advice had exactly the opposite effect on me."

Whitley listened intently, recognizing herself in his description.

"You, my dear, are definitely a chip off the old block in that regard," Lucas continued with a knowing smile. "I know you feel like you constantly have to prove yourself in this male-dominated industry, and to some degree that's unfortunately true. Not to me personally, I should add—you proved your business worth to me long ago. But unfortunately, the business world is still largely run by men like Ron Jenkins, with their outdated attitudes and prejudices."

"But?" Whitley prompted, sensing there was more to his thoughts.

"But now you have Layla in your life, and that changes everything."

Whitley cocked her head with curiosity. "I've had serious partners in the past, Dad. What makes this different?"

Lucas nodded thoughtfully. "Yes, you have had relationships before. But none of them ever lit a genuine fire in your heart the way she does. As I said, you're a chip off the old block, and I know this is true because I experienced exactly the same transformation when I met your mother."

Whitley felt her expression soften as she thought about Layla's impact on her life.

"Layla truly gets you. She's different from anyone you've ever been with—outspoken, authentic, unafraid to challenge you."

Whitley smiled and chuckled softly. "You're definitely not wrong about that."

"She reaches a part of you that no other person has ever touched," he said with certainty. "That's exactly why you found the strength to stand your ground today and establish some healthy boundaries. You're finally ready for balance in your life."

Sighing deeply, Whitley dropped her head back and stared at the ornate ceiling. "We haven't seen each other properly in an entire week, Dad. A whole week."

"Then you have to make the time, Whit," Lucas said firmly. "The work isn't going anywhere. It'll still be here tomorrow and next week and next month. I think you've more than earned some personal time, even if it's just leaving the office early occasionally."

"But Layla has her own demanding life too," Whitley protested. "She's constantly rehearsing with the quartet and spending hours busking to earn money."

Lucas shrugged with the wisdom of experience. "So go watch her perform. Be part of her world instead of expecting her to always fit into yours."

Huh. Why hadn't she thought of something so simple? Whitley genuinely loved hearing Layla play; it was magical to witness her talent and passion.

"Sweetheart, don't leave it until next December before you make another significant change in your priorities," Lucas said, his tone teasing but carrying obvious sincerity beneath the humor.

"December is our special month, Dad," Whitley replied with a soft smile, thinking of their annual Christmas encounters.

"Then capitalize on *this* December while you have the chance," he advised warmly.

26

Serenades & Office Romance

Smiling with warmth and gratitude, Whitley strode over to where her father sat. "Thank you for understanding," she whispered softly as she bent down and wrapped her arms around him in an affectionate hug from behind.

After a few more moments of comfortable silence and paternal support, Whitley finally broke away and began collecting her things from around the conference table. Lucas gave her an encouraging wink and headed off toward his office, leaving her alone with her thoughts and newfound determination.

Now that the confrontational meeting with the board was finally over and resolved in her favor, Whitley could race through the last few essential bits of work that absolutely had to be finished before she could justify leaving the office. If she really concentrated and focused her efforts, she'd be able to get out early enough to catch Layla rehearsing with the choir at the foundation.

Next week was their first care home performance, and it warmed Whitley's heart to see how seriously all the kids were taking this opportunity. They approached every performance, no matter how small or intimate the audience, with the same level of dedication and professionalism.

Armed with purpose and a fresh cup of strong coffee, Whitley settled at her desk and began working with laser focus. The office buzzed with its usual symphony of animated chatter and constant keyboard clicking. Diane, Whitley's incredibly efficient personal assistant, updated her calendar as she did every day, but for the first time in her professional career, Whitley didn't automatically accept all the proposed changes and additions.

"Is everything alright, Ms. DuPont?" Diane asked with obvious concern as soon as Whitley finished systematically rearranging some of the proposed appointments and declining several scheduled meetings.

"Everything is perfectly fine, Diane. But going forward, I won't be accepting any meetings scheduled after four o'clock in the afternoon," Whitley announced decisively. "Most of these late-day meetings could easily be handled through email anyway. There will also be days when I choose to work remotely from home."

She had to suppress a laugh at the astonished expression that spread across her assistant's face. Diane looked like she'd just witnessed something impossible, like gravity suddenly working in reverse.

"Right, of course. I'll make a note of these new parameters immediately," Diane replied, though her voice carried a note of bewilderment.

Diving back into her work with renewed energy at the thought of leaving the office early and going to Layla, Whitley initially missed the sudden shift in the office atmosphere around her. It was only when the beautifully haunting sound of a violin began echoing through the open workspace that she snapped her head up in surprise and recognition.

Through the glass walls of her office, she could see every single head in the building turned toward the elevator bank, faces filled with curiosity and wonder.

The achingly beautiful notes played out again, longer this time, with more complexity and emotion woven into the melody.

Pushing back from her desk on unsteady legs, she made her way toward the main office area, her heart beginning to race with anticipation. Several heads turned her way as she moved, but Whitley only had eyes for the person creating that gorgeous sound that was filling the entire floor.

Her heart hammering against her ribs like a caged bird, she took a deep, steadying breath before stepping into Layla's direct line of sight. The woman was currently standing in the center of the office space with her violin perfectly positioned and her eyes closed in complete concentration. She wore her regular ripped black jeans that deliciously hugged her legs, paired with a coat that looked like it had been borrowed from a Dickensian novel—thick wool with ornate brass buckles serving as fasteners. No signature top hat this time, though. Just Layla's wonderful mass of dark curls, as wild and untamed as ever. Her makeup was dramatically dark, almost gothic in its intensity, making her look like some kind of beautiful, mysterious musician from another era.

A shuddering breath escaped Whitley's chest as she watched Layla completely lose herself in the music. Layla was clearly in her zone; that magical place where nothing existed except the melody flowing from her instrument. The hauntingly beautiful tune vibrantly sprang to life as Layla continued to play with obvious passion and skill. It wasn't a song Whitley recognized from any classical repertoire, but it was utterly mesmerizing and seemed to cast a spell over everyone within hearing distance.

Layla swayed gracefully with the sound she was creating, taking the entire office full of surprised workers on an unexpected musical journey. Suddenly, her eyes flew open and immediately found Whitley across the crowded space, as if drawn by some invisible magnetic force.

The tempo of the music suddenly changed, becoming more dynamic and energetic, and so did Layla's movements. She regarded Whitley with love and affection as she stepped forward and began to dance, her body moving in perfect harmony with the music flowing from her violin. The choreography appeared to be completely improvised yet looked perfectly planned, as if she'd rehearsed this exact performance countless times. How in the world she managed to navigate around desks and office furniture without missing a single note or stumbling was absolutely beyond Whitley's comprehension.

Tears began forming in Whitley's eyes as she watched this wonderful, extraordinary woman serenade her in the middle of her workplace, surrounded by colleagues and coworkers. No one had ever done something so spectacularly romantic and public for her before. The gesture was so bold, so unapologetically dramatic, so perfectly Layla.

However, if any of her previous boyfriends had attempted something like this kind of grand public display, she would have been absolutely mortified and furious rather than swept completely off her feet. She would have been embarrassed by the attention and concerned about maintaining her professional image.

Is that what her father had been talking about when he mentioned balance and finding someone who truly understood her?

Of course it was. Everything Layla did made Whitley feel weak in the knees with love and desire. She was completely, utterly, hopelessly smitten. Even during her most serious relationship with Anthony, when things had progressed to discussions of marriage and shared futures, Whitley had never once considered slowing down her work pace or prioritizing personal time. They had both been perfectly content to spend extended periods apart, focused on their individual careers and ambitions.

But this was entirely different. This was *Layla*.

Leaning against the closest desk, needing some physical stability, she watched with rapt attention as Layla drew the impromptu song to a gradual, elegant close. Her heart hadn't stopped its frantic racing since the very first note had rung throughout the office space. Whispers and murmurs began to seep into the growing silence as Layla slowly withdrew her bow from the strings and stood there looking directly at Whitley with obvious affection and satisfaction.

Tears clouded Whitley's vision, and shock had rendered her completely mute. She was stunned by the beauty and boldness of what had just happened.

"Hey there, babe," Layla finally said, her voice carrying clearly across the quiet office. "I missed you something fierce."

Swallowing hard around the emotion clogging her throat, Whitley managed to stand up straight and find her voice. "So, you thought you'd just pop by my office and play me a song?" Could Layla hear the wonder and amazement in her tone?

"Well, yeah, obviously," Layla replied with characteristic, matter-of-fact simplicity, as if serenading someone at their workplace was the most natural thing in the world.

Layla's completely straightforward answer made Whitley emit a sound that was part sob and part laughter. It was a weird combination of emotions, but she couldn't stop the sound from spilling out of her chest. Without hesitation, Layla handed her prized instrument to the closest person. "Give that to one of the DuPonts, would you?" and stepped confidently into Whitley's personal space.

"Want to get out of here?" she asked softly, her eyes dancing with mischief and invitation.

Standing on suddenly steady legs, Whitley draped her arms around Layla's neck without caring one bit about professional propriety or office gossip. Sure, it wasn't exactly professional to start passionately making out in the middle of the workplace, but Whitley was so far beyond caring about appearances that potential issue wasn't even a consideration.

"Yes, I desperately want to get out of here," she murmured, right before descending on Layla's plump, inviting lips with hungry enthusiasm.

If Layla was embarrassed or concerned about the sudden public display of affection, she certainly didn't make it known. In fact, she was the one who deepened the kiss by adding her tongue into the mix, much to the obvious delight of their audience.

Wolf whistles and enthusiastic clapping suddenly shattered their intimate bubble. William and Aubrey stepped out of the elevator with perfect timing, making complete nuisances of themselves as they always did when they wanted to embarrass their sister.

Finally, the blush that should have appeared much earlier crept its way up Whitley's neck and face. "Let's go right now," she whispered urgently against Layla's lips.

Layla gave her one last quick peck before stepping back with obvious reluctance. "Go grab your stuff, love. I need some quality time with my girl, and I need it immediately."

How did every single word that came out of Layla's mouth turn Whitley into complete emotional mush?

Scampering back to her office like a lovesick teenager, Whitley hastily threw her cell phone into her bag and practically ripped her coat off the standing rack. Most of the office workers had returned to their desks and computers, though they were chatting excitedly about the unexpected musical performance they'd just witnessed.

Some were still crowding around Layla, asking her all manner of questions about her music and her relationship with their boss.

Whitley caught sight of her father leaning casually against his office door frame, watching the entire scene unfold with obvious amusement and approval. She grinned back at him with pure happiness.

"Ready to go?" Whitley asked, placing her hand gently on the small of Layla's back to get her attention and extract her from the growing crowd of admirers.

"Sorry, good folks of the DuPont empire," Layla announced to her impromptu audience with theatrical flair, "I'm afraid I must take my leave now and attend to more pressing matters. But feel free to stop by Cedars Retirement Home next week if you want to see more of this musical magic. The choir will be involved in that performance too, and it's going to be spectacular."

She paused dramatically before continuing with a wicked grin, "But right now, I have a beautiful woman to properly woo and seduce. Toodles, everyone!"

Layla had barely finished her flamboyant farewell when she whirled around with impressive speed, firmly grabbed Whitley's hand, and marched her toward the elevator with obvious determination and purpose.

The automatic doors closed behind them, creating a private sanctuary, and Whitley immediately pounced on her girlfriend with desperate hunger. Hopefully, the building's security guard wasn't paying too much attention to the elevator cameras, because he was *definitely* about to get quite an eyeful of executive-level romance.

27

Soft Jazz & Emergency Calls

S oft jazz music gently played in the background, creating an intimate atmosphere in the dimly lit penthouse. Layla lay sprawled on her back, chest rising and falling as she tried to catch her breath. Whitley had her head resting comfortably on Layla's stomach, breathing just as hard from their passionate encounter. The fireplace flickered and danced, casting the entire living room in a warm orange and red glow that made everything feel magical and romantic.

They'd been frantic with desire in the elevator after leaving the office, hands roaming and lips meeting in desperate kisses. The sexual tension had continued during the car ride back to the penthouse, with Ryan doing his professional best to ignore the heated whispers and soft moans coming from the back seat. But as soon as they'd stumbled through Whitley's front door, everything had naturally slowed down and become more tender. Their kisses had become softer, deeper, more meaningful. They'd made love with exquisite slowness on the plush shag carpet in the living room, taking their time to explore and savor every moment together. Everything about the evening had been absolutely perfect.

"I still can't believe you actually came to my office and serenaded me in front of all my colleagues," Whitley said with wonder in her voice, her fingers tracing lazy patterns on Layla's bare skin.

Folding one hand under her head for support, Layla shrugged with characteristic casualness. "I couldn't stop thinking about you, no matter what I was doing. You were constantly on my mind."

Whitley lifted her head, shifting to lean on Layla's stomach with her chin, her eyes sparkling with curiosity and affection. "So you decided the logical solution was to play a beautiful song for me? It was gorgeous, by the way. I've never heard that particular melody before. What was the piece called?"

"That's because I literally just finished writing it," Layla replied with a shy smile.

"What do you mean?" Whitley moved again, this time positioning herself directly over Layla's body so they were face to face, giving Layla the perfect opportunity to take in every inch of Whitley's beautiful, flushed countenance.

"I wrote that song myself. From scratch."

"For me?" Whitley's voice shot up an entire octave, and her eyes grew wide with amazement and emotion. "You wrote an original composition for me?"

Smiling softly, Layla lifted her head just enough to place a gentle peck on Whitley's lips. "I wrote it about you, actually. The melody and the emotions behind it reflect exactly how I feel when I think of you, which is pretty much constantly these days."

"Layla..." Whitley's voice was thick with emotion.

"Is that too much?" Layla asked, suddenly uncertain. "I know we haven't been together very long, and I don't want to overwhelm you."

This was truly the first time Layla had ever found herself in this particular position with anyone. She couldn't seem to keep Whitley from occupying her thoughts, no matter how busy she was with rehearsals, teaching, or busking. The song had come to her gradually, over the space of several days, starting as a persistent earworm that she simply had to work out on paper and develop into a full composition.

Earlier today, she'd finished her rehearsal session with the quartet and had been struck by an overwhelming, almost visceral urge to see Whitley immediately. The need had been so intense that instead of waiting patiently for one of their rare scheduled moments when their busy lives might align, Layla had impulsively hopped into a taxi and headed directly to the DuPont offices without any real plan.

Her nerves had been completely out of control during the entire journey across the city, which was particularly strange because Layla never experienced performance anxiety. She'd performed for thousands of people without breaking a sweat, but the thought of playing for Whitley had made her palms damp and her heart race. She'd gradually recognized her nervousness was less about the actual musical performance and more about simply being close to Whitley; about expressing her feelings so publicly and vulnerably.

With every passing minute, every shared conversation, every stolen glance and tender touch, Layla was becoming painfully aware she was falling deeply, conclusively in love—the kind of all-consuming love that turned entire worlds upside down and inside out, that changed everything about how you saw your future.

"No, it's not too much at all," Whitley assured her with conviction, her voice warm with emotion. "It's the most romantic thing anyone has ever done for me."

Whitley's leg slipped naturally between Layla's thighs and brushed against her already aching center, sending sparks of renewed desire through her entire body. Layla sucked in a sharp breath as the delicious pressure began building again. Lifting her head with purpose, she captured Whitley's bottom lip between her own, giving it a playful tug that made Whitley moan softly.

"You're so incredibly beautiful, Whit," Layla whispered against her lips. "Inside and out."

Instead of replying with words, Whitley dipped her head and placed an open-mouthed kiss on the sensitive skin of Layla's neck. Layla instinctively arched her back as Whitley continued the sensual journey down her body, leaving a trail of fire in her wake. Layla immediately missed the intense pressure of Whitley's leg between hers, but that loss was quickly forgotten when it was replaced by the warm, firm press of Whitley's talented tongue against her most sensitive areas.

Clawing desperately at the soft fibers of the expensive rug beneath them, Layla let her head drop back, surrendering to the incredible sensations. Her entire body bowed like a drawn string as Whitley's ministrations quickened with obvious skill and confidence. She felt that delicious tongue tease her opening with assertive precision, exploring and tasting with clear enthusiasm.

Whitley was no shrinking violet in the bedroom, despite her sometimes-reserved public persona. She approached lovemaking with the same focused intensity she brought to everything else in her life, and she consistently took Layla to previously unknown heights of pleasure with every intimate encounter they shared.

Two fingers spread her wide with gentle but firm pressure, rubbing in slow circles on either side of her swollen clit. The newly exposed nub felt the cool air keenly, sending jolts of electricity racing up through Layla's abdomen and making her entire body tremble with anticipation.

"Oh, God, yes," she sighed, her voice breathy with building pleasure.

"I can't get enough of you," Whitley replied between long, languid licks, her voice muffled but filled with obvious desire and devotion. "I could spend hours just tasting you."

"Lay on your side," Layla said with sudden urgency, her need to reciprocate becoming overwhelming. She desperately needed to have her mouth on Whitley immediately, to give back even a fraction of the pleasure she was receiving.

The second her clit popped free from Whitley's plump, kiss-swollen lips, Layla quickly maneuvered herself so she was lying on her side too, but facing the opposite direction. Lifting one leg to provide better access, she exposed herself again to Whitley's waiting mouth while positioning herself to return the favor.

"You too," she urged breathlessly. "I need to taste you."

They arranged themselves in a classic sixty-nine position, lying top to tail with their glistening centers tantalizingly close to eager mouths. Both women stilled for a moment as they took in the erotic sight of their respective prizes, the anticipation building to an almost unbearable level.

Whitley broke first, diving back in to recapture Layla's sensitive clit with hunger and enthusiasm. Growling with her own desperate need to get her mouth on Whitley, Layla wasted no time in mirroring Whitley's passionate actions. She couldn't seem to get close enough, even after she grabbed Whitley's perfect arse with both hands and buried her face so deep between Whitley's legs that she could barely breathe properly.

All the while, the melody of Whitley's song played on repeat in her head like a soundtrack to their lovemaking, the notes seeming to match the rhythm of their movements and the inevitable crescendo of their shared pleasure.

Her hips began thrusting forward instinctively, riding Whitley's tongue with increasing desperation. The sensation was exquisite, especially when Whitley began making those incredible keening and mewling sounds as her pleasure continued building towards its predictable peak.

As soon as Whitley entered Layla with two fingers, hard and sure and perfectly angled, Layla was completely gone. The orgasm took over her entire nervous system like a lightning strike, every nerve ending firing at once in a symphony of sensation. It was honestly a miracle she was able to keep Whitley's clit in her mouth and continue the rhythmic sucking and licking she knew would push her lover over the edge.

Layla's vibratory moan of release rang out through the room, echoing off the high ceiling. Whitley's entire body began shaking violently as she followed Layla into bliss just moments later, her cries of pleasure muffled against Layla's sensitive flesh.

They'd barely caught their breath and begun to come down from their shared high when Layla moved with renewed energy until she was positioned on top of Whitley, straddling her hips. The kiss they shared was slow and deep and tasted of their combined essence. Layla simply needed to keep Whitley close for a little while longer, to maintain this intimate connection that felt more precious than anything she'd ever experienced.

The sudden, jarring sound of Layla's phone buzzing insistently from somewhere across the room cut through their post-coital bliss. She had zero intention of answering the intrusive call, wanting nothing more than to stay wrapped up in Whitley's arms for the rest of the evening. But after the fourth consecutive call in as many minutes, she huffed with annoyance and reluctantly rolled off Whitley, who stretched her satisfied body with a contented smile etched across her beautifully flushed face, and retrieved her phone from the pocket of her discarded jeans.

"Hello," Layla answered breathlessly, snuggling back into Whitley, not bothering to check the caller ID in her irritation.

"Layla, love? Is that you?" The familiar voice immediately caught her attention.

Sitting up abruptly, Layla furrowed her eyebrows with concern and confusion. "Dad? What's wrong?"

"Hello there, Button." Her father's voice came through the phone, using her childhood nickname with obvious affection.

"Is everything okay?" Layla asked, her heart beginning to race with worry. It wasn't that her parents never called her, but they usually scheduled their conversations for Sunday evenings when they could all relax and chat properly. The only other times they'd randomly and unexpectedly called were when Layla's beloved grandfather had passed away, and later when their family dog had to be put down.

"Everything's okay, love. No one died," her father assured her quickly, clearly recognizing the panic in her voice.

Chuckling with relief, Layla settled back against the sofa, her eyes automatically finding and admiring a still-smiling Whitley stretched out on the carpet like a satisfied cat. God, she was ethereally angelic in the firelight.

"Did you hear me, Button?" Her father's voice brought her back to the conversation.

"Shit, sorry, Dad. I was a bit distracted," she admitted sheepishly.

"Oh, aye! You've got a young lady with you, have you?" There was obvious amusement and approval in his tone.

"I do indeed. Sorry, what did I miss? You were saying something important."

"Your mum and I got into a small accident earlier today," he said, his voice becoming more serious.

Broken Legs & Family Meetings

"Accident?" Layla's breath caught painfully in her throat, and all the color drained from her face. Whitley's contented smile immediately vanished as she registered the shift in Layla's tone. She sat up quickly and reached over to take Layla's free hand, offering silent support and comfort.

"Yes, a little car crash, love," her father explained, trying to keep his voice calm and reassuring. "Your mum has a broken leg, and I've got a bit of a concussion, but I'm feeling perfectly fine, all things considered."

"Jesus Christ, when did this happen?" Layla asked, her voice rising with panic and concern.

"This morning, around ten o'clock. We popped into town for a bit of extra shopping. Your mum's got herself a lovely pink cast on her leg—she insisted on the color, of course. The doctors are keeping her overnight for observation, but I'll be taking her home tomorrow afternoon if everything continues to go well."

"What about you? Don't you need medical supervision for the night, too, with a concussion?" Layla pressed, her medical knowledge from various first aid courses kicking in.

"Aye, they did suggest it, but they're not officially admitting me to the hospital," her father replied with his usual stubbornness. "I told the doctor he can bloody well check on me from the visitor's chair if he needs to. I'm not leaving your mother alone in this place overnight. I don't care what that old battle-ax at the reception desk has to say about visiting hours."

Layla listened to her father's characteristic grumbling, but all her mind could really process was the terrifying fact both her parents had been injured in an accident. The thought of losing them, of being so far away when they needed her, was overwhelming.

"I'm coming home," she announced suddenly, jumping to her feet and immediately beginning to search for her scattered clothes. "I'm on the next available flight."

Whitley followed her lead without question, also rising and starting to gather her own clothing from around the room.

"You don't need to come all the way here, Button," her father protested, though his tone lacked real conviction. "We'll be perfectly alright. It's just a bit of a bump, nothing more."

"I don't care what you say, Dad. I'm already mentally packing," Layla said firmly, pulling on her jeans with shaking hands. "I'm getting on the next flight home, and that's final. Give Mum a kiss from me and tell her I'll be there as soon as humanly possible."

"Okay, love. We'll see you soon then," her father conceded, and the fact he hadn't fought harder for Layla to stay in New York told her everything she needed to know about how worried he actually was.

"Are they going to be okay?" Whitley asked with clear concern, her eyes wide as she watched Layla struggle with her emotions.

Layla swallowed hard and closed her eyes tightly, trying to keep the threatening tears at bay. When she opened them again, she nodded and reached out desperately for Whitley's comforting presence. "Yes, they're going to be okay. Mum's just a bit banged up with the broken leg, and Dad's being his usual stubborn self. But Whitley, I have to go to them. I'm so sorry."

"What on earth are you apologizing for?" Whitley asked, looking genuinely confused by Layla's words.

"Because I'm completely ruining our perfect evening together by having a family emergency," Layla explained, her voice thick with guilt and unshed tears.

"Well, if it's alright with you, I'd like to come along," Whitley said without hesitation, as if it were the most natural thing in the world.

"To England? You want to come with me to England?" Layla asked, hardly daring to believe what she was hearing.

"Of course. We can take the family jet, which will be much faster than commercial flights," Whitley replied practically. "You shouldn't have to deal with this alone."

The relief and gratitude that washed over Layla was so intense that she immediately broke down sobbing. She knew, logically, that her parents weren't in life-threatening danger, but the shock of the news and the fear of being so far away from them when they were hurt had completely overwhelmed her emotional defenses.

"Just breathe, baby," Whitley said softly, wrapping her arms around Layla's trembling form. "Everything's going to be fine."

Layla felt Whitley's soothing hands tracing slow, comforting paths up and down her bare back, grounding her and helping her regain some measure of control. She'd managed to get her trousers and one sock on, but her emotional state was making it difficult to focus on the simple task of getting dressed.

"Okay...I'm okay now," she said, taking a deep, shuddering breath. "Let's go."

"Shower first, Layla," Whitley suggested gently but firmly. "We both smell distinctly of sex, and I absolutely cannot meet your parents for the first time smelling like I've just made love to their daughter."

Nodding in agreement, Layla dragged Whitley towards the luxurious bathroom. They washed each other quickly but thoroughly, the intimate act providing comfort rather than arousal, under the circumstances. Layla continued to struggle with keeping her emotions in check, and a few more tears escaped despite her best efforts, but Whitley was right there to catch them—to catch her when she felt like she might fall apart completely.

After leaving Whitley's penthouse in record time, Ryan rushed them through the city streets to Layla's far more modest apartment. She burst through the front door and gave a rushed, breathless explanation to Puck, who immediately understood the gravity of the situation. He hugged her tightly and told her to give her parents a big kiss from him, his own eyes misting with concern for the people who had become like surrogate parents to all of Layla's friends.

She packed a small overnight bag with essentials, her hands shaking slightly as she tried to think of everything she might need for an indefinite stay. Within minutes, she was sprinting back to the waiting car, her heart pounding with anxiety and the urgent need to be with her family as she listened to Whitley on the phone with the private airfield, asking the pilot to ready the jet.

Ryan definitely broke several traffic laws on the way to the private airstrip, and Layla couldn't have been more grateful for his willingness to bend the rules.

If Layla weren't so consumed with panic over her parents' condition, Whitley's family jet would have required much more detailed exploration and appreciation. The aircraft was visually stunning, with leather seats and polished wood fixtures that screamed luxury and privilege.

Instead of lingering and marveling at her surroundings, she allowed Whitley to guide her to a plush seat in relative silence, her mind too focused on her parents to take in the opulent details.

Whitley settled into the seat directly next to her, buckling both their seatbelts with gentle efficiency. "Try to get some sleep, baby. It's going to be a long flight, and you'll need your energy when we get there."

After a couple of hours of restless tossing and turning, sheer physical and emotional exhaustion finally won out, and Layla managed to close her eyes and drift into an uneasy sleep. The captain's announcement about their imminent descent woke her abruptly, leaving her feeling disoriented and groggy for several moments until Whitley's gentle touch brought her back to full awareness.

"We've landed safely," Whitley said softly, caressing Layla's face with tender fingers before placing a gentle kiss on her mouth.

"Right. Christ, I feel like I've been fucked in the skull by a jackhammer," Layla groaned, rubbing her temples where a pounding headache had formed.

Whitley laughed despite the circumstances, the sound providing a moment of lightness in the heavy atmosphere. "That's certainly a delightful way to put it.

Would you like some water or orange juice to help you feel more human?"

"Yeah, juice would be brilliant, thanks."

They shared a quick breakfast of fresh orange juice and buttery croissants before the aircraft doors opened to reveal the typical gray of an English morning. A sleek black car was waiting for them on the tarmac, and Layla felt a wave of relief at not having to navigate public transport while in her current emotional state. The privilege gap had never been more apparent than right now, and maybe Layla should be worried, but then she looked at Whitley and knew it didn't matter. She was just Whit. Kind, funny, beautiful Whit, who had moved Heaven and Earth to get Layla to her parents' bedside.

Bursting through the hospital's automatic doors with barely contained urgency, Layla felt even more frantic. The combination of stress, lack of proper sleep, and overwhelming worry had left her feeling wired and dangerously close to a complete emotional meltdown. She knew as soon as she saw her parents with her own eyes and confirmed they were truly okay she'd be able to breathe normally again.

Once again, Whitley slipped her hand into Layla's and squeezed gently, providing the same silent comfort and support she'd been offering ever since that first devastating phone call.

After getting somewhat heated with the officious woman at the reception desk—who Layla immediately presumed was the "battle-ax" her father had mentioned—she finally managed to extract her mother's room number and directions to the correct ward.

Before pushing through the door to her mother's room, she turned to face Whitley with a mixture of gratitude and apprehension. "I honestly can't thank you enough for being here with me through all of this. It means more than I can possibly express. But I should probably warn you about something."

"Warn me about what?" Whitley asked, looking curious rather than concerned.

"I'm sorry in advance for whatever my mum says," Layla said with a rueful smile. "She has absolutely no filter, especially when she's been given pain medication. Come on, let's get this over with."

The hospital room was small and sterile, filled with that distinctive antiseptic smell that made Layla automatically scrunch up her nose in distaste. She first caught sight of her father slumped in the uncomfortable visitor's chair, his usually neat hair sticking out at odd angles from running his hands through it. His characteristic mustache twitched slightly as he softly snored, and a small white plaster was stuck to his forehead where he must have hit his head during the accident.

Then her eyes found her mother sitting up in the narrow hospital bed, a colorful silk scarf wrapped around her head in an attempt to contain her wild curls, though several rebellious ringlets were still poking out in various directions.

"Layla!" Beverly exclaimed with obvious delight, her face lighting up at the sight of her daughter.

Breaking into what had to be the shortest jog in history due to the cramped space, Layla threw her arms around her mother and squeezed her as tightly as she dared, breathing in the familiar scent of her perfume, though it was now mixed with hospital soap.

"Are you really okay, Mum?" she asked, pulling back to study her mother's face for signs of pain or distress.

"Of course I am, love. Just got a little jostled about, nothing more serious than that," Beverly replied with characteristic stoicism, though Layla could see the fatigue in her eyes.

"You've got a broken leg, Mum. That's not exactly nothing."

"Better a broken leg than a broken neck, I always say," Beverly replied pragmatically. "Oh...and who might you be, dear?"

Layla stepped back and gestured towards Whitley, who moved forward with clear nervousness. Whitley extended her hand with perfect politeness and said, "I'm Whitley DuPont. It's wonderful to meet you, Mrs. Simmons."

"Pfft, less of that formal nonsense, thank you very much." Beverly waved dismissively. "Call me Beverly, love. So tell me, are you my Layla's paramour?"

"Girlfriend," Layla corrected quickly, feeling her cheeks warm. "She's my girlfriend, Mum."

"Is she now?" Beverly beamed with delight and approval. "Well, it's absolutely lovely to meet you too, Whitley."

"So when can you actually go home?" Layla asked, purposefully redirecting her mother's attention away from Whitley before she could start with the embarrassing questions.

"I'm just waiting for the discharge papers to be processed, love. Shouldn't be much longer now."

"I'll go make sure the car is ready and waiting," Whitley discreetly whispered in Layla's ear, clearly recognizing the family needed a moment alone together.

As soon as Whitley had stepped out of the room, Beverly immediately pinched Layla's side playfully, her eyes twinkling with mischief. "She's a bloody gorgeous one, kiddo. Very nicely done indeed."

"Thanks, Mum." Layla laughed, feeling some of her tension finally beginning to ease.

"She's the one, isn't she?" Beverly asked with the intuitive knowledge that only mothers seemed to possess.

Beverly's delighted squeal of excitement caused Layla's father to startle awake and nearly topple out of his chair. Like a shot, he stood up with the reflexes of a much younger man, looking around the room with wild eyes as he searched for whatever emergency had caused the commotion.

"What's happening? Where's the danger?" he asked, his hair even more disheveled than before.

Layla and Beverly dissolved into giggles at his confused expression. When he finally came fully awake and oriented himself, the first thing he did was pull Layla into one of his bone-crushing embraces.

"Oh, it's so good to see you, Button," he said, his voice thick with emotion.

"Wait until you see who she's brought with her, Rog," Beverly said with noticeable excitement.

"Who have you brought with you, kiddo?" he asked, looking around the small room expectantly.

"Her girlfriend!" Beverly announced before Layla could respond.

"Mum, he asked me directly." Layla laughed, shaking her head at her mother's enthusiasm.

The door opened at that moment, and Whitley stepped back into the room looking slightly apprehensive. Her face immediately flushed deep red as three sets of curious eyes focused on her with inquisitive interest.

Layla wanted to rush over and rescue her from the awkward attention, but she was beaten to the punch by her father, who displayed his typical complete lack of personal boundaries.

Whitley didn't even have time to offer her hand for a greeting because she was already being enveloped in an enthusiastic bear hug by Roger Simmons, who had never met a stranger he couldn't immediately treat like family.

29

Hospitals & Horn Tooting

Who knew meeting the parents so early in a relationship would be this incredibly stressful? Whitley certainly knew now. But what real option had there truly been? The sheer look of panic in Layla's eyes when she received that phone call about her parents' accident was enough to make Whitley set aside any of her own uncomfortable feelings. Her heart had demanded she go with her girlfriend, leaving no room for hesitation or doubt over her decision to accompany her to the English countryside.

Throughout the journey, she'd done her best to keep Layla calm through small, strategic touches. Whitley instinctively understood Layla wasn't the type of woman who appreciated being smothered or overwhelmed when she was feeling emotionally raw. Instead, Whitley had offered quiet support, gentle hand-holding, and occasional soft kisses that communicated more than words ever could.

The flight itself had been remarkably smooth, thanks to the family's private jet. Layla had spent the majority of the journey asleep, which allowed Whitley some precious time to make necessary phone calls to her parents and her professional team. They would have to manage the business without her for a while, and surprisingly, that prospect didn't stress her out nearly as much as she would have expected.

Nothing mattered more than being with Layla right now—not her career, not her professional responsibilities, not even the carefully constructed life she'd built for herself. She'd shaken her head and emptied an entire glass of champagne upon fully realizing this profound truth.

Whitley DuPont was utterly and completely in love with Layla Simmons.

She'd known they shared something special from their very first unexpected encounter, but after their week apart, after hearing the beautiful song Layla had composed specifically for her, after the incredible time they'd spent making love and exploring each other's bodies and hearts, Whitley knew with absolute certainty this was it. Layla was her person, her future, her everything.

And now here she was, awkwardly standing in a small hospital room with the entire Simmons family staring at her after Mr. Simmons had hugged her within an inch of her life. Her own family was certainly tactile, but they usually had the decency to refrain from such intense physical displays within the first ten seconds of meeting someone.

"Sorry about that." Mr. Simmons chuckled, looking only slightly embarrassed. "Just excited to see my little Button and meet the woman she's dating. Probably should have led with an introduction rather than a bear hug, huh?"

Whitley cracked a genuine smile, finding his enthusiasm endearing rather than overwhelming. "It's absolutely fine, Mr. Simmons."

"Roger," he corrected immediately. "Call me Roger."

Whitley nodded, her professional politeness softening into something more genuine. "Roger. And I'm Whitley. It's truly wonderful to meet you both."

"Oh, likewise!" Roger replied with his usual gusto. "We've never actually met one of Layla's girlfriends before."

Whitley shot a quick glance at Layla, who was turning an adorable shade of red and studiously looking everywhere except at her or her parents.

"Then it makes this moment even more special," she added smoothly, hoping to ease Layla's obvious embarrassment.

The hospital room door opened again, and the same stern-faced woman from earlier waltzed in with an official-looking clipboard. "You're free to go, Mrs. Simmons. Do you have transportation arranged?"

"The car is waiting," Whitley supplied helpfully. The nurse gave a stiff, professional nod and left as quickly as she had entered.

"Blimey, I'll be glad not to have to see her cheery face again," Roger mumbled, absently smoothing out his mustache. The gesture did little to tame it, and Whitley suddenly understood exactly where Layla had inherited her larger-than-life, uncontrollable hair.

Roger's own hair was shorter but still had distinct curls that seemingly refused to lie flat, and Beverly had several big, rebellious curls escaping from beneath her headscarf. Whitley would have bet the entire DuPont family fortune that Layla's mother had the same wild, untamable coils as her daughter.

Layla began gathering her mother's belongings with efficient, loving movements. "Come on, let's get you two home," she said, her voice carrying a mixture of concern and practical determination.

Whitley hovered near the door, unsure whether she should offer assistance or stay out of the way. Roger helped Beverly out of the hospital bed with gentle care, and Layla efficiently hauled their bags out of the room.

Pointing somewhat awkwardly toward the door, Whitley cleared her throat. "I'll just...give you some privacy..."

"Okay, dear. We won't be long," Beverly replied breezily, already untying her hospital gown with complete lack of self-consciousness. It was clear that modesty was not a significant concern for the Simmons family.

Hurrying down the hospital corridor, Whitley spotted Layla and quickened her pace. "Wait up!" she called.

The smile she received in response sent delightful shivers cascading down her spine. Layla looked at her like she'd personally hung the moon or invented Christmas—a gaze filled with such pure, unadulterated adoration it made Whitley's heart skip several beats.

"Sorry about my dad," Layla blurted the moment Whitley was by her side. "He's a big, happy goof sometimes. Did he make you uncomfortable?"

"Not at all," Whitley assured her. "Your parents are absolutely lovely."

Layla let out a bark of laughter. "Let's see how you feel after spending some extended time with them in close quarters."

"Oh, are we staying at their house?" The thought about where they'd stay hadn't even occurred to Whitley until that moment.

"Um, I was planning on it," Layla replied, a hint of uncertainty creeping into her voice. "But if you'd prefer to find a hotel, that's completely fine too."

Whitley didn't need to be Sherlock Holmes to deduce how the idea of staying anywhere other than with her parents was causing Layla some underlying stress. The accident had clearly shaken her more deeply than she was letting on.

Clasping Layla's hand firmly, she pulled them to a stop just outside the hospital entrance. "Not a chance. I'm more than happy to see your childhood home and get to know your parents better. In fact, I'm hoping they'll tell me all your most embarrassing childhood stories. Maybe even break out the photo albums."

Snorting with laughter, Layla pulled her close and placed a soft, intimate kiss just under her ear. "You don't need to ask them anything. I'll tell you whatever you want. No shame here. My childhood pictures are cute as fuck. I was absolutely adorable."

"And modest?" Whitley teased.

"Pfft. Ain't nobody gonna toot my horn for me."

Grinning mischievously, Whitley let her hands drift down to playfully squeeze Layla's butt. "I'll be more than happy to toot it for you, if you'd like."

Layla let out a low, sensual chuckle that sent immediate heat racing through Whitley's body. "I'll definitely hold you to that. Although I wonder how you'll feel when you see my actual childhood bedroom."

"I can't wait," Whitley replied honestly. She wanted to learn everything possible about Layla—her past, her family, her dreams, her entire world.

30

Graffiti & Mince Pie Declarations

T he driver quickly jogged over and took their bags to the car. The automatic hospital doors swooshed open, revealing Roger pushing a squealing Beverly in her wheelchair, performing dramatic wheelies that made the hospital staff look both amused and slightly concerned. Whitley couldn't help but laugh at their playful dynamic.

"Alright, get in the car before they call security on you two lunatics," Layla called out, shaking her head with a mixture of exasperation and love.

The car ride took about an hour, during which Whitley silently observed Layla reuniting with her parents. It was immediately clear how much they adored their daughter. The pride in their eyes was unmistakable as they caught up on everything that had happened since Layla's last visit.

Listening to Beverly, Whitley quickly understood *exactly* where Layla had inherited her direct communication style. Beverly pulled absolutely no punches, grilling Layla about everything from her busking experiences in New York to the specific skin products she was now using—because Layla needed to be careful with her sensitive skin in the cold weather.

"Let's get inside. The heating's been on all night, so it'll be lovely and warm," Roger called over his shoulder as he helped Beverly navigate the path leading up to their wreath-covered front door.

The house was indeed warm—almost stifling. Layla immediately raced over to the thermostat, grumbling about energy consumption and climate change in a way that made Whitley giggle. Roger and Beverly disappeared into another room, leaving Whitley once again hovering awkwardly near the entrance.

The Simmons' home was cozy and totally saturated with Layla's essence. Pictures and framed newspaper clippings hung on every wall, telling the story of Layla's life through visual snapshots. There was a distinct smell of Christmas—cinnamon and pine—and with the sun already setting, the home looked incredibly inviting. Twinkling fairy lights curled around the banister, creating a warm, magical atmosphere.

"Are you coming in?" Layla asked with a smile that made Whitley's heart skip a beat.

Toeing off her boots, Whitley took Layla's hand and let herself be pulled into what turned out to be the kitchen. Beverly sat on a stool, directing Roger, who was now wearing a Mrs. Claus apron that looked slightly ridiculous and completely endearing.

"Rog will get some hot chocolate going," Beverly announced. "Why don't you two settle your bags upstairs? I'll call you when it's ready."

Excited to see Layla's childhood bedroom, Whitley followed close behind as they ascended the stairs. She also made sure to appreciate the view of Layla's perfectly fine ass the entire way up, because why not?

"Okay, are you ready?" Layla asked with a mischievous smile as they stood outside a nondescript white door.

"I'm definitely intrigued," Whitley replied.

Pushing the door open with dramatic flair, Layla let Whitley enter first. Whitley's feet came to an abrupt halt as she took in the room's extraordinary decor. Every single wall was covered in graffiti—but not the cheap, messy tags typically seen on bridge underpasses. This was genuine graffiti art at its finest.

"Oh, wow," Whitley breathed, completely stunned.

"Pretty funky, right?" Layla asked casually.

"Who *did* this?" Whitley turned in a full circle, trying to absorb every incredible detail. There wasn't a single patch of wall space left blank.

"My dad. He's a pretty talented artist," Layla explained.

"*Pretty* talented?" Whitley choked out. "This is phenomenal. How old were you when he did this?"

Layla squinted her eyes, thinking back. "About ten, I reckon."

"And he just happily graffitied your walls? No questions asked?"

Shrugging, Layla placed their bags by the wardrobe and sat on the bed. "They were always cool with things like that. They wanted me to express myself. I think they realized early on that trying to suppress me wouldn't work. I was a bit of a tearaway, remember?"

One particular section caught Whitley's attention. "Is...is that you?" She stepped closer to the wall beside the bed, her face just inches from the surface as she studied the painted version of her girlfriend.

"Yup. That's me busking for the first time," Layla confirmed.

"At ten?" Whitley asked, astonished.

"Mum and Dad took me. I'd been bugging them for weeks. It was Christmastime, as you can see from the artwork. I stood on that street corner for three-and-a-half hours, playing. Mum and Dad were frozen solid by the time I finished, but they never complained. They said they'd never seen me so happy."

"That's beautiful," Whitley said softly, moved by the story.

"Hot chocolates are ready!" Roger called from downstairs.

Whitley didn't want to leave the bedroom. She wanted to spend more time examining the incredible artwork, and if she were being completely honest, she also wanted Layla. Alone, and preferably naked. Her thoughts must have crossed her face because Layla smirked knowingly.

"I promise you can do whatever is going through your mind right now in a few hours," Layla whispered. "Let's go drink some hot chocolate and eat mince pies. It's nearly Christmas, after all."

The approaching holiday raised an unspoken question: Where would they be spending Christmas? Whitley had never missed Christmas with her own family before. But she suspected Layla wouldn't be thrilled about leaving her family so soon after their accident.

Silencing her worry, Whitley followed Layla downstairs. Beverly and Roger were in the living room, which twinkled with multicolored lights. The Christmas tree was comically too tall for the ceiling and bent at a funny angle, but still looked absolutely charming.

"I added a little tipple to the hot chocolate to get us in the mood," Beverly announced, wiggling her eyebrows.

"In the mood for what?" Layla laughed.

"Christmas games, of course!" her mother shot back.

Roger slurped loudly on his drink, earning simultaneous scowls from both his wife and daughter. Whitley was already highly entertained. That was, until Beverly turned her laser-focused attention directly on Whitley with a look that suggested an imminent interrogation.

"So, what do you do, Whitley? You're definitely not a musician," Beverly stated more than asked.

"Oh? And why's that?" Whitley asked, intrigued.

"Because our Button wouldn't date a musician if they were the last person on Earth," Roger interjected.

Beverly nodded in agreement. "Exactly. So, what's your occupation? Not that it matters. Don't go thinking we're going to judge you based on that."

"No," Roger added. "We'll judge you based on how you treat Layla."

Clearly, Layla had inherited her direct communication style from *both* parents.

"I work for the family company," Whitley explained. "Mainly in finance, but my real passion is the work I do with our nonprofit foundations and charities."

Roger whistled. "Sounds intense. You work a lot then?"

"I do," Whitley admitted. "But I'm actually attempting to lighten my workload."

"You are?" Layla asked, suddenly very interested—though her attention was momentarily divided between Whitley and a mince pie she seemed to be eyefucking with considerable enthusiasm.

"I am," Whitley confirmed.

"Why's that?" Beverly asked, though her knowing look suggested she already had the answer.

"Because I want to spend more time with Layla," Whitley said simply. "As much time as I can, actually."

The mince pie was immediately forgotten, and Whitley found herself face to face with an intensely focused Layla, her eyes boring directly into Whitley's soul.

"Do you mean that?" Layla asked, her voice a mixture of hope and vulnerability.

Whitley was acutely aware of Beverly and Roger watching their interaction. She would have preferred to have this conversation in private, but at this point, she was beyond caring about propriety.

"Yes, I mean it," she said firmly. "I...well, I'm in love with you, Layla. I want to spend all my time with you."

Silence settled over the room, and Whitley's heart rate shot up. She couldn't—*wouldn't*—believe her feelings weren't mirrored by Layla. Not after everything they'd shared. She willed herself to remain calm and vulnerable.

"I love you too," Layla whispered, her confession barely audible but filled with profound emotion, before capturing Whitley's lips in a searing kiss.

Whitley felt Layla's tongue brush her lips seeking entrance, and even though they were in the company of her parents, Whitley was powerless to refuse. She breathed Layla in and sucked delicately on her tongue, lost in the moment.

"Huh. Well, looks like the inquisition's off, Bev," Roger commented dryly.

Whitley pulled away from Layla, smiling. Layla rested her forehead against Whitley's and took a deep, centering breath.

"I'd say so, Rog," Beverly replied. "Right, mince pies all around. Welcome to the family, Whit!"

31

Early Mornings & Electric Violins

I t felt incredibly good to be home. Now the initial shock of her parents' accident had worn off, and Layla knew they were truly okay, she could fully enjoy her visit with Whitley.

They hadn't ravaged each other as originally promised the night before, primarily because both were far too stuffed with mince pies, boozy cocoa, and Quality Street chocolates to even consider any passionate encounters. Layla had laughed to herself, imagining they would have looked like beached whales attempting to roll on top of each other if they'd tried anything remotely sexy in their current state of post-feast lethargy.

Now, Layla lay awake with Whitley tucked into her side. They'd been forced to sleep closely due to Layla's childhood bed being barely larger than a double. The curtains remained open all night, just as Layla had always preferred, allowing her to watch the stars. Now the morning sun shone through, casting warm golden rays over their intertwined bodies.

Turning her head, Layla breathed in Whitley's distinctive scent. It wasn't the first time she'd had a woman in her bed—she'd been young and reckless once. She softly scoffed to herself, acknowledging she was probably still somewhat reckless. But not when it came to women. Especially not when it came to this specific woman.

There was no room for recklessness where Whitley was concerned. Layla knew, with absolute certainty, that she had something truly special.

A warm breath skated across her neck as Whitley softly sighed in her sleep. The swell of emotion was sudden and profound. Layla had never felt this strongly about anyone before, not in her entire life. Her mind drifted back to the previous night and Whitley's nervous declaration of love.

Layla probably should have taken her aside privately instead of responding in front of her parents. But in that moment, she hadn't been thinking rationally. She had been so desperately eager to hear and reciprocate Whitley's feelings that appropriateness had been the furthest thing from her mind.

To their credit, her parents had simply hugged them both and continued with their evening as if such conversations were the most natural thing in the world. Layla had spent every subsequent moment plastered to Whitley's side as they ate and played silly family games. It had been beautiful to watch Whitley integrate so seamlessly with her family.

Beverly had pulled Layla aside at the end of the night and shared how much she and Roger liked Whitley. Her mother had tearfully confessed they could see how deeply in love they were, and that this was all they had ever wanted for their daughter.

Whitley's song played through her head as she lay there holding her, her gaze roaming the art-covered walls of her childhood bedroom. She remembered all the times her dad had patiently painted over a wall with white whenever

Layla felt a sudden burst of creative inspiration. He had never complained, always happy to provide a fresh canvas for whatever artistic vision she wanted to explore.

The only section that had remained unchanged throughout the years was the painting of Layla's first busking scene—a testament to the significance of that moment in her life.

An overwhelming need to play music suddenly surged through her body. Sucking in a sharp breath, she rolled gently, inadvertently dislodging Whitley from her comfortable position.

Whitley grumbled sleepily, "Mmm, no, let's stay asleep."

"Babe, I'm taking you busking!" The idea seemed like the most brilliant plan in the world. Yes, Layla would take Whitley to the exact corner where she had first performed as a young girl, and play. She would spread some festive cheer and share this deeply personal moment with the woman she loved.

"What?" Whitley's eyes blinked rapidly, trying to process this sudden announcement.

"Busking!" Layla exclaimed, jumping out of bed with infectious enthusiasm. She quickly shoved on a pair of old jogging bottoms and a comfortable T-shirt. "I'll grab you some coffee and a slice of toast."

She was out of the room before Whitley could even formulate a response.

Beverly sat at the kitchen table, her broken leg propped up on a chair, looking amused by her daughter's sudden burst of energy. Layla skidded to a halt in front of her.

"Coffee? I need some toast and coffee for Whitley," she announced.

"There's a fresh pot, and you know where the bread is. There's also a teapot stewing," Beverly replied dryly. "Where's the fire?"

"I'm taking Whitley busking. I can't believe I didn't think of it sooner!"

Beverly laughed. "Surely she's seen you play in New York."

Layla nodded, grabbing a mug of coffee to stir Whitley to life and a mug of authentic English tea for herself. "Of course she has. But this is different."

"Ah, you want to take her to *your* corner," Beverly observed, eyeing Layla over the rim of her coffee mug. "That's very romantic, honey."

Rolling her eyes, Layla popped bread into the toaster, carefully setting it to the precise setting that would produce the golden-brown crust Whitley preferred.

"I know it's romantic, Mum. I know how to woo a woman," she said with a confident swagger.

"She takes after me." Roger grinned, entering the kitchen. He pecked Beverly on the lips and then pulled Layla into a tight hug. "What's got you looking so wired?"

"She's whisking her lady love off to do a spot of busking," Beverly explained.

"Oh, lovely," Roger said. "Ask Whitley to take some pictures. I could update the mural."

"No!" Layla protested immediately.

Roger chuckled. "Alright. Take pictures anyway. Right, I'm off to the shops. See you all later."

"Okay, I need to rouse a very grumpy Whitley. Wish me luck," Layla announced.

Beverly snickered as Layla carefully juggled two mugs and a plate of buttery toast. Whitley hadn't moved a muscle and was now lightly snoring.

Setting the cups down on the nightstand, Layla wafted the plate of toast under Whitley's nose, causing it to twitch adorably.

"Is that..." Whitley mumbled.

"Buttery toast, just how you like it," Layla confirmed.

"Okay, I'm waking up."

Layla stifled a laugh as Whitley struggled to pry her eyes open. The jet lag was clearly hitting her hard. After several minutes of face scrunching and eye flapping, Whitley finally sat up, eyes wide open.

"Layla. Why...I mean, thank you for the coffee and breakfast, but why so early?"

"Because we have places to be, things to do," Layla explained with enthusiasm. "Starting with breakfast, then a bus ride into town, followed by brunch, and then some music. It's not snowing like in New York, so the wintery wonderland I'd envisioned isn't going to happen, but I think I can still make it magical."

Whitley chewed on her toast, licking the butter from her lips in a way that momentarily distracted Layla from her mission of getting her out of bed as quickly as possible.

"You didn't bring your violin," Whitley mumbled through a mouthful of food.

Layla bounced off the bed and headed to the wardrobe. It had three drawers at the bottom and a cabinet top. Turning the small brass key, she whipped open both doors and turned back to Whitley, who sat slack-jawed in surprise.

"What kind of musician would I be if I didn't have backups?"

In fact, Layla had four extra violins displayed in the cabinet. Two electric and two acoustic. One was the very first violin she had ever picked up.

"Wow!" Whitley exclaimed, getting out of bed with the last piece of toast hanging from her mouth. She stepped up to the cabinet, eyeing the instruments closely.

Layla swallowed hard, trying to ignore the fact Whitley was completely naked. If she touched her now, they wouldn't leave her room at all, and she really wanted to busk with Whitley by her side.

Leaving Whitley to her perusal, Layla grabbed her robe from the back of the door and draped it around Whitley's shoulders. "Here. I need you to cover up before I do indecent things to you."

Chuckling, Whitley placed a quick kiss on her lips. "These are beautiful, Layla. Which is your favorite?"

"That one is my first, so it will always hold a special place in my heart," Layla explained, "but for showmanship, the neon-blue electric is my go-to choice."

"Don't you need a speaker?"

"Amp, and yes. I have a portable one."

Whitley draped her arms over Layla's shoulders. "If you're dragging me outside in the freezing cold at an ungodly hour, can I choose which one you take?"

"Sure," Layla agreed.

"The electric one. I haven't heard you play one yet."

"Deal. Now, get dressed."

Whitley reluctantly released her hold on Layla and began rummaging through her suitcase for appropriate busking attire. "What exactly does one wear to perform on street corners in December?" she asked, holding up one of her many cashmere jumpers that probably cost more than most people's monthly rent.

"Something warm that you don't mind getting a bit scruffy," Layla replied, carefully lifting the electric violin from its wall mount. The instrument gleamed under the morning light, its vibrant blue finish catching the sun streaming through the window. "And definitely not that jumper. You'll freeze your tits off, and I quite like those tits exactly where they are."

"Charming as always." Whitley laughed, tossing the expensive jumper back into her case. "How about this?" She held up a thick wool coat and dark jeans.

"Perfect. Very street musician chic."

As Whitley dressed, Layla tested the violin's tuning, her fingers dancing across the strings with practiced ease. The familiar weight of the instrument against her shoulder felt like coming home, even more so than being back in her childhood bedroom. The violin was her first love; her constant companion through every major moment of her life.

"Right, then," Layla announced once Whitley was bundled up appropriately. "Time to show you where it all began."

They made their way downstairs, where Beverly was still stationed at the kitchen table with her leg propped up, now working on what appeared to be a crossword puzzle.

"Off on your romantic adventure then?" she asked without looking up from her paper.

"Something like that." Layla grinned, slinging the portable amp over her shoulder. "We'll be back after lunch."

"Take your time, love. Your father's gone to the shops, so I'll just be here solving seven down...'musical performance in public spaces for donations'."

"Busking," Whitley and Layla said simultaneously, causing all three women to burst into laughter.

"Clever clogs, the pair of you." Beverly chuckled.

Following Layla to the door, Whitley observed her girlfriend. "You were really just a child when you started doing this?" she asked, as they stepped out onto the frost-covered street ready to make their way to the bus stop. Layla had point blank refused Whitley's offer of calling a car.

"Ten," Layla confirmed. "Mum was terrified I'd get kidnapped or worse, but Dad convinced her that music was meant to be shared, not hidden away in practice rooms. He said the streets would teach me things no fancy conservatory ever could. Plus, Dad had the locals in the village keep an eye on me, so even when my parents couldn't come, I was never truly on my own."

"He was right, wasn't he?"

"Absolutely. Playing for strangers teaches you to read a crowd, to adapt your performance based on their energy. It's completely different from playing in a concert hall where everyone's obligated to sit quietly and politely applaud at the end."

Gammon Sandwiches & Street Corners

Ah, Layla missed riding double-decker buses. The distinctive smell—a unique blend of worn leather seats, diesel fumes, and the faint traces of countless passengers' perfumes and aftershaves—transported her back to many memories of traveling around town, applying for gigs, and making music on the streets. The rumble of the engine beneath her feet and the gentle sway as the massive vehicle navigated winding roads also felt like coming home. Sitting in the familiar seat was a reminder of her journey as a musician, filled with hope and determination, when every bus ride represented another opportunity, another chance to share her music with the world.

Whitley seemed to be thoroughly enjoying herself too, her eyes bright with curiosity as she gazed out the large windows at the bustling streets below. One of the things Layla loved most about her was how genuinely down-to-earth she was, in the way she could find wonder in the simplest experiences.

The DuPonts were possibly some of the wealthiest people on the globe, their name synonymous with luxury and privilege, but Whitley never came across as a snob. She never turned her nose up at Layla's penny-pinching lifestyle and never made her feel inadequate for choosing second-hand clothes or counting coins for bus fare. Instead, she embraced and appreciated Layla's approach to life with an enthusiasm that made Layla's heart swell with affection.

Sure, Layla would love to make a consistent living from her music, to not worry about rent or whether she could afford groceries that week, but her goal had never been about becoming rich. It was about the pure joy of creating and sharing music with the world; about that magical moment when a melody could stop someone in their tracks and make them feel something profound.

They exited the bus onto the familiar cobblestone street. The crisp December air immediately nipped at their cheeks as they headed towards Layla's favorite local pubs. The warm glow spilling from its frosted windows promised refuge from the biting cold.

"You're about to have a mouthgasm!" she announced dramatically, her breath forming small clouds in the frigid air.

Whitley laughed, the sound melodic and infectious in the quiet street. "Okay. Care to put that into context? Otherwise, I'm going to think you're planning some kind of serious public display of affection."

Layla wiggled her eyebrows mischievously, her dark eyes sparkling with playful intent. "Hmm, I do enjoy a bit of risk. But no, I didn't mean that. This time."

Closing the space between them with deliberate slowness, Whitley brushed her nose against Layla's, the intimate gesture sending warmth spreading through Layla's chest despite the cold. Layla's wild, untamed curls, freed from their usual constraints and dancing in the winter breeze, tickled her cheek, causing Whitley to giggle and bat away the errant strands with mittened hands.

"So, about this mouthgasm?" Whitley prompted, her voice dropping to a husky whisper that made Layla's pulse quicken.

"Right. Julie, who runs the pub, is a master of Christmas food. She absolutely smashes it every single year." Layla's voice took on the reverent tone she reserved for truly exceptional things. "Her turkey dinner is delicious, perfectly seasoned and tender enough to cut with a fork, but nothing—and I mean nothing—beats her gammon sandwiches. The meat is glazed with honey and mustard, slow-cooked until it practically melts in your mouth, and served on thick-cut bread that's still warm from the oven. It's like a tradition in my family to have at least one sandwich at Christmas. It's something we've done since I was small enough to need a booster seat. I've missed a few now, living away and chasing gigs, so this is going to be extra good."

Whitley laughed at Layla's enthusiasm. "Well, I have no idea what gammon is, so I'm excited. Lead the way."

They entered the cozy pub, immediately enveloped by the welcoming warmth and the rich aromas of roasting meat and mulled wine. The interior was everything a proper British pub should be: dark wood paneling, brass fixtures polished to a warm gleam, and mismatched chairs that had clearly hosted decades of conversations and celebrations. Fairy lights twinkled around the bar, and a crackling fire cast dancing shadows on the walls. They headed to the bar, weaving between tables occupied by locals nursing pints and sharing quiet conversations.

Layla smiled when Julie noticed her from behind the bar and made a beeline over, her face lighting up with genuine pleasure. They hugged warmly, Julie's embrace carrying the comforting scents of kitchen spices and the faint sweetness of baking bread.

Layla made introductions with the pride of someone presenting a treasured friend to family. Julie was as lovely to Whitley as she was to Layla—welcoming her with the same warmth she'd always shown the Simmons family—and there had never been any doubt she would be. Julie was essentially the town's nicest woman, with always perfectly styled silver hair and laugh lines that spoke of decades of genuine joy. Julie loved the Simmons family as much as they loved her.

They placed an order for two gammon sandwiches to go. Julie promised they'd be ready in just a few minutes and refused to let them pay full price despite Layla's protests. As much as Layla would have loved to linger in the pub's cozy atmosphere, soaking up the warmth and the familiar comfort of home, she was desperate to get her impromptu busking session underway.

They walked the rest of the way through the town center, their footsteps echoing off the ancient buildings, with Whitley happily listening to Layla's stories and interesting local facts. Layla pointed out the music shop where she'd bought her first guitar pick, the bookshop where she'd spent countless rainy afternoons reading music theory, and the corner where she'd first heard a street musician and realized what she wanted to do with her life.

"We're here," Layla announced when they reached her special corner—a spot where two busy streets intersected, creating natural acoustics that made even a whispered song carry.

She placed her portable amp on the ground with the reverence of a ritual and began setting up her violin with practiced efficiency, her fingers automatically moving through the familiar motions. People walked past, bundled in winter coats and focused on their destinations, oblivious to her presence—which was typical until she started playing. The anticipation built in her chest, with that familiar flutter of nerves and excitement that never quite went away, no matter how many times she'd done this.

"Okay. I'm going to start. I hope you enjoy it," Layla said, a hint of vulnerability creeping into her voice despite her confidence. This mattered—Whitley's *reaction* mattered more than she wanted to admit.

Whitley didn't respond verbally. Instead, she gave Layla a deep, passionate kiss that tasted of winter air and promise before stepping back to watch, her eyes already shining with anticipation.

Closing her eyes, Layla lifted her violin, letting it settle snugly under her chin in the familiar embrace she'd known since childhood. She breathed in deeply, experiencing the nostalgic scent of the town—a mixture of old stone, woodsmoke from chimneys, and the faint sweetness of chestnuts roasting somewhere nearby. It made her heart incredibly happy, filling her with a contentment that added to her sense of coming home after a long journey.

Lifting her bow with the ceremony the moment deserved, she felt the same giddy excitement she had experienced all those years ago when she first started busking as a pre-teen, nervous and hopeful and desperate to share her music with anyone who would listen.

Letting her passion flow like water finding its course, Layla played as though she were performing in front of a stadium full of people instead of a handful of passersby.

Her eyes remained closed as she lost herself completely in the music, letting it carry her to that place where nothing existed except melody and rhythm and the pure joy of creation.

Her body began to move and sway—something that always happened when she played, and an involuntary response to the music flowing through her. She couldn't stop herself from reacting to the tempo, becoming one with the song. The music possessed her entirely, body and soul.

Song after song went by in a whirlwind of magic, each piece flowing seamlessly into the next as if they were all part of one continuous story. She could feel the enchantment in the air, that electric moment when music transcended mere sound and became something transformative. The effect was confirmed when she finally opened her eyes and scanned the large crowd that had gathered around her like iron filings drawn to a magnet.

There were couples dancing together, swaying in warm embraces with eyes only for each other, families twirling their children and moving to her melody with unconscious grace, and elderly people standing with tears in their eyes as her music awakened long-buried memories. And then there was Whitley, standing at the front of the crowd with tears streaming down her cheeks, clutching her chest as if trying to hold her heart in place.

Coins littered her open violin case like scattered stars—more money than she'd ever made at this very special busking spot, even more than when she'd spent entire afternoons playing here growing up. Layla pulled the bow across the strings for the last time, the final note hanging in the air like a benediction, and took a deep, theatrical bow as she finished. The crowd clapped and cheered with genuine enthusiasm, with more money dropping into her case as people showed their appreciation in the most practical way possible.

When the people dispersed, returning to their lives but carrying a piece of her music with them, Whitley was upon her instantly, pulling Layla into a soul-consuming kiss that tasted of salty tears and overwhelming emotion. Her tongue pushed into Layla's mouth, devouring her completely, their bodies pressing together as if they could merge into one person. Their hands began to roam desperately, seeking contact and connection, the intensity of the moment making them forget where they were.

A wolf whistle from a man across the street finally pulled them apart, reality crashing back in with jarring suddenness.

"You are spectacular," Whitley said breathlessly, completely ignoring the catcaller like he didn't exist.

"Did you enjoy it?" Layla asked, though the answer was written clearly across Whitley's face in tear tracks and wonder.

Whitley nodded emphatically, her hair bouncing with the motion. "Now I understand why you love busking so much. It's absolutely intoxicating—the way you can just create magic out of thin air and share it with complete strangers."

Layla smiled, her heart full to bursting. "It's the best feeling in the world. Everyone should have access to music, regardless of who they are or how much money they have. That's one of the reasons I could never gel with the classical music crowd. Too rigid, too snobby, too concerned with pedigree and proper technique instead of just letting the music speak."

"People do deserve music," Whitley agreed, her voice fierce with conviction. "Especially music as special as yours."

"Come on. Let's pack up. We've got some sandwiches to eat." Layla paused, suddenly self-conscious. "Although you didn't have to wait for me to eat yours."

"Oh, no," Whitley replied firmly, helping to coil cables and pack equipment. "This is something we have to do together. It's a tradition, right? And traditions are meant to be shared."

God, Layla wanted to be alone with Whitley, to explore this feeling building between them without the distraction of crowds and public spaces. After the quickest pack-up in history, her hands moving with efficient urgency, she deposited her earnings in the closest charity donation pot.

They headed to the bus stop and took a seat on the cold metal bench, the adrenaline from the performance slowly fading into a warm glow of satisfaction. Handing over a sandwich wrapped in brown paper that was already spotted with grease, they unwrapped them with the ceremony of a sacred ritual. Layla's mouth watered in anticipation, the rich aroma of honey-glazed gammon making her stomach audibly growl.

"Ready?" she asked, holding her sandwich like it was a treasured artifact.

"Ready," Whitley confirmed, her eyes sparkling with delight.

Layla took a giant bite, savoring every single flavor—the sweet glaze, the smoky meat, the tang of mustard, the soft bread that had soaked up all the delicious juices. It was as good as she remembered, maybe even better, because she was sharing it with someone who mattered. Whitley made an obscene noise of pleasure that sent heat shooting through Layla's body.

Laughing, Layla wiped away a glob of mayo from Whitley's mouth with gentle fingers, the simple touch electric between them. "I told you it was good."

Taking another bite, Whitley nodded and smiled, her expression radiating pure contentment. "Everything about this is good, Layla." Her eyes conveyed far more than her words could express—promises and possibilities and a future that suddenly seemed bright with potential.

Layla agreed completely, her heart full of music and love and the perfect simplicity of a shared sandwich on a cold December morning.

Everything was good.

Sketches & Oral Appreciation

"**A**re you on the jet?" Aubrey demanded the second the call connected, her voice sharp with urgency. "Because Mom is getting that infamous frown line between her brows every time the family dinner is mentioned. She's picked up your place marker at least twenty times already."

Whitley sighed deeply. She hated the idea of her mother being upset, but what could she realistically do?

"No, I'm not on the jet. I'm still in Layla's room at her parents' house. I don't know what to do. Layla's so happy to be home, I don't think she'll want to head back to New York until after the holidays."

And I don't want to leave her.

Aubrey sighed back, matching Whitley's tone of frustration. "Mom isn't going to like that, Whit."

"It's not Mom's choice," Whitley snapped before quickly settling down and moderating her tone. "Of course I want to be home. I love our Christmas Day tradition, but Layla is a part of my life now, Aubs. We've already done one too many separately."

Last year had been the hardest. Even though she'd vowed to take some time to figure out her feelings for Layla, the holiday had felt fundamentally wrong—incomplete and empty without her in some inexplicable way.

"You weren't a couple then—" Aubrey started to argue.

"Maybe not the first year," Whitley interrupted. "But last Christmas there were definitely feelings. If I hadn't had to go to London, who knows what might've happened between us?"

She heard Aubrey mutter something in the background to William, presumably discussing potential solutions. Rolling her eyes, Whitley decided to check her email while her siblings continued their hushed conversation.

"Aubrey!" she finally shouted, growing impatient. "Shall I just hang up?"

"No! We were just brainstorming," Aubrey replied quickly.

"Did you both strain your brains?" Whitley teased.

"Burn!" William shouted from somewhere behind Aubrey, causing Whitley to chuckle and shake her shoulders with laughter.

"Shut up, Will," she retorted. "What were you brainstorming?"

"How we can make Mom happy and keep Layla happy at the same time," Aubrey explained.

"Video chat on Christmas Day?" Whitley suggested halfheartedly.

"No, dumbass," Aubrey scoffed. "Bring Layla's parents with you. Who wouldn't love a surprise trip to New York City at Christmas?"

"Plus, they'd get to see where Layla lives, and all that," William added helpfully.

Huh. Why hadn't Whitley thought of that herself? "Isn't that crossing a line?" she mused aloud, but Aubrey cut in immediately.

"I think you're solving a problem, Whit."

Nibbling her lip, Whitley tried to think through all potential outcomes. The only scenario she wanted to absolutely avoid was upsetting Layla. Then she thought back to Layla's unexpected appearance at her office—how she would have carefully weighed her options before showing up. Layla hadn't known exactly how Whitley would react to her turning up uninvited at her workplace, but she did it anyway because she wanted to give Whitley something beautiful.

"Aubrey, call the pilot and let them know there will be four passengers on the return flight," Whitley announced decisively.

"And when should I schedule the return flight?" Aubrey asked.

"Tomorrow morning. As early as possible."

William hollered enthusiastically in the background, causing Whitley to smile at her brother's excitement.

"Okay. I'm going to break the news," she told her siblings.

"Aww," Aubrey whined. "That's killing the surprise!"

"How the hell do I get them packed and ready to go if I don't tell them?" Whitley countered logically.

"Shove them in the back of a car and take them to the airport," Aubrey suggested mischievously.

Tutting, Whitley shook her head. "That's called kidnapping. No, I need to tell them. There might be a reason they can't come."

"Fine, fine," Aubrey conceded.

After cutting the call, Whitley sent a few more emails before nervously heading downstairs. Layla was in the kitchen with Beverly, gossiping and sharing a cup of tea.

"Hey, babe. Everything okay?" Layla asked.

Whitley smiled reassuringly. "Fine. Nothing urgent. Um...where's your dad?"

"Here, love," Roger sang as he waltzed through the door, his ever-present smile lighting up the room, especially when he looked at his wife and daughter.

Whitley remained standing as Roger joined Layla and Beverly at the table. Her hands shook slightly with nerves—something Layla immediately noticed. Whitley gave her a reassuring smile and took a deep breath.

"In the DuPont family, we always trade one gift on Christmas Eve, which is tomorrow," she began, realizing her words might make Layla feel bad about being in the UK instead of with her own family.

Continuing quickly, she added, "But, if you don't mind, I would like to give you all a present right now."

Beverly smiled and looked from Roger to Layla. "That's very sweet of you, love. But you really didn't have to get us anything."

"It's my pleasure. So, may I?" Whitley asked.

"Of course." Roger chuckled. Layla remained silent, her eyes filled with confusion. They hadn't discussed gifts and had actively avoided any conversations about the rapidly approaching holiday.

"Um, do you have a pen and paper?" Whitley asked.

The question made all three Simmons furrow their brows, but Roger reached into the drawer closest to him, retrieving a small pad and pen, which he laid on the table.

Reaching over, Whitley took them with a shy smile. Instead of simply blurting out she'd booked Beverly and Roger on the return flight, she wanted to make the moment a little more special. She was no artist, but after a few minutes of careful sketching, Whitley had to admit she'd done a decent job drawing a plane ticket on the pad. She'd even included the Simmons' details.

"Okay, it's ready," she announced.

Layla grinned, though her eyebrows still portrayed her underlying confusion. Handing the pad to Beverly, Whitley did her best to rein in her nerves. The wait was excruciating as Beverly studied the drawing, her eyes gradually widening. She passed the pad to Roger, who studied it carefully.

"Bloody hell," he whispered.

"What? What's happening?" Layla asked, straining to look at whatever Whitley had drawn, her curls bouncing with her animated movements.

Clearing her throat nervously, Whitley addressed Beverly directly. "Um, is that something you would enjoy?"

Beverly slapped the table with pure glee and scrambled from her seat—slowly, due to her cast—hobbling around to Whitley with obvious excitement.

"It's the perfect gift. Thank you, love," she said, pulling Whitley into a warm embrace.

"Would someone *please* tell me what the bloody hell is happening?" Layla shouted, her frustration evident as her curls bounced even more with her gesticulations.

"Well, Button," Roger started, his eyes twinkling as he looked at Whitley, "your wonderful girlfriend has booked us onto your flight home for Christmas. We'll be heading to New York with you, if that's okay."

Layla's eyes immediately snapped to Whitley. She remained silent for several long minutes, which did absolutely nothing good for Whitley's blood pressure. The silence stretched uncomfortably.

"Would you excuse us for a moment?" Layla finally said, her tone completely unreadable. But surely this couldn't be good, right?

Oh no. She'd messed up royally, and now Layla was going to be furious with her. Schooling her features into a neutral expression, Whitley smiled politely at Layla's parents before following Layla out of the room. Halfway up the stairs, Whitley thought she was going to vomit from anxiety. Whatever Layla was planning to say must be harsh enough she didn't want her parents overhearing.

Ready to defend her decision and explain her reasoning, Whitley was taken completely off guard when Layla pushed her firmly against the bedroom door the moment they stepped over the threshold and closed it. Layla's tongue immediately licked at Whitley's lips, asking for entry. Still thoroughly confused by this unexpected response, Whitley opened her mouth and welcomed her girlfriend in. Their breathing quickened rapidly as the kiss intensified with desperate passion.

Suddenly, Layla's thigh was positioned between Whitley's, and she almost slipped to the floor as her legs turned to jelly with the first roll and thrust of Layla's hips. Dropping her hands instinctively, Whitley grabbed Layla's ass, pulling her closer. The friction was fantastic, and she could already feel the beginnings of an orgasm stirring in her lace panties.

"Oh, yes," she mewled breathlessly.

Layla pulled away from Whitley's lips and began kissing her neck with fervent intensity. Heat radiated from both their bodies as they rubbed against each other with increasing desperation. But then something changed dramatically. It took Whitley a second to realize the delicious friction was suddenly gone. She opened her eyes just in time to see Layla drop gracefully to her knees. A second later, Whitley's yoga pants were stripped from her legs, taking her underwear along with them.

Layla was clearly on a mission, and Whitley was absolutely here for whatever she had planned. She instinctively opened her legs wider. Layla wrapped her hand under Whitley's right knee and lifted it up and over her shoulder with practiced ease.

The firm, confident swipe of Layla's tongue through her folds had Whitley immediately slapping a hand over her own mouth. The sound trying to escape her throat was indecent at best. Her girlfriend was relentless, silently taking her apart with every expert lick and suck.

"I'm coming...I'm...co—Oh, God, yes!" she gasped against her palm.

Her thighs quivered uncontrollably, and she felt the rush of liquid spill out as the climax shook her very bones. Layla held Whitley's hips firmly, anchoring her to the spot as she bucked and cursed through the intense waves of pleasure.

Whitley's vision was blurry as she came down from the incredible high. Her chest rose and fell rapidly, and her abs ached from tensing so hard during her release. She felt Layla stand and lean into her body, placing a gentle kiss on her neck that made Whitley turn and snuggle into Layla's shoulder.

"That was... I thought you were bringing me up here to yell at me," she admitted breathlessly.

Layla pulled away slowly, cupping Whitley's face tenderly with both hands. "What you did for me and my parents was so wonderfully thoughtful. Are you sure about this?"

Kissing her softly, Whitley nodded with conviction. "I don't know why I didn't think of it sooner. Actually, it was Aubrey and William who suggested it."

"You called them?" Layla asked.

"Aubrey called me. Mom was having a complete meltdown over table settings and place markers."

"I'm sorry," Layla said, guilt evident in her voice.

It was Whitley's turn to grasp Layla's face gently. "I'm here because I *want* to be here with you. But then my irritating siblings made me realize we could all be happy together. I didn't want to leave you or ask you to come back with me when it was clear you wanted to be with your parents. But I admit, the thought of missing my family over the holidays was a little upsetting. This way, we all get to be happy, right? You *are* happy that I invited them, or should I have asked first? Damn, did I cross a line?"

Layla pressed two fingers firmly over Whitley's mouth, effectively shutting her up.

"You're absolutely adorable when you ramble, but I need you to hush up and listen," Layla said with a loving smile. "I am fucking ecstatic that you gave me this gift. I felt so torn, knowing you wanted to be at home with your family, and me feeling like I had to be here with Mum and Dad. I don't want to do another December, or even another day, without you, Whit."

"Oh, thank God." Whitley laughed with relief, immediately claiming Layla's lips in a passionate kiss.

"To be fair," Layla huffed with amusement, "I would've thought that excellent display of cunnilingus would've given away the fact that I was happy with your decision."

Rolling her lips to suppress a grin, Whitley delved both hands into Layla's wild curls. "It was definitely an impressive display. I wouldn't mind a repeat performance."

Layla immediately went to drop to her knees again, but Whitley hooked her under the armpits before she could touch the ground. She laughed at Layla's disappointed pout.

"But...we need to get your mom and dad packed and ready," Whitley explained practically. "The plane leaves early tomorrow morning."

"There's plenty of time," Layla grumbled, her eyes dropping hungrily to Whitley's still-uncovered sex.

"Maybe for you and me, but we have no idea if they need anything picked up beforehand. The stores are still open for a few more hours."

"Ugh, fine. You win! I shall not eat you out again right now...happy?" Layla sighed dramatically.

"You're so theatrical." Whitley giggled. "I love you."

Layla's eyes immediately softened, and a sappy smile spread across her face. "Yeah, you do. How did I get so incredibly lucky?"

"You rescued me from a dark alleyway," Whitley reminded her.

"You should know that's become my favorite part of New York now," Layla said with a grin.

"Not the diner?" Whitley asked, surprised.

"Nope. The alleyway where you were hulking out with Christmas baubles. You were so gorgeous in your fury."

Blushing furiously, Whitley playfully pushed Layla away. "We're going to end up in bed if you keep up all that sweet talk."

After pulling up her clothes and making herself presentable, she took Layla by the hand and led her back downstairs to face her parents.

"I looked it up on the NHS website," Beverly announced as they returned to the kitchen. "I'm perfectly okay to travel with my cast."

"Excellent. Is there anything you need fetching from the shops?" Layla asked.

Beverly eyed them both with a knowing twinkle in her eye. "Well, now that you've finished thanking Whitley properly, I wouldn't mind a trip to Marks & Spencer."

Whitley blushed furiously while Layla smirked with obvious pride. "I am very good at showing my appreciation."

"Layla!" Whitley spluttered in embarrassment.

Beverly and Layla tittered with shared amusement.

"You take after me, Button," Beverly retorted with a wicked grin.

"Beverly!" Whitley choked out, her face burning red.

Whitley had a distinct feeling the DuPonts were in for a very different kind of Christmas this year.

Rescuing Rudolph & NYC

Layla's face hurt from all the laughing and smiling she'd done over the past several hours. Her parents' wonder through every stage of their travel was overwhelmingly sweet, and she had Whitley to thank for it.

The winter light in New York had a particular quality—soft and diffused, casting long shadows across the cityscape and creating an almost ethereal atmosphere. The DuPont town car navigated smoothly through the snow-dusted streets, a testament to the family's commitment to comfort and style.

"Oh, is that Central Park?" Beverly shrieked, her face smushed up against the car window. Ryan was laughing, as were Whitley and Roger.

The park stretched out before them, a pristine white landscape dotted with bare trees and bundled-up New Yorkers moving like small, colorful dots against the snow.

"It is. I'll take you if you want, Mum," Layla offered.

"Now? Can we stop now?" Beverly asked with childlike excitement, her enthusiasm infectious and filling the car with warmth.

Whitley nodded to Ryan, who promptly pulled over. The car came to a smooth stop, steam rising from its exhaust in delicate plumes that quickly dissipated in the cold air.

"Will you be okay walking with your crutches, Beverly?" Whitley asked, her concern evident in the gentle way she leaned forward.

"Yeah, it's probably slippy, Mum," Layla added, her protective instincts showing through as she studied the snow-covered pavement.

"Nonsense," Beverly scoffed, her determination unwavering. "We'll just go slow."

Roger gave an almost imperceptible nod to Layla, a silent communication that spoke volumes about their close relationship and shared understanding. "Aye, let's go for a stroll. It'll be like Home Alone."

Layla narrowed her eyes, trying to figure out what her dad was banging on about; his movie references often lost on her music-focused mind.

"There *are* a lot of pigeons," Whitley answered helpfully, her knowledge of movie references apparently extending far beyond Layla's musical world.

"See, that's how I know you're a keeper. You know movies. Unlike my philistine of a child," Roger said with obvious pride in his voice.

"Hey!" Layla protested, her wild curls bouncing with indignation.

"Is he wrong?" Beverly commented with a knowing smile that crinkled the corners of her eyes. Years of watching her daughter prioritize music over popular culture evident in her amused expression.

"Um, I was a tad busy mastering the violin to sit and watch movies," Layla explained, her hands unconsciously mimicking the graceful movement of drawing a bow across strings.

Whitley turned to her, wide-eyed with genuine disbelief. The winter light caught her profile perfectly, making her look like a Renaissance painting—all soft edges and dramatic shadows framed by golden hair. "You haven't seen Home Alone? Any of them?"

"Nope. Not a one."

"We'll have to rectify that immediately," Whitley stated with conviction, her voice taking on that authoritative tone that made Layla's pulse quicken. It was kind of hot, and Layla *definitely* felt it in her knickers. She imagined Whitley at work, bossing people around in her perfectly tailored pencil skirts and crisp white blouses, commanding boardrooms with that same confident energy.

The car's interior seemed to grow warmer with Layla's sudden surge of desire, the winter chill forgotten in a moment of pure, heated attraction.

"Layla!" Whitley's voice cut sharply through her increasingly vivid daydream.

Snapping out of her sexy reverie, she noted everyone looking at her expectantly, their faces showing varying degrees of amusement and curiosity.

"Sorry, what?"

"Bloody hell. I asked if you're ready to go," Beverly chided, already scooting towards the car door with practiced efficiency, despite her cast. Ryan was already out of his seat, walking around to the passenger door.

They all staggered out of the car and entered the park, the cold air hitting them like a refreshing slap. Beverly was a whiz on her crutches, navigating the snowy paths with surprising agility. The snow didn't slow her down one bit; her determination to explore overrode any physical limitations.

The park was transformed into a sight suitable for any Christmas card—pristine and unusually quiet for New York. Snowflakes drifted lazily from the overcast sky, catching the weak winter sunlight and sparkling like thousands of tiny diamonds scattered across the landscape. The bare trees created intricate silhouettes against the gray sky, their branches etched with delicate frost that made them look like nature's own artwork.

Layla took a deep, cleansing breath, the cold air filling her lungs and clearing her mind. She loved the park with a passion that went beyond simple appreciation. Playing there was one of her favorite places to busk, the acoustics perfect and the audiences always receptive.

It meant a lot to be sharing this special place with Whitley and introducing her parents to a piece of her New York life.

"Oh, it's like a winter wonderland!" Beverly gasped, her eyes bright with marvel and her cheeks already pink with the cold, making her look years younger.

Layla looked at the park through her mum's eyes, seeing it fresh via someone else's perspective. It really was gorgeous in its winter dress. People walked hand in hand, in thick coats and colorful scarves, their breath creating small clouds in the frigid air. New Yorkers had a well-deserved reputation for their nonstop attitude and relentless pace. It was described, after all, as "the city that never sleeps," but in that moment the city seemed to quiet down, as if the snow had muffled not just sound, but the usual urban urgency. People slowed down, taking time to appreciate the beauty around them. Layla slowed down too.

Ever since getting involved with Whitley she'd started finding it easier to slow down, pausing and appreciating what she had rather than constantly chasing the next performance or opportunity—cheesy, but undeniably true. Before Whitley entered her life, Layla's sole focus had been on her music—obsessively so, to the exclusion of almost everything else. That single-minded dedication was why she'd only had fleeting encounters instead of meaningful relationships, never allowing anyone to get close enough to matter.

Maybe she'd been unconsciously waiting for the woman to come along who could mean more to her than music, someone who could share that coveted place in her heart. Whitley was that woman, without question. Just like music, she felt Whitley's importance in her very marrow—in the deepest part of herself. Layla would commit to Whitley with the same fierce dedication she'd always reserved for her music.

"Are you okay?" Whitley whispered in her ear, her warm breath creating a pleasant contrast to the cold air. Layla's parents were just up ahead, laughing and chatting animatedly as they explored.

"I'm perfect," she replied honestly, taking Whitley's gloved hand in hers. They'd spent time in the city together before, but this was the first time they'd roamed the park hand in hand as an official couple. It meant more to Layla than she could possibly express in words. So, instead of voicing her overwhelming feelings, she gripped Whitley's hand a little tighter, letting the pressure communicate what words couldn't.

Whitley watched Beverly and Roger with a fond smile, clearly charmed by their enthusiasm. "I'm surprised we're all still standing. None of us got much sleep on the way here."

"Amazing what adrenaline can do," Layla replied, admiring her parents' energy. "I haven't seen them this wound up in ages."

"That's a good thing, right? Being wound up?" Whitley asked, wanting to understand the family dynamics.

Layla grinned, her face lighting up with genuine happiness. "In this instance, yes. What time are we expected at the DuPont mansion?"

Rolling her eyes with theatrical exasperation, Whitley dropped Layla's hand and snuggled into her side instead, seeking warmth and closeness. "You make it sound like Batman's house."

"Does it have a secret cave?" Layla teased, enjoying the playful banter.

"It has a cellar. Is that close enough?" Whitley quipped, her eyes sparkling with mischief.

"Hmm, depends on what's in it," Layla responded, playing along with the game.

"Wine, and lots of it." Whitley laughed, the sound bright and musical in the crisp air.

Layla scoffed with mock disappointment. "Well, that's no fun. Anyway, what time do we need to leave? If I don't give Mum a deadline, she'll have us stomping all over the city."

"Layla, look," Beverly suddenly shouted, her voice cutting through their conversation. Layla pulled Whitley along until they were by her parents, who were staring with fascination at a man dumping stuff into a large garbage can near the park's edge.

"He's binning Rudolph!" Roger stated unnecessarily, his voice filled with outrage. The man was, in fact, stuffing a four-foot Rudolph ornament into the bin with obvious frustration. New York saw it all, and not one local was paying the man any attention, too accustomed to the city's endless parade of oddities.

"Roger, go and rescue it," Beverly commanded with the authority of a general issuing orders.

"Mum, you are *not* making Dad rummage through the garbage to fetch a bloody manky Rudolph statue," Layla protested, already knowing she was fighting a losing battle.

"I'll be right back," Roger said, completely oblivious to Layla's objections, already rolling up his sleeves for the rescue mission.

Whitley pulled on Layla's hand, seeking clarification. "Babe, what is happening?"

"Oh, you know. Dumpster diving for Christmas decorations," Layla replied with resigned acceptance.

"Yes, I see that. But why?" Whitley asked, genuinely bewildered by the scene unfolding before them.

Layla pondered how to explain her mother's unique worldview. "Mum likes to assign feelings to inanimate objects. She took one look at poor Rudolph over there and instantly had to help him."

"And what will they do with it when they've saved it from certain death?" Whitley asked, equal parts amused and concerned.

Layla laughed, already anticipating the inevitable outcome. "I'll end up having it in the apartment until they go, and I can bin it again."

"He's a handsome fella, Bev," Roger shouted triumphantly as he wrangled the thing free from a stray banana peel and various other pieces of garbage. "Just needs a quick wipe down."

"If you insist on taking it, we need to get going," Layla huffed, checking her watch and realizing they were cutting it close.

Beverly hobbled around until she was facing the way they'd come from, her mission accomplished. "Off we go then."

Whitley giggled, the sound infectious and delightful. "We can leave him in the car. Mom just messaged and asked if we were en route."

"Did you hear that?" Layla called to her parents, hoping to establish some boundaries. "Rudy is staying in the car!"

Beverly waved her off dismissively, which never boded well for anyone hoping to maintain order or logic.

Fine Champagne & Awkward Wagers

After an uncomfortable ride to the DuPont residence, with the garbage Rudolph wedged in between Beverly and Roger, Layla was ready for a bucket of alcohol. This year was already a little fraught with tension due to the fact Layla was attending her first family-only event in an official girlfriend capacity. Add on Beverly, Roger, and now, bloody Rudolph, and Layla had a film of sweat forming on her upper lip due to her mounting anxiety.

The DuPont mansion stood as a testament to generations of wealth and refinement, its elegant façade adorned with tasteful holiday decorations that sparkled softly in the winter evening light. Intricate wreaths hung from perfectly positioned windows, and carefully placed spotlights illuminated the snow-covered landscaping, creating a scene that looked like it had been lifted straight from a luxury magazine's holiday spread.

"Relax, baby," Whitley murmured as they headed to the front door, her hand providing a gentle, reassuring pressure against Layla's lower back.

Easy to say. Impossible to do. She ignored her parents' bickering behind her and surged forward. Whitley led them inside, and thank the universe, they were met by a tray of Champagne, the crystal flutes catching the warm light of the grand foyer's chandelier.

"Darling, you're here," Lucienne cried, gliding over in a very formal dress. The Simmons family was definitely underdressed.

"Mom, you look radiant."

After a long, drawn-out hug, Whitley turned to introduce Layla's mum and dad. With no surprise to

Layla, Beverly stood there with her mouth agape, staring at the mansion's impressive...everything. Roger stood next to her, beaming at Lucienne. All quite normal if you didn't count Rudy tucked under her dad's arm like he was hugging an old friend. Beverly had clearly won the argument regarding Rudolph's accommodation for the evening.

Layla stuffed down the urge to snort. God, she loved her daft parents.

"Mom, this is Beverly and Roger Simmons, Layla's parents."

Impressively, Lucienne didn't show any signs of confusion as she stepped over and offered her hand. Layla rolled her eyes, because she knew what was coming.

Instead of shaking the proffered hand, Beverly hobbled forward and pulled Lucienne into an awkward hug. Awkward, because Beverly was at least a head shorter than the willowy DuPont matriarch. It took Lucienne only a second to adjust. A warm smile crept onto her face as she settled into the embrace.

"It's an absolute pleasure to meet you, Beverly."

"You too, love. Heard lots about you. Fab house, by the way."

Chuckling, Lucienne turned to Roger next, who shoved out his hand, having learned from the Whitley tackle-hug kerfuffle at the hospital.

"Ta very much for the offer to join your family today. Bloody brilliant surprise."

Lucienne dipped her head. "It's truly our pleasure."

"Have you got any wet wipes?" Beverly interjected. "I need to give Rudy a wipe down."

Layla chuckled as Lucienne eyed the statue and then turned her gaze to Whitley, who simply shrugged with a beaming smile on her face. Gosh, she took Layla's breath away.

"In the guest bathroom. I'll show you. Whit, darling, would you take everyone else through to the dining room? Layla sweetheart, we'll catch up soon."

Layla gave her best confident smile, but she knew Whitley saw through it. Did Whitley also see how important this was for her to get right?

Beverly hobbled off, gabbing away to Lucienne. Roger heaved Rudolph up and motioned for Whitley to lead on.

A cacophony of noise greeted them as they entered the dining room. Roger spotted Puck and almost launched Rudolph across the room in excitement. "Puck, my lad. Get over here."

Aubrey and William were the first to reach Whitley and Layla. It was a mess of limbs as everyone vied for attention and hugs.

"Dad, this is Roger...and Rudolph."

Lucas laughed. "Pleasure to meet you, Roger. He's a fine looking fellow."

"Me or the statue?" Roger quipped.

"Tough call." Lucas grinned.

Roger belly laughed. "Nice to meet you, too. Sorry about him," he said, jiggling Rudolph. "Rescue mission."

As if that cleared it up.

Layla busied herself with Reena and Simon. It was so lovely of the DuPonts inviting them all, especially knowing it was a sacred family tradition. Surely that had to be a good sign, right? Lucas and Lucienne must see her as part of the clan. But was it still as the wacky musician?

"Baby, you're doing it again." Whitley's body slid behind Layla's, her hand dancing delicately across her girlfriend's lower back. "Please relax."

Gripping Whitley's hand, which now rested on her hip, Layla nodded. The tray of Champagne that'd greeted them upon arrival and been ignored was passed around. Taking two flutes, Layla drained one and then the other, earning a laugh from her girlfriend.

"Thanks for saving me some," she joked.

Layla turned until they were nose to nose. "Extreme circumstances, babe."

"You're ridiculous."

"And you love it."

Their noses brushed, and Layla felt the ever-indulgent wave of heat pool in her knickers.

"All right, lovebirds," Aubrey muttered, passing by. "Save it for later."

The clink of a glass brought Layla back to the room. Beverly and Lucienne had returned, wet wipes in abundance.

"Can I have your attention?" Lucas called over the noise. The small crowd fell silent. "I'd like us all to raise a glass. Today is a very special tradition in the DuPont family. We always spend the day together drinking fine Champagne and eating. It's indulgent, and worth the wait. We're a busy lot, you know." That earned a laugh. "Today, however, I am over the moon to have so many fresh faces joining us. Beverly and Roger, welcome to our home. Puck, Layla, Reena, and Simon, welcome to the DuPont empire."

They were all about to drink from their flutes when Layla's mouth acted before her brain. "Hold up." Ten pairs of eyes turned her way. "Just need to clarify something."

Layla couldn't suffer through an evening like this. It meant everything to be accepted as Whitley's partner, and she'd be damned if she waited for it over alcohol and buttered rolls. She'd do what she did best: face it head-on.

"Before we get the festivities underway, I just need to settle something. Whitley and I are together, you all know that. So me being here today, isn't as a musician under the DuPont name. It's as her loving girlfriend. I need that recognized."

Silence fell. The soft clink of champagne glasses and the distant twinkling of holiday decorations seemed to pause in anticipation. Whitley's hand laced their fingers together, a silent show of solidarity and support.

"I told you!" Aubrey suddenly laughed, breaking the tension. "Pay up, suckers."

Layla furrowed her brow in confusion. Lucienne, Lucas, and William were all digging into their respective pockets, fishing out dollar bills. Aubrey collected them with a devilish grin that spoke of long-standing family traditions and inside jokes.

Layla looked at Whitley. "What's happening?"

She shrugged but smiled. "My family likes to place silly wagers."

"Christmas tradition," William supplied helpfully.

"And what was the bet?" Layla asked, curiosity piqued.

"That you would make a grand statement before dinner," William explained.

"I wouldn't call it grand," Layla mumbled, feeling slightly self-conscious.

"Close enough." Lucas laughed, his eyes twinkling with genuine amusement and affection.

Lucienne stepped in front of Layla, her elegant dress swirling with the movement. "We really didn't think you'd have any doubt that you're a part of this family, Layla, or that you needed our blessing. Which you have, by the way. Wholeheartedly. You love our daughter, and she loves you. That's all we've ever wanted for any of our children. I apologize if you've felt under pressure."

"I just want you to like me," Layla said with raw honesty, the vulnerability in her voice a stark contrast to her usually confident demeanor. Her parents had instilled this directness in her growing up, and now they were holding each other, staring at their daughter with unmistakable pride.

"We love you," Aubrey said. "Have since you brought that weird English pudding to a nightclub."

"Trifle," Layla clarified for her parents, a soft smile playing on her lips.

"Bloody good pud, that," Roger noted, raising his champagne glass in a toast.

Layla breathed a sigh of relief. "Okay then. Emotional crisis over with. Let's drink this outrageously good champers."

She received a gentle face squeeze from Lucienne and a playful bonk on the nose from Aubrey. Everyone guzzled their Champagne, her mother opting for a second one in quick succession. A muttered, "Jesus, that's the best alcohol I've ever had in my mouth," was followed by several titters of laughter.

"You just take the bull by the horns, don't you?" Whitley observed, her voice a mixture of admiration and amusement.

Layla smiled, turning into Whitley's body, her hands circling Whitley's waist, drawing her close. "When something's important, I don't want to wait and find out."

"Hmm. You waited years," Whitley pointed out, referencing their long journey to this moment.

Shaking her head, Layla nipped Whitley's lower lip. "No, you were straight as far as I knew. I would've made a move sooner if I'd thought there were a chance."

Whitley's eyes sparkled with love and mischief. "Would you now?"

Their lips met softly, a tender moment amidst the family chaos. "Or maybe not. I love our story. I've loved every second of our time together. Getting to know each other."

Whitley sighed, her breath warm against Layla's skin. "God, I could just eat you up."

"Later," Layla promised, her voice low and filled with potential.

"Oh, gag." Aubrey's voice, which was far too close, pulled them apart. "I want some food this century."

The room erupted in laughter, the tension of Layla's earlier declaration dissolving into the warm, comfortable atmosphere of a family celebration. Whitley and Layla remained wrapped in each other's arms, their connection both a private moment and a public declaration of their love.

36

Morning Delights &
Unexpected Calls

Whitley woke to the most wonderful sensation: thick dark curls tickling the top of her thighs. The early morning light filtered softly through the curtains, casting a warm, golden glow across the bedroom. Soft winter sunlight danced across the luxurious DuPont family home, promising a magical Christmas Day ahead.

Sighing contentedly, she shuffled her hips, letting Layla know she was awake.

"Morning," Layla cooed between soft kisses and light grazes of her teeth on Whitley's skin. Her touch was both tender and provocative, a delicate balance of passion and affection.

It was Christmas Day. The family party the night before had gone beautifully. Her parents had gotten along with Beverly and Roger like they'd known each other for years.

They'd all drunk, eaten, and played silly games late into the night. The rescued Rudolph statue had somehow become another member of the family by the end of the evening. Whitley couldn't have been happier.

Well, that wasn't quite right. She was happier now with Layla's tongue teasing her. A shiver of pleasure rippled up her spine, electric and intense. "Layla, stop torturing me," she murmured, her voice a mixture of desire and playful frustration.

Layla responded with firm sucks, sliding down the bed until she was just below where Whitley needed them most. Gripping the sheets, Whitley tried to subtly move her hips to position Layla more precisely. A throaty chuckle emanated from beneath the covers, warm breath sending additional shivers across her skin.

"Will you behave? I'm trying to unwrap my Christmas present carefully."

Whitley flared her nose and settled her hips. It was possibly the hardest thing she'd ever had to do. If Layla wanted to take her time, she'd let her. Hell, she'd let Layla do anything.

"You smell divine." Layla's muffled statement heightened Whitley's want by a factor of ten. Layla was the master of edging. She'd never had a person want her and worship her so thoroughly, with such complete and unabashed appreciation.

Pinching her own nipples in an attempt to take the lead, Whitley moaned deeply. She was dripping with anticipation, every nerve ending alive and sensitized. "Please, Layla, I'm begging you to unwrap me a little quicker."

"As you wish."

There was no more teasing. Layla swiped her tongue along the full length of Whitley's slit. The added flick at the end almost had her climbing the walls. Her clit was practically buzzing with sensitivity, every touch sending waves of pleasure through her body.

"Yes...more."

"More" involved two of Layla's fingers spreading her wide and a blast of warm breath directly across her sex.

Whitley was a gibbering wreck. She was getting Whitley to the point of breaking at record speed this morning.

Unable to stop her hips from joining in, Whitley pressed her head back into the pillow and pushed herself further into Layla's mouth. She was effectively fucking her girlfriend's face now, lost in a haze of pleasure and desire.

With her panting breaths becoming louder, she had to shove a hand in her mouth to stop herself from alerting the rest of the house that she was about to climax. The thought of her family hearing her in the throes of passion only added an extra layer of forbidden excitement.

Rolling her hips faster, she sucked in a breath when two fingers curled into her. Whitley realized Layla had one goal in mind now: making Whitley's Christmas wish come true. Her pussy clenched and quivered in response, every muscle tensing with anticipation.

Whitley's breath was completely stolen from her lungs as she succumbed to the orgasm ripping through her lower body, radiating to every extremity. Wave after wave of pleasure washed over her, leaving her breathless and trembling.

Through a fog of pleasure, she felt Layla shift and crawl up her body. A bundle of dark curls popped out of the covers, tickling her stomach. Layla's piercing eyes were next, full of heat and love, watching Whitley's face with intense devotion.

Unfurling her fingers from the sheets, Whitley carded them through Layla's luscious mane. Her fingernails scraped across her scalp, causing Layla to groan with pleasure.

"That was the best Christmas morning I've ever had," Whitley murmured into Layla's ear, her voice still husky.

"That was just the beginning. We've got a lot more morning to enjoy," Layla promised, her eyes sparkling with mischief and love.

"Guys, are you awake?" William shouted through the door, his voice carrying the characteristic mix of excitement and impatience typical of Christmas mornings. "Mom's got mimosas started, and Dad's cooking. Layla, we need someone competent to stop the house from burning down. We usually cater, but—"

"Will, Jesus," Aubrey interrupted, her exasperation evident. "I asked you to wake them up, not perform a monologue sending them back to sleep."

"I just wanted them to know why we need them up," William grumbled, sounding like a chastised child.

Aubrey scoffed loud enough for Whitley and Layla to hear. They snickered quietly, sharing a moment of private amusement at the siblings' familiar bickering.

"We're awake. Just give us five, okay? Make sure Dad isn't working with an open flame!" Whitley called back, her voice a perfect blend of reassurance and mild concern.

Receding footsteps signaled her siblings' retreat. Puffing out a breath, she pulled Layla closer, the warmth of their bodies creating a cocoon of intimacy.

"I can be quick," Whitley whispered, her meaning clear. She had every intention of reciprocating the morning's incredible pleasure, her mouth already watering for the chance to taste Layla.

"I can wait. Plus, I want to give you your present," Layla replied.

"When did you have time to buy presents?" Whitley asked, curiosity piqued.

"I didn't," Layla said with a mischievous grin.

Whitley smiled, understanding immediately. "You're going to play for me, aren't you?"

Layla jiggled her upper body, smushing her boobs against Whitley's. "Well, the morning muff dive was part of it."

A bark of laughter left Whitley. Her shoulders shook with amusement. "That's so crude."

Layla waggled her eyebrows. "I'm impressed you know what muff diving means."

"I've picked a few things up on my travels," Whitley responded, playing along.

"And who exactly taught you that phrase?" Layla asked, a hint of playful jealousy in her voice.

Grinning, Whitley ran a finger over Layla's bottom lip, pushing it into her mouth. Layla groaned and sucked on the digit, the intimate gesture sending a spark of desire through both of them.

"No need for jealousy, Layla," Whitley teased.

Whitley could have put Layla out of her misery and confessed she'd learned a few silly English phrases from a gay guy working in the London office last year, but she liked this side of her jealous girlfriend a little. Was that wrong?

"Mmm. Well, I guess I have you now," Layla murmured.

"You do. I'm yours, Layla. In every way."

"Get your asses out of that bed!" Aubrey's voice was one octave away from deafening them all.

The kitchen was a hive of activity, filled with the warm chaos of a large family gathering on Christmas morning. The air was rich with the scents of coffee, bacon, and something slightly burned that had clearly been

Lucas's attempt at breakfast. Beverly and Lucienne sat comfortably at the kitchen island with mimosas in hand, happily chatting away about everything from the previous night's festivities to their shared experiences as mothers of strong-willed children. Their laughter punctuated the morning air like music.

Meanwhile, Lucas and Roger peered intently at something on the stove, both men looking slightly bewildered and more than a little out of their depth in the culinary arena.

"I just don't understand how you charred it so quickly," Roger commented, scratching his head in genuine confusion as he examined what appeared to be the remains of scrambled eggs.

Lucas also scratched the back of his head, matching Roger's perplexed expression perfectly. "Me either. I swear I only looked away for thirty seconds."

The kitchen's marble countertops were scattered with the evidence of their culinary misadventure—eggshells, spilled milk, and what looked like the remnants of several failed attempts at breakfast preparation. The expensive Viking range, normally a thing of beauty and precision, seemed to mock their efforts with professional-grade capabilities neither man could properly harness.

Layla playfully squeezed Whitley's ass before heading over to the two confused men and ushering them out of the way with confident determination and barely suppressed amusement.

"Make room, gentlemen. I'm gonna save Christmas breakfast. Dad, would you grab me a new box of eggs from the fridge?"

Her movements were efficient and purposeful as she surveyed the damage, already mentally cataloging what needed to be done to salvage the morning meal. The sleeves of her borrowed pajama top were rolled up, revealing the graceful lines of her forearms as she began clearing the counter space.

Whitley knew full well she had a dopey, love-struck grin plastered across her face, watching Layla take control of the kitchen situation with her characteristic efficiency and unflappable poise. There was something incredibly attractive about watching her girlfriend command a room, whether it was a concert hall or a chaotic family kitchen.

"Whit, sweetheart, sit yourself down and have a drink," Lucienne called out, looking several mimosas deep already, her cheeks flushed with holiday cheer and Champagne. The glass in her hand caught the light streaming through the kitchen's windows.

"What time did the party start?" Whitley laughed, joining Beverly and Lucienne at the marble-topped island, accepting the offered mimosa with grateful hands.

"It didn't really finish, love," Beverly declared with a mischievous twinkle in her eye and a slight slur to her words that suggested the night's festivities had indeed continued well into the early morning hours. "You young'uns are absolute lightweights. Lucy, me, Rog, and your dad have been at it all night, haven't we, Lucy?"

Lucienne nodded enthusiastically, raising her glass in a mock toast. "Guilty as charged. We discovered we have quite a lot in common, including a shared appreciation for fine Champagne and embarrassing stories about our children, isn't that right, Bev?"

There was definitely a lot to unpack in that sentence, but Whitley was momentarily distracted by the sound of footsteps and voices in the hallway, followed by Puck, Reena, and Simon tumbling through the kitchen door like a small avalanche of sleepy musicians.

"Sorry we're late," Puck said through a massive yawn that seemed to encompass his entire face. "Those guest room beds are absolutely impossible to leave. I think I've been spoiled by luxury."

Reena stretched dramatically, her arms reaching toward the ceiling. "I may never sleep in a regular bed again after experiencing whatever thread count those sheets were."

Simon nodded in agreement, his usually perfect hair sticking up at odd angles. "I'm pretty sure I dreamed I was sleeping on a cloud made of silk and down feathers."

With everyone finally assembled in the kitchen, the morning progressed with increasing amounts of laughter, mimosas, and perfectly prepared food thanks to Layla's intervention. The room filled with the sounds of family—multiple conversations happening simultaneously, the clink of glasses, the sizzle of eggs in the pan, and the underlying current of contentment that came from being surrounded by people you loved. Whitley was going to need to join a gym in the new year to work off all this holiday indulgence.

After gifts were opened in the living room—much to the continued protests of the Simmons family, who insisted they couldn't possibly accept the DuPonts' generous open offer to fly out to New York whenever they wanted to visit—Whitley settled into the single leather armchair by the fireplace, eagerly anticipating Layla's promised musical performance.

The living room had been transformed into an intimate concert venue, with everyone arranged in a comfortable semicircle around the space where Layla would play. The Christmas tree twinkled in the corner, its lights reflecting off the various crystal glasses and creating a magical, almost ethereal atmosphere.

Puck and the other members of the quartet had already treated them to a mini concert earlier, filling the room with beautiful holiday music that seemed to perfectly capture the spirit of the season. Their harmonies had blended seamlessly, creating moments of pure musical magic that left everyone slightly breathless with appreciation.

The anticipation in the room was palpable as everyone settled into their seats, drinks refreshed, with attention focused on the space where Layla would soon stand with her violin. Whitley felt her heart rate increase slightly, knowing that whatever Layla was about to play had been written specifically for her; another piece of their love story set to music.

Just as Layla was about to take her position in the center of the room, her phone rang with an insistent buzzing that cut through the expectant quiet. Apologizing profusely to her "adoring fans"—which immediately earned her a decorative throw pillow launched directly at her abdomen by an indignant Aubrey—she glanced at the screen and answered the call.

Layla's eyes widened dramatically as she listened to whoever was on the other end, her expression shifting from casual curiosity to intense focus. Her gaze shot straight to Whitley with an intensity that made Whitley's stomach flutter with sudden nervousness.

Something important was happening. Something that would change everything.

Gesturing urgently for Whitley to follow her, Layla quickly stepped out of the living room and into the relative privacy of the hallway. The curious glances from their assembled family and friends had Whitley shrugging helplessly in response. She honestly had no idea what was going on, but the serious expression on Layla's face suggested it was significant.

Whatever this phone call was about, Whitley had a feeling their perfect Christmas morning was about to take an unexpected turn.

37

Opportunities & Celebrations

In the hall, Layla sat on the bottom step of the grand staircase, the phone balanced precariously on her knee. The hallway was quieter than the living room, but they could still hear the murmur of conversation and laughter from their family gathering. Sitting next to her on the carpeted step, Whitley cocked her brow questioningly. Layla responded by pushing the loudspeaker button with a decisive tap.

"Could you repeat all that? My girlfriend is here and I'm not deciding anything without her input," Layla said firmly into the phone, her voice carrying that familiar note of determination Whitley had come to love.

"Certainly. As I said, my name is Miller Barnes."

Whitley reared back in shock, her eyes widening with recognition. She'd heard of Miller Barnes alright. Hell, most people in the United States had heard of him. He was the go-to man if you wanted a serious career in the entertainment industry; a legendary figure known for his ability to transform talented unknowns into household names—a kingmaker, or in this case, a queenmaker.

"I want to work with you, Layla. You've gotten a lot of attention recently," Miller's voice crackled through the phone speaker, professional and confident.

"Really?" Layla asked, genuine surprise coloring her voice.

"Yes. You've been anointed by the DuPonts. That turns people's heads in this industry."

Whitley felt her cheeks flush with a mixture of pride and slight embarrassment. She hadn't realized her family's endorsement carried such weight in the entertainment world.

"Just FYI, Miller, Whitley DuPont is my girlfriend," Layla stated matter-of-factly.

"No shit!" Miller's professional composure slipped momentarily, revealing his genuine surprise.

Layla cringed visibly and quickly muted the call, panic flashing across her features. "Fuck, I just outed you publicly. I'm so sorry, Whit."

"I literally couldn't care less," Whitley replied immediately, reaching over to squeeze Layla's hand reassuringly. "I'm proud to be with you, and I don't care who knows it."

Layla unmuted the call, relief evident on her face. "What do you mean by 'work with me', Miller?"

"I want to take your Christmas concert concept wide. Not just at DuPont charity events, but to venues across the country and eventually internationally."

Layla narrowed her eyes, her expression becoming more guarded. "The money from those concerts does a lot of good for people who need it. It kinda feels like you want me to prioritize profit over helping people, Miller. If that's the case, we're not a good fit."

Whitley placed a supportive hand on Layla's leg, pride swelling in her chest. This was exactly why she loved this woman: her unwavering commitment to her values, even when faced with potentially life-changing opportunities.

"Not at all, and I appreciate your directness. I'd heard you were a straight shooter," Miller replied, his tone respectful.

"I am. I'd rather call a spade a spade," Layla confirmed.

"Good. Then let's get real. Take the concerts wide, give the money to charity. It's about getting your name out there before we launch your world tour."

"World tour?" Layla's voice rose an octave, disbelief and excitement warring in her expression.

"Yes. I've seen your work, Layla. It's fresh, exciting, innovative. You draw in a younger crowd while still appealing to traditional classical music lovers. That's a rare combination."

"I do love connecting with audiences. But I have rules," Layla stated firmly.

A throaty laugh echoed through the phone speaker. "Not to toot my own horn, but I've usually got people clamoring to work with me, begging for the opportunity. I've never had so much resistance from the get-go."

Layla shrugged and looked directly at Whitley, seeking support and understanding. "Music is in my soul. I do it because I love it, because I want people to learn to love the violin like I do. I'm not compromising my artistic integrity for a few quid. So, if I agree to this, I have full creative control. What I say goes, musically. You can sort out the financial and technical logistics. But the artistic vision is mine."

"That's quite the ask," Miller replied, though his tone suggested he was intrigued rather than put off.

"I'm quite the musician," Layla responded with quiet confidence.

"Deal. We'll meet in the new year and discuss contracts in detail. I'm envisioning a European tour next December, building up to it throughout the year."

Whitley tried to stop the panic from rising in her chest, but the mention of December—their special month—hit her like a physical blow. It was ridiculous to feel this way. Layla had an amazing opportunity to see the world and inspire people with her incredible gift. Getting upset they wouldn't be together next December was selfish and small-minded.

"We can talk about all that later," Layla said. "Send me the details of our meeting. I need to get back to my family."

"Sure, sure. Go enjoy your Christmas. We'll catch up soon, and Layla? This is going to be big."

The line went dead, leaving them sitting in sudden silence on the staircase. Neither Whitley nor Layla moved for several long moments, both processing the magnitude of what had just happened. Whitley was a complicated mix of emotions—overwhelming pride for Layla's success, excitement for the opportunities ahead, but also a growing dread about what this might mean for their relationship.

It had been hard enough last year when they weren't even together, spending most of December apart. How would they manage months upon months of separation for the foreseeable future?

"Whit...what are you thinking?" Layla asked softly, studying Whitley's face with concern.

Stuffing down her worries and forcing a bright smile, Whitley turned and took both of Layla's hands in hers. "I'm so incredibly proud and excited for you. This is huge, baby. Miller Barnes is the real deal. He will make your dreams come true."

"I know all that," Layla replied, her eyes searching Whitley's face. "I want you to tell me what was really running through that beautiful head of yours when he mentioned next December."

"You caught that, huh?" Whitley asked with a rueful smile.

Layla leaned her head against Whitley's, their foreheads touching intimately. "I did. You're worried about us being apart?"

"I'm just being selfish, baby."

"Not wanting me to leave you isn't selfish, Whit. I completely get it. The thought of being away from you again, especially in December, makes my stomach hurt too."

"But this is the chance of a lifetime, Layla. You know you need to take it, right?"

Layla gently stroked Whitley's jaw, her touch tender and reassuring. She leaned in and kissed her slowly, pouring all her love into the contact. "So come with me."

Whitley pulled back, startled. "Baby, I can't just take off on a world tour. Dad's actively prepping me to take over the company."

"Just for a few weeks in December," Layla clarified. "We'll deal with the world tour if and when it actually happens. I'm not going anywhere for another year. That's plenty of time to figure everything out."

"I love you, Layla," Whitley whispered, overwhelmed by the depth of her feelings.

"Right back at ya, baby. We've got this. We'll figure it out together."

Taking Layla by the hand, Whitley pulled her up and into her arms. "Ready to get back in there and show off those beautiful fingers of yours?"

Layla grinned mischievously. "Not sure your parents would appreciate that particular demonstration."

Batting her playfully on the butt, Whitley leaned in and lightly bit Layla's earlobe. "That demonstration comes later. Right now, I want to celebrate with you properly. Your parents are going to be so pleased when they hear about this. Hell, everyone is going to be thrilled."

Everyone was indeed ecstatic when they shared the news. Puck nearly fainted when Layla announced she had every intention of bringing him, Simon, and Reena along for the journey. After all, they were family and had started this musical adventure together.

Beverly and Roger cried loud, proud tears while hugging Layla and the other members of the quartet. Whitley's family immediately rolled out more Champagne, just as excited about the group's success as if it were their own children achieving these dreams.

Finally, when everyone had calmed down and were suitably lubricated with celebration, Whitley got the rest of her Christmas present. Layla stood in the middle of the living room, backlit by the roaring fireplace, with her violin poised elegantly at her neck.

"Shhh," Whitley hissed, effectively shutting up Aubrey and William's continued bickering over who got the last mince pie that Beverly had whipped up earlier in the day.

Layla shot her a grateful nod and a sexy wink that made Whitley's pulse quicken. She bit her bottom lip in response, not caring if anyone saw the lustful gaze. Layla deserved every bit of her admiration and desire.

"Before I begin, I'd just like to say how very grateful I am to have spent today with all the people I love most in this world," Layla announced, her voice carrying clearly through the room. "Now, that's enough talking. Let's get to the good bit. Without further ado, I'd like to play you a set of songs I intend to add to next year's concert series. I call it 'Once Upon a Time in December.'"

Whitley felt the rush of love in every cell of her body as she watched Layla take her performance stance. The music poured out, filling up the DuPont house with melody and magic. She watched the woman of her dreams play for their friends and family, performing songs she'd written specifically for Whitley. The medley was their love story set to music.

Their life ballad was only just beginning, but Whitley knew with absolute certainty that Layla would be with her until the very last note played, no matter where in the world that might be.

The Final Bow &
Happily Ever After

Layla sped through the snow-covered streets of New York. Her scarf flailed perilously behind her, whipping through the cold air and occasionally catching unsuspecting pedestrians across the face. The city was alive with its characteristic energy, even in the depths of winter.

There were several grumbled protests from people she'd accidentally struck with her scarf, but Layla didn't have time to stop and apologize. Not when she was running late on the most important night of her life.

The city buzzed with a winter's vitality that Layla had missed deeply during another year of international touring. There was no snow in the UK, and only a light dusting in Germany and France. But here in New York City, winter hugged every surface with a passionate embrace. The roads were barely passable, and Layla loved it—okay, maybe not the sleet stinging her face, but she'd be warm soon enough. Only one more block to go.

The gala venue came into view as she *literally* slid around the corner, her expensive Italian leather shoes finding just enough traction on the icy sidewalk to keep her upright. She was already dressed in her finest suit—a stunning green outfit with barely visible silver Christmas trees sewn in a random, artistic pattern. It was festive as hell and had earned her more than a few curious looks when she'd bolted out of her taxi seven blocks back.

Twenty-foot ferns guarded the entrance, their decorations elegant and perfectly portraying the evening's theme. A classic red, green, and gold color palette transformed the space into a sophisticated holiday wonderland. A plush red carpet lay in wait, but Layla didn't have time to stand and pose for photographers. She was three minutes away from her performance and still needed to wade through the crowd, deposit her belongings, and tune her violin.

If she hadn't gotten so excited and forgotten the goddamn ring—which had forced her to turn around, go home, and then set out again—she would have already been stationed in the wings, ready to take center stage.

"You're cutting it fine," Puck called out, his voice a mixture of concern and exasperation.

Layla held back her eye roll. "No shit! I forgot the bloody ring," she hissed back.

Puck *did* roll his eyes dramatically. "I told you to give it to me. You're bloody useless when you get overexcited."

"Duly noted. You can berate me later. I have roughly thirty seconds, and I haven't even tuned my violin."

"I did it for you. It's ready to go. The sound system goes live in twenty seconds. Take a few deep breaths. You're going to be great."

The memories of the past four years washed over Layla like a complex musical arrangement. Four years since she'd received that life-changing offer to tour the world. Years where Layla and Whitley had battled through challenging times, but always emerging stronger, more connected.

"She's here, right?" Layla asked, with a sliver of anxiety pinching her heart.

Puck scoffed. "Yes. She's been watching the entrance like a hawk."

A wave of guilt washed over her. Whitley would be worried. This wasn't the plan. She was supposed to have arrived ages ago, shared a glass of Champagne with Whitley, and then discreetly slipped away to prepare for her surprise performance.

Unlike in previous years, Layla had opted out of joining the main concert as a headliner. Instead, she had dedicated her time to helping up-and-coming musicians practice and rehearse in between her own shows. The back and forth had been brutal but worth it. She knew intimately what it was like to perform in front of important people who could open up entirely new worlds of opportunity. She wanted to ensure that as many young musicians as possible got the chances she'd been given four years ago.

Teaching over these last few months, even under such exhausting conditions, had also opened Layla's eyes to the fact that she was tired of touring. Layla was done. She had reached her dream of making music and sharing it globally. Now she wanted something different. Layla wanted to pass on her knowledge, but more importantly, she wanted to make music just for Whitley, to build a life together. In the same damn city, and what better day to make this declaration than on their anniversary? Eight years to the day since they'd first met.

Whitley had given Layla everything she'd needed to succeed, consistently putting her own dreams on hold. She was now the official CEO of the DuPont empire, having taken over from Lucas two years ago when he decided to retire and travel with Lucienne. This transition had made their long-distance relationship even more challenging, as neither could travel on a whim.

That had been an incredibly trying time for them, filled with late-night video calls, careful scheduling, and an unwavering commitment to making their relationship work.

But Layla knew the dream Whitley truly held onto was marriage and family. They had spoken of children many times over the years, but there was always something interrupting their plans. First, it was Layla's continued world tour—a resounding success that led to another contract, and then another tour.

All their carefully made plans had been perpetually pushed to the back burner.

Enough was enough, though. Layla missed Whitley so much that her heart ached daily. She refused to spend another day, let alone another December, away from her.

Now, Layla wanted to give Whitley *her* dream.

The lights dimmed, which was Layla's cue. Lifting her violin, she began playing the song that held the most profound meaning in her life—the very first melody she'd written for Whitley. It had been a showstopper during her tour, but it meant so much more when played specifically for her girlfriend.

Still standing in the wings, Layla drew her bow down and away for a dramatic pause. The crowd of nearly three hundred people was silent, hanging on every note. A chuckle graced her lips as she heard Whitley's distinctive voice state, "That's Layla. I'd know her sound anywhere. What's going on?"

She must be close to the front of the stage. Layla made a mental note to thank Aubrey, who was in on the plan. Whispers rippled through the audience, the curiosity palpable. But Layla had to refocus. She played on for another minute, hidden from view. The crowd was suitably intrigued.

Finally, she stepped out. A round of applause followed but quickly stopped. They wanted to hear the music more than their own hands clapping. Layla's gaze instantly found Whitley's stunned face.

Walking to the edge of the stage, she dropped until she was sitting directly in front of Whitley, her violin continuing its haunting melody.

Playing with her eyes fixed on her girlfriend, Layla couldn't stop the memories from rerunning in her mind—all the times she'd woken up next to the love of her life. Each kiss, whether a simple peck on the cheek or a passionate make-out session. How their bodies knew each other so well as they made love. The quiet nights when they managed to find time to unwind in the same time zone.

Everything flooded her mind and heart—their journey, their struggles, their unwavering adoration.

Whitley was outright crying, which made Layla want to throw her violin aside and take her into an embrace. But there wasn't much of the song left, so she played on, each note a testament to their love story.

As soon as she pulled her bow away for the final time, Layla asked the question she should have asked years ago: "Whitley, will you marry me? Have kids with me, and grow old disgracefully with me?"

The answer was more of a gurgled "Yes!" than a coherent response, but Layla got the gist of it as Whitley threw herself into Layla's waiting arms. Thankfully, Puck had been ready to catch her violin, preventing any potential damage to the instrument.

Layla hadn't held Whitley in nearly three months. She wrapped her arms around her and buried her head in Whitley's neck, breathing her in deeply. The familiar scent of Whitley's perfume, the softness of her skin, the warmth of her embrace—it all felt like coming home.

"I'm home, Whit," she said into Whitley's hair, her voice thick with emotion.

"I can see that." Whitley laughed, drawing back. Their eyes glistened with tears, reflecting the stage lights and the raw emotion of the moment.

Layla shook her head. "No, I mean, I'm back for good. No more tours, no more leaving. I'm here, in New York with you every day. Every December. We're going to get married and pop out a few musically and financially gifted kiddos. Maybe get a dog. We're going to celebrate every anniversary at our diner and attend this gala every year. We're going to host our own family Christmases and travel to the UK. Everything we spoke about, Whit. It's time. I've missed you so much."

Whitley palmed Layla's face, stroking her cheeks with tender fingers. The touch was both a caress and a confirmation—a physical manifestation of their reconnection.

"I want all of that, Layla. But are you sure? You've still got so much music to give to the world," Whitley asked, a hint of concern mixing with her overwhelming joy.

Layla's response was immediate and heartfelt. "My music is for you and our future family. The only time I want to be in concert is for you, in our living room. Possibly naked."

Whitley threw her head back and laughed, the sound filling the space around them with pure, unbridled happiness. "Not when those kiddos are in existence."

Layla waggled her eyebrows mischievously. "Okay, then you'll get a separate, private gig."

"Is this real?" Whitley whispered into Layla's mouth as they kissed again, the words barely audible but laden with disbelief and wonder. "It feels like a fairytale."

"It's real and it's a fairytale, babe," Layla murmured back.

"Mmm." Whitley smiled. "How does it start again?"

Wrapping her arms around Whitley, Layla brushed their noses together and smiled, the familiar gesture speaking volumes about their connection. "Once Upon a Time in December…"

Afterword

Thank you for reading & reviewing Once Upon a Time in December.

Spill the Tea (in a Review)!

If this book gave you butterflies, made you swoon, or kept you up way past your bedtime, I'd love to hear about it! Reviews help indie authors like me reach more readers who are searching for their next sapphic romance obsession. Drop a review on Amazon, Goodreads, or wherever you love to share your bookish thoughts. Even a quick "loved it!" makes a huge difference.

You're the best!

Stay Connected

Don't Miss Out!

Love steamy sapphic romance? Join my newsletter for new release alerts, promotions, book recommendations, and special reader-only perks. Sign up now: https://alysonroot.com/

<u>Become a VIP Member</u>

Want the ultimate insider experience? My VIP membership gives you early access to new books, exclusive bonus content, behind-the-scenes insights, member discounts, and a front-row seat to my creative process. Plus, you'll be part of a community of readers who love these stories as much as I love writing them. Join the VIP club:

VIP MEMBERSHIP

Let's Talk About Pleasure

I write characters who own their desires, communicate openly, and prioritize their pleasure—because that's how it should be in real life, too.

As a sex-positive author, I'm all about breaking down stigma and celebrating what feels good. That's why I'm thrilled to partner with *Wet For Her*, a queer-run online adult toy store that's as inclusive and empowering as the stories I write.

I use their products myself, and I can vouch for their quality, care, and commitment to the community. Ready to explore and get 10% off your purchase? Visit them through my affiliate link:

Web link: Toys

or

Checkout Code: ALYSONROOT

Your pleasure matters!

Transparency Corner: Yep, this is an affiliate link. If you make a purchase, I get a little kickback. Think of it as buying me a metaphorical coffee while exploring some fun products. Win-win!

Other Titles By Alyson Root

A Dance Towards Forever

Diving Into Her

Always Emilie

Broken Parts Included

Love & Other Wild Things

Finding Molly Parsons

Keeping Carmen Ruiz

The Wisdom of Bug

Sleigh Bells Ring

Risking Immortality

Waiting for Eternity

Fighting for Infinity

Mob's Seduction

Playing Her Heart

Welcome to Ero-TEA-Ca: We're Open!

About the author

Alyson was born and raised in the heart of England. She moved to Paris in 2015 when she met her wife. Together they moved to the west of France, where they now live with their two dogs. Alyson spends her time reading sapphic fiction books, writing and Scuba Diving.

Alyson discovered her love of writing in her mid-thirties. Her debut book, *A Dance Towards Forever,* was inspired by her wife and their very own love story. Alyson wrote *Diving Into Her* and award-winning *Always Emilie,* which added with her first book, created The French Connection series.

www.alysonroot.com

a.rootauthor@alysonroot.com